Hickory Flat Public Library
2740 East Cherokee Drive
Canton, Georgia 30115

**ALSO BY NANCY HOLDER
& DEBBIE VIGUIÉ**

Unleashed

• • •

The WICKED series

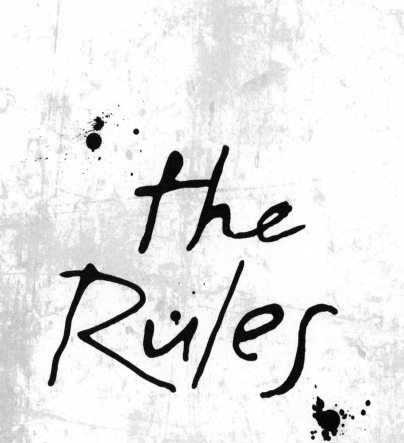

the Rules

NANCY HOLDER & DEBBIE VIGUIÉ

DELACORTE PRESS

Text copyright © 2015 by Nancy Holder & Debbie Viguié
Jacket art copyright © 2015 by Svein Nordrum/Getty Images and iStockPhoto

Visit us on the Web! randomhouseteens.com

Educators and librarians, for a variety of teaching tools, visit us at RHTeachersLibrarians.com

Library of Congress Cataloging-in-Publication Data
Holder, Nancy.
The rules / by Nancy Holder & Debbie Viguié. — First edition.
pages cm
Summary: High school junior Robin Brissett accompanies her best friend, Beth, to the hottest party of the year knowing there will be alcohol, drugs, sex, and a scavenger hunt designed to scare and thrill, but this year the school's elite are not the hunters but the hunted.
ISBN 978-0-385-74100-2 (hc) — ISBN 978-0-375-98980-3 (glb) —
ISBN 978-0-375-98347-4 (ebook)
[1. Parties—Fiction.   2. Treasure hunt (Game)—Fiction.]   I. Viguie, Debbie.
II. Title.
PZ7.H70326Rul 2015
[Fic]—dc23
2014006478

The text of this book is set in 11.75-point Fairfield.
Book design by Heather Kelly

Printed in the United States of America
10 9 8 7 6 5 4 3 2 1
First Edition

To Howard Morhaim, my agent and friend.
Words fail me, ironically enough.
Thank you for everything,
all these years, every time.
—Nancy

. . .

To Nancy Holder, my friend and cohort.
—Debbie

Everyone has Rules.
The Rules they play by.
The Rules they live by.
Here are your Rules:

Don't run.
Don't scream.
Play the game.
Break the Rules . . .
And you die.

PROLOGUE

THE NEW RULES ACCORDING TO ROBIN BRISSETT

NEW RULE #1:

Keep running.

Flames raged along the cliff. Pine trees and manzanita bushes ignited with a whirlwind *whoosh*, the steam rising off Robin's sopping-wet jeans as she zigzagged toward the beach like a desperate rabbit inches ahead of the fire. Salt and embers clogged the air. Her tongue was blistering. Her lungs burning. The hitch in her side ached as if she were being smacked over and over with a baseball bat. Everything stung and burned. She really, really had to stop.

Ringlets of her rich red hair dangled in her eyes as the blood dripped off the tips. She couldn't see, and she batted at the crazy corkscrews that insisted on bouncing right back. She was still stunned from crashing into the shell wall, lurching drunkenly left and right, fighting her hair, her exhaustion, and her panic.

If she stopped running, she would die.

NEW RULE #2:

Never surrender.

Robin's family had sworn not to let her dad's accident break them. The hit-and-run had shattered their dreams. Crushed their plans, just like his spine. *"It doesn't matter,"* her mom said. *"It's up to us. No one's going to come to our rescue. We are defined by how we react to setbacks."*

NEW RULE #3:

*People you know kill
other people you know.*

Setbacks send some people on murderous rampages.

No one's coming. No one's coming. No one's coming, Robin thought as a large pine limb split off a tree trunk, plummeting to the ground inches in front of her. She leaped over it, the heat singeing the bottoms of her boots.

But that wasn't true.

The killer was coming.

Robin might be limping. Gasping.

But Robin was still running.

And she would not surrender.

Because if she did, someone she knew would kill her.

1

AUGUST IN
THE CEMETERY

AUGUST'S RULE #1:

Don't get caught.

August DeYoung and his sister, Alexa, who had been barely one year older than he, had grown up with just one rule: don't get caught. Some kids grew up with parents who cared and paid attention. Others had parents who handed down so many rules it was impossible to keep them straight. All August and his sister had learned from their parents was to steer clear of blame. Their last name gave them a free pass. Money smoothed out . . . situations. Use both to get out of trouble. That was how the rule worked.

Until it didn't.

Almost three years earlier, back in New York, Alexa had broken the rule—resulting in expulsion, addiction, and a serious breakdown—so their mother and father had yanked August and Alexa out of private school and rehab, respectively, and "moved" to Callabrese, California, a town so tiny that it shared a country club with three other agricultural pit stops also stinking of manure. Although they opened a fine-dining restaurant called DeYoung's, they hired staff to run it . . . just as they hired staff to raise their children while they spent ninety percent of their time back in New York.

Alexa tried so hard. But she got caught in the worst way possible.

She had died exactly one year ago today.

And their parents managed to disapprove even of that. August couldn't remember if they had cried at her funeral.

He stood in front of her crypt, wondering if it would be for the last time. Set on a grassy hill overlooking the San Francisco Bay, the DeYoung tomb looked like a little marble Roman villa, an eight-foot-tall rectangle topped with an angled tiled roof. Four fluted columns anchored the corners, and a sad marble angel drooped on top of each one. The door was black as death and the brass fittings gleamed like halos. The little villa had cost the equivalent of a year's tuition at Harvard, which Alexa had been expected to attend. But the crypt was a bargain, really, because there was room for a dozen more dead DeYoungs inside it.

They hadn't buried Alexa in New York or Callabrese.

San Francisco was a good address as cemeteries went, and it helped them keep the whole mess quiet.

August was fiercely glad that Lex was finally out of Callabrese, which was nothing but grapevines and torment. Their parents had dumped them in a hellhole. That horrible, hopeless town had killed his sister. And it had been the people she knew, her *friends*.

They had betrayed her.

He remembered Alexa from the good days, when her light blond hair had glittered and her skin had not been sallow, and whenever you looked at her, she was smiling in a way that made you smile. Tiny and mischievous, like a little mouse. That was the Alexa he missed. But the one he mourned had been nothing like that. Dull eyes, hair of straw, scary thin. No mischief. The trap had sprung on the little mouse.

Once the tomb had been completed about a month after her murder, August had started driving to San Francisco every Saturday morning in his new Porsche. His parents had bought him the car in the hopes of cheering him up. That was their answer to everything: more possessions, more stuff.

It took about an hour to get there. He would buy a bouquet of miniature roses wrapped in tissue paper at Fisherman's Wharf. He and Alexa used to ditch school and cruise the wharf, eating cracked crab on sourdough bread and guzzling Anchor Steam beer even though they were underage. They'd feed the seagulls and talk about moving to San

Francisco once they could leave without being reported as runaways. Lex begged August to just blow it all off and bail out of Callabrese. Not to wait any longer. She couldn't bear it. She said their parents would never report them because of all the hassle it would cause. He wished to God he'd listened to her.

They used to get their pictures taken in the photo booth and go to the wax museum and send each other on little scavenger hunts all over San Francisco. He didn't know how many times she had made him find the Yoda statue in the Presidio or pick up something with a sea lion on it. He still had her sea lion collection.

That was how the scavenger hunt tradition had been born. Just for fun. Just to be goofy. Until August got his driver's license—Lex never learned to drive because she was afraid of cars—they hitchhiked to San Francisco and zoomed all over the city via cable cars and taxis. Alexa causing scenes, leaping into fountains and singing "What Does the Fox Say?" at the top of her lungs in the lobbies of all the exclusive hotels. August trailing behind, handing out money with his apologies, smoothing it over. She wasn't hurting anybody. Not when she was with him.

But back in Callabrese, the fun faded quickly. She got into the kind of trouble that money could not fix. And her "friends" just made it worse.

Her *friends*. She had never had friends in Callabrese. She had users, the so-called cool of the school, taking her down after they watched her flail for a few months to gain their acceptance. She didn't see that at first she scared them, and then they got off on letting her think they'd given her a place among them, when really, it was just to wind her up and watch her spin.

He learned by example. When she died, he did not have one single friend at their school. Correction: not one single *betrayer*.

God, he hated them.

"You're getting payback, Lex," August promised her, his fingers closing around the bouquet that dangled at his side. "Tonight."

And to execute it, he had a better weapon than knives or guns: an IQ of 160, which made him a certifiable genius. After what had happened to Alexa, he was certifiable, all right. He had spent hours planning his revenge, and it would be sweet.

And they didn't even have a clue that he was using them, manipulating them. Every smile he had flashed, every joke he had laughed at—all lies to throw them off the scent. All a part of his big scheme.

After tonight, they would know exactly what he thought.

But truthfully? Realizing he was about to cross that line scared and saddened him as much as the horrible police visit he'd received one year ago this very night. It had been three a.m. His parents were in Manhattan as usual, so it had been just him and Alexa, two feral children raising each other because their parents couldn't be bothered.

Only, Alexa hadn't been home. She wasn't asleep in her

room, as August had assumed. She'd snuck out, not because she had been "wild," like everybody would say later. She'd just wanted to go to a party. She'd wanted so badly to fit in. She would have done anything.

He was standing beside Abbie Meyers, one of a string of ineffectual housekeepers his parents had hired, when two police detectives rang the bell. They stood there grimly, and the tall one said, "We're afraid we have some bad news."

Down at the morgue, he had seen what she looked like dead. The place was ice-cold, and they had a viewing room, where he stood panicking in front of a window. They drew back the curtains like he was there for a slow-motion magic trick, and there she was. Lifeless and gray. She looked like a rotted rubber doll.

He nodded before throwing up. They took that as a positive ID.

August knew he was in a spiral, going down, down, down. He needed help. His parents made extremely halfhearted attempts to make sure he was coping—appointments with one of the most highly regarded shrinks in San Francisco, a couple of dinners together where they mostly checked their cell phones for messages. He thought about telling them he was in trouble. But when he thought about therapists and locked-up wards and all the crap Lex had gone through and died anyway . . .

She had been found floating facedown, naked, in the country club swimming pool after a night of partying.

Someone had taken her there. Someone had left her there. As far as he was concerned, they had killed her.

Back then, August was just a shadow of his former self; he had no one he could talk to. He could die just like Alexa, and no one would even notice. If he was to get to the bottom of what had really happened to her, he needed to be part of the social scene that had rejected them from the start. But he had no idea how to do that.

Then someone came to his rescue.

Her name was Beth Breckenridge, an okay-looking, average sophomore. A girl who got Bs and Cs and wasn't a standout in anything. She wasn't beautiful, athletic, artistic, or witty, but somehow she got through his armor. One day she walked up to him and asked how he was doing. He still didn't really know why he'd even answered her— "Shitty, if you must know"—but he did. They had an actual conversation and began to hang out.

She understood these people. She knew their rules. And she grasped very quickly that he didn't but that he wanted to. He didn't tell her why, and she assumed that he simply wanted to be popular. He knew that was what mattered to her, especially because they were older than her. But his wealth mattered even more to Beth, and she was completely up-front about it: he would pay for her mentoring skills with the lovely things only money could buy.

He agreed.

The Pact was born. And with it came the rules.

THE PACT RULES

1. Beth and August are not boyfriend and girlfriend or friends with benefits.

2. Beth and August are partners in the acquisition of social real estate.

3. Beth and August will trust each other, and only each other.

For ten months, the Pact had worked great. They were inseparable. Scheming, ruthless. Relentless and focused. Beth paved the way, making friends and influencing August's targets by lending an ear or a shoulder, finding out secrets (vulnerabilities), saying what they wanted to hear, doing favors. Doling out the occasional gift that was nothing but a disguised bribe, or as Beth liked to call it, positive reinforcement.

The *friends* they gave stuff to would give them stuff back: secrets, confidences, gossip. Once you knew how to do it, it was shockingly easy. August became devious and calculating, like Beth. In bits and pieces, he started figuring out what had happened to Alexa the night of her death. He uncovered secrets the others were so desperate to hide. They broke all kinds of rules, including laws and commandments. He had so much dirt on them he could put half of them in jail.

He became popular. And so did she.

Then came the fateful night when he discovered that Beth had broken the rules of the Pact. All this time, he'd thought someone finally had his back, and that was exactly where Beth had been stabbing him. *His* dirt, *his* confidences, *his* secret hopes: she'd been dishing all of it to *other* people who could help her out— out of Callabrese. Out of his life. And in with better-looking suckers.

Like Larson Jones.

August had fished Beth's phone out of her purse while she was in the bathroom at his house, crunching her password—one he'd seen her punch in hundreds of times—and read through a ton of damning messages. *Albino Man. Whiner. He writes poetry & it SUX. Listen to what he did today:*

Betrayals on top of betrayals.

He had locked himself in his room for days. He didn't eat or sleep. On the fourth day, he started secretly plotting his revenge against all of them. Tonight he would enact it, even on Beth, who had no idea what was coming. He had learned a lot from her. If he could make *her* suffer, make all of them go through a tenth of what Alexa had gone through, he would count this very last scavenger hunt as his own personal win.

A single tear pearled, but he didn't let it fall. He was solid frozen steel inside. The softer side of August lay buried with Alexa, and there it would rot.

"Let the games begin," he whispered.

August placed the baby roses he had brought for her in their holder and climbed back into his car.

JACKSON'S RULE #1:

Never let anyone take what's yours.

Despite being located in wine country and surrounded by local wineries, Callabrese had seen far better days. The sea fogs could be brisk, even in late May. Although Jackson White's breath was making ghosts, his sweat was burning him like acid.

In their "clubhouse"—a burned-out brick building that had once been a bookstore—his homeys were staring at him with seventeen pairs of stone-cold killer eyes. The Free Souls had been planning to break into DeYoung's, the fanciest restaurant in Callabrese, but the cops had caught wind of it. Change of plans. Now they were all gathered together and staring at Jackson in a way that made him uneasy.

"You know we take care of our own," Macho, their leader, said. "And nobody takes what is ours. I shot this three days ago."

He handed Jackson his phone, which displayed a picture of a girl grinding on a guy. She had on a baby tee and the world's tiniest shorts, her black hair balanced on top of her head like a bubble. And that girl was *his* girl,

Thea, who had broken up with him *yesterday.* She had cried and told him she needed her space. Just until things got better at home, because her parents didn't like him. No, she said, there was no one else. She had sworn it. Staked her life on it.

While he stared in shock at the screen, he shook with shame. He was so mortified and enraged, he couldn't even look at the guys around him.

Jackson recognized that guy Thea was dancing up against. He was pretty famous around Callabrese. A-hole must figure that because he'd made it, he could do whatever the hell he wanted. Guys like him sent guys like Jackson into gangs. Because where else could he define himself?

Jackson's skull began to sizzle.

He handed back the phone and then stomped to his rusted-out electric-blue El Camino, got in, and drove off.

His hands shook. His head pounded.

I swear to God I'm going to kill her.

2

LYING UNDER OATH

ROBIN'S RULE #1:

Never cheat.

"It's the knife, isn't it?"

Robin Brissett's little brother Carter mock-stabbed the Clue board with his yellow plastic Colonel Mustard token. He pushed up his black-rimmed glasses and examined his clue list, then speculatively eyed the murder envelope in the center of the board, which contained cards naming the weapon, room, and perpetrator.

Robin kept her face carefully neutral. She had the knife card in her hand, which meant that it couldn't possibly be the murder weapon. If Carter made an accusation, he would lose, and that meant he would have to do her weekend chores. She *hated* vacuuming.

Beth leaned over to whisper into Robin's ear, "Hey, Merida, we gotta go."

Merida was Robin's old nickname because of all her wild red hair. It trailed down her back in crazy spirals. Robin hadn't cut it in years despite pressure from the girls at school to get a "look." She had her own look, and it included lots and lots of fiery red hair and very casual clothes—ripped jeans and comfy fleece sweats. You couldn't lose the fashion race if you didn't run in it.

In addition to a *Teen Vogue*–worthy cashmere sweater, peacoat, and her geometric, blue-black bob, Beth was wearing leggings, flat boots, and a raw silk plaid micromini. Robin's self-confidence faltered as she looked down at her own red Henley, jeans, bomber jacket, and hiking boots. She'd figured scavenger hunt equaled dressing down. Maybe she'd miscalculated.

They were sitting in Robin's kitchen just like old times, before Beth had dumped Robin as a friend at the end of sophomore year. Now it was almost the end of junior year, and Beth was acting like nothing had ever happened. In fact, yesterday after last period she had zoomed up to Robin in the hall and invited her to one of the legendary parties the superelite of Callabrese High threw for themselves. This one would be extra-amazing because August DeYoung was the host and that meant scavenger hunt, and they were the most fun. Despite a major quirk factor, August had become the king of the school, and Beth was the duchess. Robin had to wonder why she had been included. She never had been before.

"Motive," Robin said, tapping the Clue board. "*Why* do these people murder the victim? That's never discussed."

"Who cares?" her little brother said. "That's not the point."

Just then, Jinny Brissett, Robin and Carter's mom, walked into the kitchen. "It's so good to see you, Beth. It feels like the old days."

The better days, Robin silently translated.

Robin forced herself to smile at her mother, feeling kind of panicky. She probably shouldn't have lied about where they were going.

They say that somewhere, down deep, you always know. That voice inside your head can tell you if you're off on an adventure or headed for a disaster. That's the same voice that tells little kids there's a monster in the closet and that magical beings like Santa and the Easter Bunny bring you gifts on special days.

The thing is, the presents do arrive, right on schedule. So do the disasters.

And Robin had a funny feeling about tonight.

"It was great to see you, too. We have to get going now, though," Beth said.

"Say good night to Daddy for me?" Robin asked her mom. He was in the master bedroom, drifting in and out of consciousness on his pain medication. He'd been riding a bicycle to the mini-mart to save gas after he'd been furloughed as a coach at Callabrese High. Budget cuts. He never even saw who hit him and left him there in the foggy darkness. His spine had snapped. Now he was on disability, and the doctors were saying he'd never walk again. Her dad said differently. He said he would be walking by her high school graduation, one year and three weeks from tonight.

Robin looked at Carter. "By the way, I hid the answer cards."

He blinked comically, like a shocked turtle. Then he snatched up the packet and hefted it in his hand. His mouth forming an O in outrage.

"You *took* them! You cheater!"

"I didn't look at them. I swear it. I just removed the temptation for *you* to look."

"That's not fair!" Carter bellowed at the top of his lungs.

"Easy, honey," Jinny said.

"I'll be back tomorrow and then we'll finish," Robin reminded her brother. "And by the way? It's *not* the knife. Got it?" He looked so lost sitting there as she got ready to party. She mimicked holding a hand of cards, and his face lit up. He crossed KNIFE off his clue list.

"Knives are the second most common murder weapon." Carter had a thing for true crime statistics. "In real life."

"Sweet," she said. "I'll keep that in mind."

He grinned at her and mimicked slicing her neck with his wee tiny blade.

"And Saturday is the most common day to be murdered," he added cheerfully. "Today." He waggled his brows, slicing the air again.

Beth had already gone outside, and Robin gave Carter and her mother a farewell wave as she followed her. Cell phone coverage at Beth's had always been spotty, and Robin had told her mom that the Breckenridges had gotten rid of their landline. That would give her a cover story if her parents tried to get in touch with her since she was supposedly spending the night there. She felt guilty for lying to them, but they really were too preoccupied to notice. Anyway, she was sixteen, all grown up.

"C'mon, c'mon!" Beth said. "The last ones there die horribly!"

Across the street from the house, blurry moonlight bleached fields of twisting grapevines heavy with fruit. Thirsty vineyards lapped up moisture like vampires sucked blood. In wine country, fog was a friend.

Unless you were pedaling a bicycle through a thick nighttime mist and someone hit you. Robin had sworn to find that person someday. She used to daydream about running them over, and then she had nightmares about torturing them to death. Now the hatred had burned out of her and she just wanted them to go to jail forever.

The fog was on the move, so thick an entire army of the walking dead could be headed their way and they'd never know it. Robin thought back to all the ghost stories she and Beth used to scare themselves with. It was hard to believe that once upon a time, she had been afraid of pretend things. The real world was pretty darn scary on its own.

OPPORTUNITY

THEA'S RULE #1:

Never get caught cheating.

Thea Ward slunk out of her house in black leather pants and a fuzzy black sweater and popped into the front seat of Beth's new Beemer—new to Thea, anyway—like she was on a spy mission. Her long black hair was pulled into such a tight ponytail she looked like she'd had a face-lift. At least, that's what her little sister said.

Thea was amazed that Beth had invited her to this party. Freshman and sophomore years, Thea, Robin, and Beth had been "the three amigas," but then Beth had started hanging out with August DeYoung and Mr. Brissett got hit by a car and she'd gotten involved with Jackson.

And *nobody* but Thea liked Jackson. Crazy, that's what people said about him.

Tonight the amigas were back together again, Robin tucked in the backseat, Beth at the wheel, except they were going to the Callabrese High equivalent of the People's Choice Awards. It was like Thea was living in an alternate universe. But every time her phone dinged, her reality intruded:

"Oh God, you guys, Jackson has texted me, like, fifty times," she said with a quaver. "He's so mad that I broke up with him."

"Ignore him, sweetie." Behind the wheel, Beth glanced away from the road and held out her hand. "Better yet, give me your phone."

"You don't know what he's like when he's upset," Thea said. He was positively homicidal, but she didn't say that. "He can't help it. He had a brain injury," she added quickly.

"Oh my God. So what's *your* excuse?" Beth asked. Just then Beth's own phone trilled like a bluebird, signaling an incoming text message. "I'm betting that's our first clue!" She held her phone out to Thea. "Read it, please."

Thea grunted but did as she was told. "It's from August. It says, 'On your mark! Square root of one hundred sixty-nine?'"

"Type in *thirteen*," Beth said without hesitation.

Thea blinked. "Wow, super math woman," she said. "Unless August already told you all the answers." August and Beth were tight. They had been odd-couple besties for a year. Robin spent all her time with her family, and Thea must have lost her mind when she decided it would be a good idea to fill her empty Friday and Saturday nights by dating a gangbanger.

It's not Jackson's fault that he has a brain injury, she told herself. *And if he didn't, he'd be really sweet all the time.* It was just that he had what he called "episodes." He would go completely berserk. Everyone at school judged him for them. Jackson told her the Free Souls accepted him exactly as he was. But she couldn't. Jackson was all wrong for her.

Plus she kind of had someone cooler on the back burner.

"August didn't give me the answers," Beth replied. "He wanted me to have fun, too. This is the last hunt. And? Math makes us free."

Thea raised her brows. Beth used to hate math. But then old Beth would never have thrown herself in with August DeYoung and a cynical clique. Only new Beth liked running with the big dogs, buying August's old car from him for peanuts, and doing precalculus. Thea didn't even know what calculus was.

"Type it in," Beth insisted.

"One-three. Sent," Thea reported. They all waited.

"'Thirteen is your lucky number,'" Thea read off the phone screen. "Go you, Bethie-B! Okay, here's the clue: we're supposed to drive to Second and Vineland, then go north on Vineland for thirteen blocks and then text for further instructions."

"And we're off!" Beth cried. "This is how it works. How we find the fun, girls."

A wind chose that moment to blow strands of fog across the two-lane blacktop county road. Thea leaned back in her seat, looking out over the grape fields to the scattered houses with their glowing porch lights. *You are sixteen and free. And you are going to find the fun,* the little voice in her head promised her. *Especially if you-know-who is in the mood.*

She quirked a half smile, feeling both guilty and sad at the same time.

MICK'S RULE #1:

Practice makes perfect.

Mick, Stacy, Drew, and Hiro were Maximum Volume and had been for almost three years. All their blood, sweat, and song stealing were finally going to pay off: they had one more gig in Callabrese, and then they were moving to Los Angeles to record their first album with a major label. August DeYoung had told Drew that only Maximum Volume would do for his hush-hush party, and he had backed up that statement with some serious cash. Now they had arrived at the cannery right on schedule. But where was their audience? And why the heck was the party going to be held *here*?

"Whoa," Stacy murmured from the backseat. "Look at *that.*"

Mick braked too hard, and Drew dropped his dark blue

Bic lighter into his lap. The van reeked of Drew's weed and Stacy's clove cigarettes. If there was any justice in this world, Drew's nads would catch on fire.

Maximum Volume had played some crazy venues on their way to the top. They'd chased their sound, hopping around from grunge to power metal to operatic metal and finally to their own indie vibe, which they called "metal rhapsody." When you changed your identity as many times as they had, you learned to be flexible. One week you banged out box chords in a scummy bar in Fresno and the next week you were the darling of a fringe festival in Old Sacramento. But *this* . . .

They'd driven for two hours and had just reached their final destination. About twenty steep feet below the van sprawled the hulking remains of an abandoned cannery. What appeared to be party central—as it was the only building with lights—was a large brick factory or warehouse covered with graffiti, sliced by dozens of rows of thin, rectangular, blasted-out windows. A pitted roof featuring a drooping smokestack and a listing black metal bell tower completed the view. The building looked as unstable as Drew, the bassist and their founder. Drew had once been awesome, his dreams fueled by talent and lots of hard work. But drugs were taking him down, and fast. Their new manager, Pascha Haimes, had even hinted to Mick, the lead guitarist, that Samurai Records might be open to developing Maximum Volume as a trio: Mick on lead guitar, Stacy on vocals, Hiro on drums. They could get a studio musician to take the bass line until they found Drew's permanent replacement. That sounded great to Mick. Except that he didn't know how they could pull it off.

Beside the warehouse, a wicked Porsche was parked at an angle in a huge lot of crushed shells, as if the driver had roared in and skidded to a halt so he could get his orders from MI6 or seek shelter from the zombie apocalypse. To the right of the Porsche, midway into the lot, stood a lumpy wall made out of cement, rocks, and abalone shells that wound on down to what appeared to be a lower lot, the details lost in the thick fog. Above that turnoff, darkness poured like black paint across the landscape to a very steep cliff dotted with ice plant and weeds. Well behind the warehouse and beyond the slope to the lower parking lot, a long, low half-demolished building stood below a faded billboard that said AZUL CANNERY—HOME OF THE FINEST SALMON AND SARDINES. ASK FOR AZUL! To the left of the warehouse, the fog thinned, revealing a falling-down wooden dock stretching out over another cliff, tumbling at a forty-five-degree angle into the ocean of inky blackness. On the other side of the dock, pine trees and woody California manzanita shrubs formed a barrier that trailed on down toward the ocean.

One car. Just one. The place looked like a junkyard. Directly ahead of the van, a rusted wrought-iron sign stretched across both sides of the road. It was decorated with outlines of fish and the letters Z U L. Between the open gates, fog rolled toward them like a pack of starving ghosts.

"What the hell, Drew?" Mick said. "Is this a joke?"

"It looks like the House of Usher. I like it," Stacy said, rolling down the window. She was guzzling water from her omnipresent travel tumbler. Mick was positive it was permanently attached to her left palm. And that there was more vodka in it than water. "I am Zul, the Gatekeeper."

"Home sweet home, Morticia Addams," Mick teased her. He could see her in the rearview mirror. Little lost goth girl stuck in a time warp. Her hair was a smudge of black and her face was heavily made up. Her one arm, chest, and back were covered with super-colorful floral tattoos in red, blue, and purple. She was dressed perfectly for a haunted mansion gig: a black leather corset, matching leggings, and lace-up knee-length boots with heels so high Mick couldn't figure out why her feet never slid out from underneath her. Especially because she was loaded for twenty hours of the day.

"Hey, we're getting paid a lot," Drew pointed out. He sounded like his usual whiny, defensive self. "A *lot*. And we need moving money."

God, if only we could leave you here, Mick thought. Getting signed by Samurai Records was the big time, but only if Maximum Volume proved they were worth the investment. They'd get one chance to make good, and one chance only. Mick was ready. He'd been practicing for at least six hours a day for years. Working out. Taking care of himself. Doing everything he could to be an excellent bandmate.

But there were problems. Most of them were named Drew. Years of playing dive bars and tiny clubs would have taken a toll on any normal person. No musician was normal, but at this point, Drew was weaker than most people. It didn't show to the casual observer yet. But sooner rather than later, it would. Drew was going to flame out. It would be better if he died in some epic tragedy, like the great ones, say, in a plane crash. The band would sell a ton of records if that happened. But overdosing was far less sexy and much too cliché. Mick was sure he and Pascha agreed on that.

The problem was, Maximum Volume had gotten Samurai's attention because of the three songs Drew had written on the demo. If Drew was out, they wouldn't be allowed to play those songs. He owned them and no one could record them without his permission. And he sure as hell wasn't going to give permission if they booted him out of the band.

But here was the kicker, the thing Mick couldn't tell Pascha: Drew had stolen those songs from two tiny indie bands that had broken up within weeks of forming. Drew said no one would ever know. So far nobody had made any accusations, but Maximum Volume was a lawsuit away from trouble.

Mick couldn't come clean about the plagiarism. Samurai would drop them immediately. So would Pascha.

Better to get rid of Drew now. That would solve so many problems. But only if it happened fast. And soon.

The other problem, sad to say, was Stacy. She was burning too brightly. She loved to party. Luckily, she'd slept with him, Drew, and Hiro, so those potential strained group dynamics had already been taken care of, but she still screwed anything that moved, no questions asked. She drank like a fish, popped Ecstasy like Tic Tacs, and had no judgment, none at all. She lived in the moment. One day she was going to bring home a stray serial killer. Or show up completely juiced for a recording session at Samurai.

He and Hiro had discussed both of their problems. They'd agreed that sexy girl singers were easy to find, especially in L.A. But songwriters who could at least recognize what songs were worth stealing? Much less easy.

Somebody had to take care of business. That was supposed to be Drew, since he had founded the band. But Mick had slowly been taking control. Tonight's gig, however, was Drew's find.

It figured.

"We have a gig. We have to set up," Drew said. "That's August's Porsche. He's here and we have to be on time."

Mick sighed and looked over his shoulder at Stacy, who smiled reassuringly at him. Beside her, Hiro had his earbuds in, his head back, eyes closed. Mick was so irritated. He needed some backup in this mutiny.

"It's just a show, Micky-baby," Stacy said. "One last

show in Callabrese. We'll make good money. It's like a paid practice."

"Yeah," Drew said. "August DeYoung is connected. He said he'd give me some names of guys in L.A. to jam with. He knows the Stones, man."

What a load of bullshit, Mick thought, feeling the idling of the van through his boots. *August DeYoung does not know the Rolling Stones.* But then he looked at the Porsche. It was tricked out. Probably some kind of limited edition. Maybe August DeYoung *did* know the Stones. That was the bewildering thing about their client. It was obvious that he had tons of money, and every now and then, something amazing would happen to August, at least according to Drew. For example, he had recently gone to visit Walt Disney's family in Napa. If he was so connected, why on earth was he living in Callabrese? Was his family in the Witness Protection Program or something?

"C'mon, Mick, chill," Stacy said. "We're going to be famous, but right now, we're still broke."

That was true. Samurai was going to pay the expenses for making their first record, but that was it. When it came to food, clothing, shelter, and gas money, Maximum Volume was on their own.

Stacy's right. This is a paying gig. What's the worst that can happen?

He took his foot off the brake and the van rolled down the drive.

4

NUMERO UNO

JACOB'S RULE #1:

Look out for number one.

An electric guitar wailed as Jacob Stein coasted his motorcycle into the cannery yard and planted his feet on either side. He turned off the engine. Whoa, creepy place. Jack the Ripper scary, even. Mass murderers on every floor. August liked the dramatic and all, but he had taken it to a new level of *Final Destination*.

Jacob chortled and took off his helmet, giving his hair a rearrangement before he pulled his phone out of his leather bike pants to check the time. No cell reception here, no surprise, but he was super early for the party. August would say he'd cheated because he had not waited for his little texted riddles and then sent his answers to get the next clue like a lab monkey rewarded with bananas. But hey, it wasn't his fault that Hiro Yamamoto, the drummer for Maximum Volume, had come into the bike shop last Thursday. Hiro had been looking to buy some leather gloves and he spent a lot of time talking about this weird gig at an abandoned cannery he was going to play the following Saturday night. Jacob had been invited to August's party that Saturday and Maximum Volume was playing it. So he had listened carefully, done a Net search, and voilà.

August had announced that tonight was his last hunt *ever*. "The farewell tour," he called it. He was graduating and moving on, just like Jacob. It was going to be a party people would talk about for years. Legendary. Something like a dozen juniors and seniors had been invited. Plus August confirmed that he had summoned Thea Ward from the land of high school nobodies to be Jacob's scavenger hunt partner. Jacob's mouth watered at the thought. Thea was *hot*. He had lusted after her since last summer, when he had seen her at the pool in the world's tiniest bikini. Those scraps of string had made a thong look like an old-lady swimsuit. Somehow he had told Beth about his undying lust—*how* and *when* he wasn't sure—and now Thea was on tonight's guest list. Behold the awesome power of August.

August was pretty cool, for a head case. It was too bad about Alexa.

I should have never slept with Alexa, Jacob thought. *She thought it meant something it didn't. And I shouldn't have left her at the pool that night. I just couldn't take any more of her insanity.*

But I didn't lock that gate. I don't care what anyone says. I didn't do it.

It had been a Friday, his turn to throw a party. It was just going to be a small get-together at his house. Just the "in crowd." The coast was clear: his parents were out of town.

He was texting everyone about when to come over when he spotted Alexa DeYoung coming out of her parents' restaurant. She'd left town months ago. To go to rehab, people said. The girl was an out-of-control freak. Seriously scary. People steered clear. There's living on the edge, and then there's jumping off the cliff without a parachute.

He grinned as a plan hatched: Morgan totally hated her, and he was pissed off at Morgan because she had scraped the new paint job on his motorcycle with her car door and refused to pay for it. Time for a little revenge.

So he sauntered up to Alexa, flashed his Jacob Stein smile, and invited her to his party. He told her that Morgan had specifically asked him to invite her. She was so grateful that he actually felt guilty. He had watched her working hard to be liked ever since the DeYoungs had moved to Callabrese. They all had. She was completely clueless about how to fit in.

Hours later, he had left her crying in the country club swimming pool because she thought he had actually *liked* her, when all their hookup had meant to him was a good time. Tears running down her cheeks because he did not want to plan their future right then and there, like she did. Then the crying and screeching had begun. Calling him a bastard. Saying that he'd used her. Then after that it was as if she had forgotten how to speak English. Sounds and words just exploded out of her, and she was scaring him.

So he'd bailed.

I had nothing to do with her death, he reminded himself. *I didn't lock her in. I know I didn't. I checked. But I shouldn't have left her there.*

He wouldn't think about that. Tonight was not about regrets. It was about fun. And Thea. He would make sure she understood from the get-go that it was just a hookup.

It was also about stuff. Their jaded little in-group actually competed for the swag that August provided because it was that awesome. Last time, Larson Jones had won an all-expense-paid trip for two to watch a Mogwai recording session in Scotland. This being the last party, August was going to deliver something even better. So rather than let Albino Man know he'd arrived early, Jacob decided to have a look around. He'd see if he could find some of the objects August would have put on the list and memorize where they were. So yeah, okay, that was cheating.

Whatever.

Stabs of moonlight pierced the fog as he walked his bike out of sight before starting a methodical search of the grounds. There was a lot to cover. The warehouse itself was huge, along with an extended building with a rusted corrugated roof and two or three smaller sheds. There looked to be a cave set into the cliff opposite the warehouse, but in the watery light, he couldn't be sure. He'd check that out, too. A cave would be a perfect scary place to hide something in a scavenger hunt. August was sly like that.

Jacob's boots crunched down on the pulverized shells scattered like gravel. He could hear the tide rushing in and out, like an asthmatic giant. As he walked, generators rumbled like jackhammers and gas exhaust clung to his nostrils. The motors must be powering the lights and the band equipment.

After a few minutes, he heard someone's noisy footfalls, and he ducked behind the large brick warehouse to wait out the intruder. He prudently turned sideways so that no one would see him if they were looking through any of the windows in the back rooms.

The footsteps died away. There was nothing but the *putt-putt-putt* of the generators, the *whoosh* and rush of the water. An owl singing to prey. *Come out, come out, wherever you are.*

And the guitar. Whoever was playing it had skills. No wonder Hiro's band had been signed to a label.

Jacob started to walk on.

Then something cold and sharp slid into his back, pushing out all the breath in his body.

He didn't feel the shells stipple his face as he fell

forward, hard. Didn't feel his nose breaking. Didn't feel the serrated hunting knife being yanked out and thrust back in again.

Out.

In.

Out.

In.

Didn't feel the blood spilling into his lungs, filling them like water balloons, pouring into his esophagus.

He wouldn't feel anything ever again.

5

CRIME SCENE

BETH'S RULE #1:

Be nice. Or at least appear to be.

"This is *it*?" Thea said anxiously as Beth led the way to the door of the warehouse. Thea kept gathering up her ponytail and stroking it like a cat. "I thought we were going to some kind of mansion."

"Where would be the fun in that?" Beth grinned at the glittery, glow-in-the-dark sign August had placed above the door: INFERNO: ABANDON ALL HOPE, YE WHO ENTER HERE. Nice touch.

At first it hurt Beth's feelings when August had told her that he was going to plan the hunt alone. It was the very last one, ever. She'd helped him throw four amazing hunts and God knew how many smaller parties since forming the Pact, and she'd been looking forward to really pulling out all the stops on this one. She knew he wanted to make it super scary (although it would be hard to top Halloween) and she'd been creating storyboards and flow charts of clues for months. But then just after spring break, he'd told her he wanted her to have a chance to play. In all the time they'd known each other, she had never gotten to be a guest. So he was going to run this one on his own.

"This is payback," he'd said sweetly, and she couldn't seem to convince him otherwise. She liked playing hostess. In fact, being just a guest was a sort of demotion.

Then he reminded her that if she was a scavenger hunt contestant, he could pair her up with Larson Jones and offer a prize such as a fully crewed getaway—sailors, steward, cook—on the DeYoung yacht, *Guilty Pleasure*. That had caught her off guard. She hadn't realized he'd noticed that she'd been crushing on Larson. What *else* had he noticed?

"I don't like stuff like this," Thea said anxiously. "I hate horror movies and scary rides and those walk-through haunted houses."

"This will be totally different," Beth promised, although she had no idea if that was true. She *did* know August had specifically asked her to get Thea Wade to the party. Jacob Stein had a crush on her and August wanted something from Jacob. To her consternation, August wouldn't tell Beth what it was. It probably had something to do with motorcycles, since Jacob worked at the local motorcycle dealership.

"Maybe I'm getting something for *you* at the biker store," August had told Beth, and Beth had smiled her sweetest smile.

Not for the first time, she wondered if he suspected that for the last three months, she had been laying the groundwork for Life after August. She assumed he would be good for using his parents' connections to get her into the college of her choice—that being Oberlin—and maybe there'd be one more great summer, but after that, he'd be going away to college and their bond would weaken. It was inevitable.

She had to be practical and brutally honest with herself. People were going to pretend to like August for the rest of his life because he was rich and his family was important, and for the rest of *her* life, she might have to continue to pretend to like people like him. It all depended on how much friendship from other people she could purchase in the time allotted. So while she had the reputation of being August's friend, she had to line up social clout for senior year. Beth hoped he understood.

There were advantages to losing August, though. It would be cool to have a real boyfriend. Someone to take her to prom next year. Hopefully it would be Larson, who was also a junior. She hadn't tried to hook up with Larson because she knew that boy-girl besties could get awfully jealous if one of them hooked up with someone else. Three definitely was a crowd. Yet the fact remained that Larson Jones was incredibly hot and she couldn't stop thinking about him. She loved his curly dark brown hair and deep-set eyes, caramel with sugary gold flecks. He had adorable freckles on a slightly twisted nose that only added to his unusual looks.

As they reached the door, Thea stiffened like she was going to run away shrieking, and Beth suppressed her sigh of exasperation. Thea had been dating a guy in a gang, and she was afraid of a little bit of spooky? Thea owed Beth for talking her into breaking up with Jackson. A few serious heart-to-hearts, a couple of good cries, and Thea had finally kissed Jackson White goodbye.

"It'll be fun," Beth promised Thea, who was playing with her ponytail again. "I don't need to tell you that on the other side of this door, the cream of the social crop are gathering. You really can't imagine the things I've gotten to do because I hang out with them. Last summer I spent three weeks in Maui, and August's parents paid for *every-thing*. Then I went skiing at Lake Tahoe during Christmas break. Heather's going to invite me down to L.A. after she films her pilot. She saw Jessica Biel at the farmer's market. And Praveen's talking about a big shopping trip to San Francisco."

"Okay, okay, I get it." Thea scowled at Beth. "You have this great, fantastic life now. I'm so happy for you."

Beth blinked. Thea was so dense. "You're missing the point, sweetie. What I'm saying is just get with it and you could have a shot at all this."

"Right," Thea drawled sarcastically.

"I made up these rules for myself," Beth continued. "And they worked, didn't they?" She held up her fingers. "One: Be nice. Really nice. Two: Act interested. Everyone wants to feel special."

"That's right. *Everyone*," Thea said, crossing her arms and giving Robin a look that said *back me up*. But Robin just stood there.

"You *are* special, sweetie," Beth said, trying very hard to sound compassionate, but she could hear the patronizing tone in her own voice. "You got invited to this party, didn't you?"

"I only said yes after you told me Robin was coming," Thea said, and Robin lit up.

"Thank you," Robin said to her.

A frisson of mild alarm shot up Beth's spine. She didn't need these two comparing notes too closely. She had only invited Robin to get Thea to show, for Jacob. Robin had been an afterthought, so Beth had lied to Thea, telling her that Robin was already in.

It would pain Beth, but only a little, if Robin figured that out. What mattered is that these two girls had won the golden ticket. If they didn't make the most of it, that wasn't on her. It would just go to prove that she'd been right to leave them behind when she had moved on. What was the saying about lipstick on a pig? It was still a pig?

Time would tell.

"The third rule for this crowd is that you have to bring something to the table. You have to know things, or be able to do things, or be funny or smart. You have to have something to offer."

Thea's angry expression clouded with humiliation as if to say she would be out of the circle before the hunt even started.

"But rules one and two are more important," Beth said quickly. "If you act like these people are interesting, they'll think *you're* interesting. That's a start. Then you can figure out what's missing in the mix." She smiled brightly at Robin. "Let's think of something *you're* good at, Merida. You like to play Clue. How about gaming?"

Robin shook her head. "I play board games with my little brother. That's it."

"Well, we'll think of something. For each of you. Now let's put on our *game* faces," Beth said, chuckling at her pun. She smiled brightly. "Do I look good? No lip gloss on my teeth?"

Before either girl could answer her, the door crashed open, nearly smashing her in the face. "Hey!" Beth yelled as she stumbled backward and collided with Thea, who bumped into Robin. *Not* the grand entrance Beth had planned.

None other than Larson himself shoved past her on his way out. *Pushing* her. He didn't even seem to notice. She registered the slight and knew Robin and Thea had, too. She swallowed her heart along with her pride.

"Lar, you startled me," she said in a high, friendly tone, but he kept going.

"Dude, where you going? Party's inside," said a weed-laden voice.

Cage Preston swaggered up behind her as tall as a mountain, gorilla-huge, his arms so muscular he couldn't lower them to his sides anymore. There were raised veins like long, hard worms underneath his skin. When he went down the football field, people yelled, "Hulk *smash!*" He deserved the gaudy MVP ring he wore on the pinky of his left hand—*MVP* spelled out in glittering rhinestones, with a red enamel *C* just below the *V*, for *Callabrese*.

For a second Beth thought Larson was going to ignore Cage, too. Then he moved his shoulders and put his hands in the pockets of his Callabrese High letter jacket. "Gotta smoke," he said, then stomped off into the darkness.

"You can smoke at the party," Cage called after him. More to himself, he added, "We always smoke at the parties."

"Jerk," Thea muttered.

Beth's cheeks went hot. Larson was permitted any level of jerkiness, but a nobody like Thea could not get away with commenting on it.

"Let's go in," Beth said, leading her two lambs to the slaughter.

Even Beth had to catch her breath as they entered the warehouse. August had outdone himself—correction, outdone himself and *her*—with a huge cavern of a room that was rippling with holographic projections of hellish flames reaching to the thirty-foot ceiling. It was amazing.

41

Animatronic bats squeaked and dive-bombed from way high up in the rafters on filament wires. There was a hanging skeleton whose jaw dropped open with an ear-splitting shriek.

Prismatic tumbles of scarlet- and pumpkin-colored light spilled across the floor, where leering devil faces grinned and stabbed with pitchforks. Along the walls, glow-in-the-dark coffins held shrouded figures clutching nosegays of dead, dried roses. The figures writhed and shifted very subtly. It was like the set of a Hollywood Halloween movie.

Beth started picking out the faces of the usual suspects: Praveen, Heather, Morgan; Cage and Larson were outside. She didn't see Jacob Stein. "Prince" George Frisen was missing, too. And yummy Kyle Thomas.

A large white banner with dripping bloody letters proclaimed, WELCOME TO HELL! August was standing beneath it in a fedora, khaki trench coat, green silk shirt, and tuxedo pants. The mike of a headset curled in front of his mouth. The fedora hid his hideous bleached hair, and not for the first time, Beth considered that if he just had some pigment to his skin, let his hair grow out to its mousy brown, dyed his eyebrows, and got some permanent lash extensions, he would actually look good. He had great bone structure.

He was holding an old-fashioned stopwatch and a clipboard. Combined with the mike, he had standard Pact scavenger hunt equipment.

"Wow, this is cool," Robin said.

"It's scary," Thea whined, and Beth wanted to slap some sense into her.

"Hey, Beth, 'scuse," Cage said, scooting around the three girls to get inside. "August, my man!"

Cage ambled up to August and clapped him on the shoulder. Two large glowing purple skulls rested on a black coffin-shaped table beside him. One skull was marked HELLNOTES and the other one LIFELINES.

"Greetings, greetings, you know the routine," August said to Cage. "Don't open the envelope. And give me your phone."

Cage good-naturedly laid his cell phone in LIFELINES, which was already filled. A couple of them had the new sparkly cases that cost a bazillion dollars. Then Cage turned to the basket marked HELLNOTES and started going through a stack of black envelopes with names printed on them in red.

"Alphabetical, Cage, as usual. I know those pesky letters can be confusing. Don't break the seal. You *will* be disqualified." And then August looked at Beth's entourage. "Robin? Brissett?" he said, in complete shock.

Cage lifted an envelope out of the basket and walked away.

"Hey, August," Beth said smoothly, moving in front of Robin. "So a bit of last-minute logistics. It's a very long story, but Robin's kind of stuck with me this weekend, and the more the merrier, right?"

August's yellow brows climbed an inch as his colorless

eyes moved from Robin back to her. He was actually angry with her. Beth was astounded. But she was the other half of the Pact.

Or maybe not. Maybe she was just plain old Beth Breckenridge again, a nobody. She felt the change come over her like she was morphing into Dr. Jekyll or something. It felt awful, so she fought it down. She had the power. August wouldn't even be having this party if it weren't for everything she had done for him.

"Well, here's the deal," August said. "Jacob texted me. He's not coming. And Prince George's grandmother had a stroke, so he's at the hospital. I figured you and Thea could be a team. But now we have an imbalance."

Beth was stunned. She had assumed she would be paired with Larson. August had as much as said so. Was he *punishing* her for daring to bring her own guest?

"Robin can do the hunt with Beth," Thea suggested. "I don't really want to do it."

"Yes, you do," Beth said quickly. Thea had to play or August would be insulted. "She totally does, August."

August exhaled with the exasperation of a genius confronted by a sea sponge. "You know how *precise* I like things," he said. "I don't have a prize for Robin."

"That's no problem. She'll just hang out with us, okay?"

Beth flipped through the basket of clues and then held up the envelopes with her and Thea's names on them. "She's not even all that smart"—she flashed Robin a warning not to contradict her—"so she won't be that much of an advantage."

August's face tightened, his eyes bugging out, as if he had bitten into a lemon. He was more than upset. He was seriously angry. Beth stood her ground.

"We'll be a ménage à trois. Wouldn't you like that?" she asked silkily, which she realized immediately was the wrong thing to say. She and August didn't tease about sex. They teased other people about sex.

She dropped the act. "Hey, August, may I speak to you for a second?" she said evenly.

He very calmly led her to a spot about ten feet away. Then he looked down on her, as in *really* looked down on her, like she was beneath him. There was definitely something wrong—more wrong than simply bringing one uninvited guest.

"Why did you already pair up Thea and me? We have to play the hookup game to organize the partners. And I thought you were going to make sure I got to be with Larson."

August gazed over at Robin as if he'd never seen her in his entire life. Robin and August had AP Spanish together, for heaven's sake.

But Beth had to admit she would have done the same thing in his place—acted like he didn't know her. Because in their world, Robin Brissett was insignificant.

"Larson's been strutting around since he got here,

bragging about how he's going to nail someone. Anyone. He's a pig. You deserve better." He reached out and patted her cheek as if she were about seven years old.

"I know how to handle him," she snapped, and the back of her neck flushed hot, her cheeks prickling with panic. Things were *wrong* between them. "I just want to toy with him." She heard the frightened bravado in her voice.

He shrugged. "Trust me. I'm sparing you."

"But I don't *want* to be spared!"

His lips twitched as if at some hilarious private joke. "You say that *now*."

Sudden clapping and hooting provided some distraction so that she didn't have to say anything in reply. Maximum Volume, the soon-to-be-very-famous local band, was climbing onto a wooden stage painted with glow-in-the-dark flames. Strings of white skull lights dangled behind them like a curtain. Cut into the wall above them was a sort of loft, an empty, black space. The ends of the skull strings were drawn through it.

Mick, the lead guitarist, settled his guitar strap across his shoulder and carried his cord toward an amp on the left-hand side. Hiro, the drummer, wrapped a white bandana decorated with a Chinese ink brush character around his forehead as he sat behind his drum kit. He wore a sleeveless white T-shirt and his arms were sculpted muscles. Drew, bassist and songwriter, had on a gray Grateful Dead T-shirt with his typical shaggy grunge hair. Tucked into his pocket was a big green silk handkerchief that was very close in shade to August's shirt.

Stacy, their singer, teetered on her super-stiletto boots and would have gone down if Drew hadn't caught her forearm and held on to her. She lifted a travel tumbler over her head and waved it, pouring a little bit of liquid down over her chest, and everyone burst into cheers.

"That's my cue." August turned to go, then turned back. "You, Thea, and Robin are a team of three. But there'll be a penalty. Put your phones in the basket."

Without looking at her, he walked away, extending his arms into the air as the partiers clapped and stomped their feet. Heather and Morgan had arrived and were swaying their hips like belly dancers.

"August!" Beth called after him, but he just kept going. She watched him as if she were memorizing him. As if he were someone new and different, someone she'd never met before. Because he *was*.

He was August with balls.

I've blown it. Beth's stomach dropped to her feet as she went into total free fall. *I should have been more careful with his feelings.* She looked around the room at all the beautiful people laughing. They were already farther away, as if they were on a beach and she were in the ocean, caught in an undertow that was dragging her out to sea. She had to work fast, collect them like pearls on the half shell, before they realized that she was out.

Is the Pact dead? Did I kill it? For a second she was rooted to the spot, shaking. Her mind replayed all the long hours she and August had gossiped about their peers—correction, *August's* peers—and how smug and safe and dangerous she'd felt making fun of them and using them to get ahead. Drinking August's parents' five-hundred-dollar bottles of wine with half-defrosted Sara Lee cheesecake. Microwaving popcorn and drinking the same tequila they served Johnny Depp after hours in their Manhattan restaurant's bar.

She didn't feel dangerous now. Waves of despair were washing up and over her. She was drowning in remorse. She probably felt as vulnerable as Thea, who had just broken up with a brain-damaged criminal with anger-management issues.

"Screw you," she muttered under her breath as August climbed onto the stage. "I'll do it all on my own. I'll get Larson myself. Spare me." She sneered at him. "Dream on, August. You can't do *anything* to me."

As Mick plugged his cord into his amp, there was a crackling noise and an intense white flash as his body was flung halfway across the stage.

And all the lights went out.

6.

CONSPIRACY THEORY

Rock is a matter of life and death.

"Holy shit, Mick is dead!" Stacy screeched in the darkness.

Dude, Drew thought, but that one word was the sum total of his reaction. He was a little more wasted than he had realized.

He tracked a bobbing light that flared with shimmering rainbows as it swept across his field of vision. Shadows crashed and stumbled backward, and August raced across the stage. Drew trailed unsteadily behind. Mick was on the ground. Holy shit indeed.

Someone yelled, "Call nine-one-one! Turn on the lights! August, *where* are the phones?"

Drew automatically reached for his own phone before he remembered that August had collected them during setup, explaining it was one of the rules of the scavenger hunt. No cells. None. There wasn't supposed to be any Internet available at the cannery but you never knew. August didn't want his game contestants calling their friends for help with their clues. Drew had started to argue, but Mick agreed to it. They had to keep the customer satisfied.

"I'm okay," Mick moaned, slowly getting to his feet with an assist from a black-haired chick. Beth. Drew remembered her name. August's girlfriend. "Who the *hell* spilled water on my amp?"

"Oh," Stacy said beside Drew, her voice oozing guilt. She looked down at her tumbler. "No, wait. I *didn't*. It's nearly full, see?"

"Uh-huh. Full of vod—" Mick practically spit nails as he clenched his mouth shut. Then Drew looked out at the kids watching them. Someone had turned on a couple of electric lanterns on the tables. These guys were their public. They might not have phones to snap pix and tweet right now, but they would later. And if they talked about Maximum Volume sniping at each other and Pascha or Samurai heard . . . that would be bad for business.

August walked to the front of the stage. "There are more battery-operated lanterns on the tables. Please turn them all on. I'm going to check out the electrical."

Drew absently strummed his guitar and the sound reverberated around the room. A few people whooped. They liked that. He strummed again, struggling to clear his mind.

"Okay, we've got *some* electricity," August said.

An intense reconfiguring of plugs and cords and discussions among Mick, Hiro, and a couple of the kids who knew a thing or two about electrical engineering followed. Drew didn't follow the details. Technical and boring wasn't his thing.

Drew looked at Stacy and said, "I'm going outside."

She tottered after him in the ghoulish lantern light. "I didn't do it, Drew. Really." She brushed her bangs away from her forehead. Her skin was uncommonly white beneath her makeup and she was sweating like crazy, even though it was cold enough outside to see your breath. Drew decided to light up before they had to go back inside.

"I'm feeling bad," Stacy said. "I think I'm getting sick."

"Don't get sick before L.A.," he said, and she smiled crookedly at him. Then her smile winked out of existence. Stacy went through emotions at lightning speed. Same way she burned through guys. She looked around very dramatically, then tapped his forearm with her dragon-lady fingers.

"Drew, that was *your* amp," she said. "Not Mick's. I saw the tape with the big *D* on the back when Hiro carried it in. August helped us set up. He must have confused them and we didn't notice."

Then, as if stringing all those syllables together had exhausted her, she slumped against the railing. The dock rail creaked and she jerked backward, raising her hands as if to show the bleached, brittle redwood that she meant it no harm. Her heels clattered like someone shooting off a staple gun.

Mick and August came out of the warehouse. "We're going out to the generators to check on things," Mick announced.

"Yeah, good idea," Drew said. "Glad you weren't electrocuted, man." He knew he sounded insincere, but he didn't care. He blew the pungent smoke out of his mouth as Mick the Dick and Mr. Moneybags disappeared into the rolling fog.

"This is our last gig before L.A. and it's cursed," Stacy murmured.

"Not really," he said, but he saw her point.

She coughed and gently clutched her neck.

"God, I'm burning up."

"Don't think I don't know . . . ," he began. Then he stopped himself. Why go there? What was the point? He was not looking for a confrontation.

She looked genuinely confused. "Don't know what?"

Maybe she wasn't in on the plan to boot his ass out of the band. Hiro and Mick thought they were so cagey, but he knew they were trying to figure out how to get rid of him. Well, cage *that,* douche bags. Let *them* get decent equipment and write great songs (and if he heard the word *plagiarize* one more time . . . He had *sampled*—everyone sampled) and find half-talented musicians who didn't have *issues.* Well, okay, he sure as hell had blown *that* part. Hiro and Mick should be bowing down and kissing the toes of his Converse sneakers. They had been *nothing* when he found them. Less than dog crap. He had practically tutored

Mick in how to sound like Eddie Van Halen. And now they thought they could make secret deals behind his back? He could replace them in two hours.

Just watch me.

"Drew? What do you know?" she asked anxiously.

Stacy. Sweet. Naive. Stoned. He reached out and tousled her hair. Then he took her tumbler and said, "Let's try some good old-fashioned water, okay? August brought a ton of water bottles. He's got all kinds of munchies. Get something in your stomach."

"You're so good to me, baby," she purred, putting both her arms around his neck. "Why'd we break up?"

"We were never actually together," he said, easing her arms away. "So we couldn't really break up."

She let her head fall back so she could smile up at him and nearly lost her balance. She ran her fingers down the side of his face. "Your eyes are jittering. They look like kettle corn kernels about to pop. What did *you* take?"

"Stuff I can't even pronounce," he said. "Good stuff." It took the edge off. Made it possible to function. But he was still damn edgy. He needed some more.

"Share," she said, pouting.

"Water," he said. "I will get. You will drink. A lot. Promise?"

She crossed her heart. "Enough to drown in," she vowed. She looked out at the ocean, then turned and peered up at the bell tower. "That thing looks like it's ready to fall over." She slid back into Drew's arms and laid her head on his chest. "Someone's going to die tonight, Drew. I just know it."

She was freaking him out.

"Well, let's make sure it's not us when this deck collapses," he said, and led her back toward the warehouse.

7

THE UNUSUAL
SUSPECTS

ROBIN'S RULE #2:

Don't do anything you'll regret later.

"Why didn't you tell me I wasn't actually invited?" Robin knew she was yelling but she seriously doubted anyone but Beth and Thea could hear her.

"I invited you," Beth said coolly.

"This is August's party," Robin insisted, and Beth pursed her lips.

"Would you have come if I had told you?" Beth asked, as if that would prove some kind of point.

"Are you kidding? Now I'm stuck here with no way to call someone to come pick me up," Robin shot back, and Thea started biting her thumbnail—her nervous habit.

Beth gently pushed Thea's hand away from her mouth. "Oh my God, sweetie. All August was worried about was the logistics of the hunt. It's not as if he doesn't like you."

Robin opened her mouth for a retort, but Beth obviously didn't want to hear it. "At least you could have thanked him," Beth said.

"Oh, *right*. For his good manners. Sure." Robin narrowed her eyes at Beth and turned to do just that.

Immediately, Beth grabbed her wrist, digging her nails into Robin's arm. Painfully.

"Wait. I'm kidding." Beth smiled her plastic smile, finally letting go. "I *am*, okay? You don't need to apologize to him. We're here. He said yes. Everything is fine."

Robin didn't like Beth's version of "fine." Beth had kissed up to August and every single person here and it had sickened Robin to watch. Beth was practically starving for their approval. It was obvious to Robin that they were only playing along, acting like they liked her.

Robin was about to say something she knew she would later regret, but she was saved when the members of Maximum Volume returned, climbing onto the stage to play an electrified version of the traditional funeral march. Everything seemed to be fine now, for them, at least. The band ended their song with a flourish, and August appeared on the stage.

"Thank you, Maximum Volume!" he said into his wireless mike. "They'll be playing again in a little while, and a final set when I announce the winners. Now it's hookup time!"

Cheers rose up as Beth caught Robin's arm. "We're exempt. We're already paired up."

"Paired up?" Robin echoed. She saw three girls, two of whom she recognized from school: Heather Smirnoff and Morgan Alcina. A third girl shook her head and laughed. Cage and Larson sidled over to them as they all checked each other out. Robin's face felt warm. She wasn't sure she was going to enjoy this "hookup time."

August dangled a black bandana. "Who will do the honors? Beth?"

"Oh," Beth murmured, sucking in her breath. She beamed at August before starting to walk forward, Miss America on her way to her tiara.

"Why don't you have your friend Thea help us out?" August finished.

Beth flinched but just as quickly recovered. "Showtime," she muttered. "Do me proud, Thea."

Like a stage magician, August gestured for Thea to come forward. She took her time, looking supremely cool. August handed her the bandana, then pointed at Cage. Cage imitated Thea's runway model gait and planted himself in front of her, bending his knees so that he and Thea were closer in height. August gestured for her to place the bandana over his eyes, and she did, tying it in place.

While she was doing that, Heather, Morgan, and the third girl dashed over to their purses and pulled something out of them. Perfume bottles. Morgan gave herself a spritz, her shiny curls bouncing as she tipped her head left and right, and Heather tipped a vial over, dabbing it behind her ears. The third girl pulled out a white handkerchief and waved it back and forth in the air.

The girls moved toward the blindfolded Cage, Morgan and Heather slinking around like pole dancers while the third girl moved her hankie back and forth very, very shyly. She glanced at the band, and Robin saw a quick flare of interest on the bass player's face, followed by longing and . . . regret? Robin looked back at the girl, who was twirling in an awkward circle with both arms extended.

Larson, August, Beth, and the entire band hooted and applauded as the Callabrese girls really put their sexy on. Heather and Morgan performed full-body rolls.

"Yikes," Robin murmured, dying of embarrassment. "Um, Beth?"

"Be cool," Beth said. "It'll be fine."

Heather blew Cage a kiss and the onlookers chuckled. Cage cocked his head to sniff the air.

"You know Heather," Beth said in Robin's ear.

Robin did. Heather was one of those blondes with perfect hair, tons of makeup, and big diamond earrings. She was the queen of the drama department, literally, with a mirror in her locker that looked like one of those clapper things they used in movies when the director called "Action!"

"She's moving to L.A. after graduation. She got a part in a TV pilot," Beth said.

"Yeah, I heard," Robin replied, and she could hear

herself working overtime to sound unimpressed. "Makes sense. Guys think she's hot." Which was also kind of bitchy of her, she supposed. Heather was a good actress. She had real talent. Robin was just very nervous.

The girls circled Cage, still doing their slinky-girl dance moves. He inhaled deeply, then reached out both arms and lunged forward, nearly grazing Heather's arm.

"Hot is right," Beth whispered. "Heather is hot for a teacher. And said teacher is hot for *her*."

Robin jerked back her head, her mouth dropping open in shock. "No way."

Beth made a show of fanning her with the clue envelope. "Way. Want to know who?"

"Beth, you can't be right. Do you know how careful teachers have to be these days?" Robin said anxiously. "My father had to take sexual harassment training every semester."

"Well, it looks like someone else flunked," Beth retorted.

"You don't *know* that," Robin insisted. "If this is just gossip, it could really hurt someone. Even get them fired."

Beth threw up her hands. "Only the guilty. And I *do* know. I know it's true."

Robin was thunderstruck. She didn't know what else to say. Did her dad know? Was it someone who had been over to the house? Before her dad's accident, her parents had been very social, inviting other teachers and the lacrosse team over for dinner all the time.

Cage inhaled again. There was a big, goofy grin on his face as he held out his hands and began to advance on Heather. Blowing him a kiss for the benefit of the on-lookers, she darted out of his way.

"Morgan," he guessed.

"Nope," August said. "Try again."

Cage lurched in the vague vicinity of the third girl but she stayed out of his way. She was wearing a green top with loose sleeves with a matching sweater wrap over it.

"That's Praveen. She has the coolest clothes," Beth said reverently. She looked from Praveen to the sweater she had on, smiled, then lifted her chin. Robin translated: Beth and Praveen were wearing the same shade of green. It must be the color of the week.

"Praveen goes to Porters. It's a private school," Beth said.

"How does August know her?" Robin asked.

"Praveen used to hang out with Alexa. His sister. You know about her, right? She died."

"I heard," Robin said. It had been all over the school. Rumors had flown: that she'd OD'd, cut her wrists, been murdered. The story that stuck was that she had drowned in the country club swimming pool. Even when the news had been fresh, Robin felt bad about the level of her own ghoulish curiosity. But then her father had gotten hit and tragedy was no longer a spectator sport in her world.

The doctors told them that Brian Brissett would live . . .

but that he would be paralyzed from the waist down. *"Tough times don't last. But tough people do,"* her mom said.

But how did you get tough? What made you weak? Was it just the way you were born, like being athletic? Had Alexa missed out on the survivalist gene, or was she just unlucky? She had only attended Callabrese High for a year and a few weeks, and half the school gossip had been about her meltdowns and over-the-top antics.

I think I'm tough. Robin tried the thought on for size. *Or maybe I just know that someone's got my back. I've got my family.*

That being the family she had lied to tonight to come to Club Pervo.

"It's Morgan!" Cage shouted as he grabbed Morgan around the waist and whirled her in a circle. He buried his face against her neck.

"Yup!" she laughed. "You cheated. You could see through the blindfold!" She batted his shoulder and yanked off the black cloth.

Cage made a show of covering his mouth in horror. "Morgan, honestly. I would *never* cheat."

August guffawed into his mike. "Tickets are now on sale for Cheater Theater. We'll let it go. We'll get a new blindfold for the next round. And how about you do the honors this time, Robin?"

"No, that's okay," Robin said, waving a hand at him.

"Just. Do. It," Beth murmured. "Please."

Sheesh. "Okay, I'm in," Robin said as Larson reached up to get a bandana from August. She didn't want to touch him. She thought he was a slime bucket.

"Okay, no more lurking, bachelor number three," August said, and he turned his head toward the shadows. "Dude, you show up late and then you don't mingle."

Dark on dark—a shape glided through the black perimeter of the room and moved in front of the coffins occupied by the writhing figures. It was about six feet tall, and as it passed behind a lantern, the warm light cut out a silhouette. Slightly turned up nose, broad shoulders and chest, with almost no butt on long legs. Robin's heart stuttered. It was Kyle Thomas. She hadn't known he would be here.

"Hey, Robin," he said, smiling at her. Right at *her.*

His velvety brown, sun-bleached hair was longer now that her father couldn't order him to cut it. His letter jacket, T-shirt, and jeans looked as elegant as the tux he'd worn at this year's winter formal, to which he'd brought some girl from another school.

"Hmm," Beth murmured beside her. "Do we have something to share?"

Robin was absolutely certain there was nothing she wanted to share with Beth about her secret crush on Kyle.

Despite all her best intentions, Robin swallowed hard when Kyle smiled quizzically at her. She translated that smile: she was not a rich kid, not a hanger-on, not a partier, so what was she doing there?

Kyle, Kyle, Kyle. He was the big everything at Callabrese

High—class president, Ice King at the formal, and lacrosse team captain—a position her dad had given him before his accident. Robin couldn't get it out of her head that with a couple more team meetings at their house, Kyle would have finally realized there was more to Robin Brissett than the fact that she was his coach's daughter.

"Will this do for me?" Kyle asked, reaching over to one of the round tables covered with black tablecloths positioned around the room. He picked up an oversized black napkin and waited for Robin.

"Thea, why don't you go ahead and cover up Larson's eyes?" August asked.

"How's your dad?" Kyle asked quietly as he handed the cloth to Robin. He smelled like cinnamon, one of her favorite things. He squatted down, facing her, and as she reached up to position the cloth across his eyes, she realized she would have to put her arms around him to tie the blindfold behind his head. His face would practically be buried in her chest. Her pulse began to race. How many times had she daydreamed about being held by Kyle? Sometimes at practice, when she had waited for her father, she'd stared at him, memorizing the shapes of his muscles, the way he moved. Lacrosse was an aggressive sport—some said brutal—and she figured herself for some kind of cavewoman because it was thrilling to watch Kyle in action, playing with everything he had.

"He's good," she said automatically. He looked at her and she shrugged. "Pretty good. It was hard sitting out this season. He was really touched when the team came over after you won the CIF championship."

"Maybe he could coach from his wheelchair," Kyle said.

"He's going to walk again," Robin said. She sounded terse. She smiled to take away the sting. "And I am going to kick your ass in this scavenger hunt."

"Are you guys finished with the marriage proposals?" Heather asked, rubbing her arms. "I'm freezing . . . and tie it tight, Robin," she added.

Robin wanted to be Kyle's partner in the hunt. But August had already decreed that she, Beth, and Thea were to be a trio and there was no way she was going to play the hookup game. And besides, what if Kyle didn't wind up with her? Then she'd have to be with Larson, the man slut.

Her elbows brushed against Kyle's shoulders as she tried to secure the blindfold without getting too close. She fumbled awkwardly and Kyle reached up to help her, his fingers twining with hers and causing Robin to catch her breath. Behind them, someone whooped and the lead guitarist started playing the melody of "Go Ahead and Show Me," the love ballad that had put Maximum Volume on the fast track to rock stardom.

"They're playing our song," Kyle said, grinning.

If only, she thought.

8

NOT ALL CHEATERS
CAN WIN

KYLE'S RULE #1:

Anything worth doing
is worth doing well.

Robin finished blindfolding Kyle and moved away. He was sorry to see her go. A jumble of emotions he had not anticipated feeling tonight were flooding through him. He hadn't expected outsiders. This kind of party was way out of her league. These people were pretty despicable. If Beth had dragged her here, then she was no friend of Robin Brissett. Of course, Beth didn't actually have friends. She had people she used.

He didn't want to stumble around smelling perfume like a bloodhound. This was actually a fairly tame version of the hookup game, and Kyle wondered if August had decided to change the rating to "safe for all ages" because of

Robin and that other chick. Thea. Of course, he'd heard that Thea had been around. None of the guys talked trash about Robin except to say that she looked hot with all that curly red hair and that she was probably too smart to go to bed with any of the losers who went sniffing around her. So to speak.

She'll definitely give me a run for my money tonight.

To decrease his tension, he stuck his arms out and mimicked walking like the Frankenstein monster, which got a couple of laughs.

"Okay, never mind the blindfolds," August said. "Take 'em off. Let's just move it along."

It wasn't like August to move it along. He always seemed to get off on turning these games into contact sports. But it was fine with Kyle to switch gears. He pulled off his blindfold, to find Robin staring straight at him. She quickly looked away.

"So I don't get Morgan?" Cage said.

"Depends," August replied. "Now listen. Here are the rules."

"We *know* the rules," Cage said.

"For the new girls," August shot back. "Rule number one: No cheating. None. Cheating does not happen."

Everyone cheered and laughed as if he'd told the best joke. Everyone except Kyle. He wasn't into cheating. Never had been. And he hoped that Robin Brissett didn't think he was.

"I'm serious. No cars, no cell phones, no help. You go

past the perimeter, you are done. I have spies this time. They will report you and you will be disqualified."

"That would be horrible," Larson drawled.

August ignored him. "Rule *dos*. Once you open your envelopes, match your clue up with your partner's. Each of you has half and together you will go after one object. And, please, the object is not to fulfill your lust. So try to restrain yourselves from running off and finding a dark corner before you even solve the first clue."

"Yeah, baby," Larson said.

Kyle glanced over at Robin. As the night went on and people got loaded, she was not going to believe what she was seeing. And it would only get worse. . . .

August continued. "The answer to the clue will be a *solid* object, since Beth's attempt to use 'concepts' last time didn't pan out so well."

Beth turned beet-red. August was definitely not feeling the love for her tonight. Kyle wondered what was up.

"The envelope for your second item will be attached to your first object. Do *not* touch other people's objects. Do *not* steal or mix up their clues."

"Watch your objects, girls," Robin deadpanned, and Kyle flashed her a grin. She saw it, blushed, and looked down at her shoes. She was *adorable*.

"Rule the third: bring back your items *in the order you find them* to this warehouse. Each of you will have a clearly marked place to pile your loot. I will check it in. At that time you will get the dreaded Truth or Dare."

"I hate that part," Heather muttered.

"That's because girls with lots of naughty secrets always have to pick Dare," Larson said.

"Shut up," Heather snapped.

"That's like six rules, August," Cage said.

"Rule number *four*," August continued, ignoring him. "Everybody must follow their clues to the end. No detours or going backward."

"Rule number four is redundant," Larson said.

"Tough crowd," said Robin, and Kyle chuckled.

"Rule number five: feel free to misdirect, confuse, and lie to anyone who is not your partner."

Another cheer rose up and Thea high-fived Beth, who gave her a *please, we are not twelve* eye roll but high-fived her back.

"Rule six: do not maim anyone!"

"Damn it," Cage said. "Now it's no fun at all."

"That's *nine*!" Kyle added, and some of the others laughed. Robin grinned at him.

August was unfazed. "First done wins. I *will* be keeping track. Of *everything*. If you break the rules, you will pay."

"Wahaha," the singer slurred into her mike.

"Since this is the last hunt, I have upped the budget on the prizes, as you have all been speculating. The two members of the winning team will each get a personalized prize. Heather, for example, could meet a casting agent who is a friend of my family. He's looking for a young ingénue for a new kids' show."

Heather caught her breath. August continued.

"Cage could win a meeting with a football scout. Everyone has one. I'll think of something for you, Robin," he said, nodding in her direction. "Each person's prize is printed on their clue card. But if anyone bails out of the game, no prize.

"And for the winning *team,* there's a choice of prizes for them to share." He held up a finger. "Option A: you and a date can ride to prom in the same limo that the Rolling Stones used when my parents took them to San Francisco to check out our new restaurant."

"Oh my God, that is so cool," Thea said, and the others nodded in agreement. Kyle wondered if August was just making that up or if it really was the same limo.

"*Or* you can have what I think is the most amazing prize of all," August said. "Everyone knows I'm something of a hacker." There were nods. "Well, check this out. In their infinite wisdom, the administration of Callabrese High has created an internal computer dropbox. Into this dropbox, all the teachers of all the classes at our school are busily uploading their final exams. *And* their answer keys."

Over the ensuing hubbub, August raised his hands. "Yes, my friends, that means *every single final.* And, of course, Mr. Blanchard, our IT teacher, has added the seven deadly rings of security." He snickered. "Which I, of course, hacked past. I have the security protocol, *including* the numerous passwords, and I will give it all to two lucky winners . . . unless you would rather have the limo."

Kyle frowned, super pissed. He had studied his butt off for weeks. Ms. Amaya and a couple of the other teachers graded on a curve, and he couldn't afford to get knocked down because people were cheating. It was so typical of August, who cut corners every chance he got just because he *could*. And typical of their friends to take the easy way out.

It was not typical of Coach Brissett's daughter, apparently. Beth and Thea were hopping up and down in utter ecstasy, but Robin looked as shocked as he felt, and he watched her arguing with them. He and Robin were the only two honest people in a den of thieves.

"When I give the signal, you will rip open your clue envelopes and find your partners," August said. "So tank up on food now. It's going to be a long night."

Kyle wandered over to the overflowing refreshment table. As usual, August had put out an amazing amount of food. And not just cheap munchies, but cracked crab on sourdough bread, clam chowder, little Japanese bento lunch boxes packed with sushi, and a massive cake that looked like a bottle of Anchor Steam beer. The table was decorated with at least six different colors of miniature roses and two enormous ice sculptures of sea lions. Random.

Robin came over. There was guacamole and chips, and she got a little skull-shaped plate and took some. He knew that even though she wasn't looking at him, she was conscious of his presence, and he moved closer and snagged a chip off her plate.

"So, this is your first August party," he said. He loved her eyes. They were blue, like his, but a bit greener. She had a cute nose. And a great body. He liked girls with athletic builds. She didn't do sports at school, but he knew she was a runner, like him. He wasn't sure if she was more into speed or endurance. This hunt location was so spread out that he would probably get to find out.

"And my last," she said, munching on a chip. "The grand finale."

"Or the bitter end. Do you want a beer? Or something stronger?"

She made a little face. "I think I'd better stick to soda. My teammates are out for blood, and I'm not a very good drinker. Plus we're getting a penalty because we're a team of three, so I need to maintain every advantage."

He handed her a can of Diet Coke and got himself a water bottle. "I don't drink, either," he said, unscrewing the cap. "August designs these hunts himself. Usually Beth helps. Why didn't he just pair you with Thea? It's not fair to clump you up and then penalize you for it."

She jerked her plate away playfully when he reached for another chip. "He didn't know I was coming. Beth invited me and I guess she forgot to tell him. Which is weird, considering . . ." She trailed off. "Anyway, I'm glad I'm the odd girl out because there is no way I'd take the test answers, and Thea and Beth are over there dancing a jig at the very thought."

"So you're not a rule-breaker," he said.

"Not usually, no. But I *will* help Beth and Thea win." She looked dubious. "It's not up to me which prize they pick."

"But you girls won't win," he said very seriously. "You know that." She lifted her brows and he reminded himself not to underestimate her.

"I already said I'd kick your ass." She grinned at him.

"Hah. I could beat you *all* without the penalty. Me and my partner," he added. If it was Heather, she'd probably wander off somewhere and hook up. That would be fine with him. Give him room to maneuver. Otherwise she'd be a total boat anchor.

"Wow, lacrosse captain, are you ever so competitive."

"You got that right." He feinted to the left as if to steal a chip, and as she batted her hand at him, he snatched away the plate, and held it above her head. He scooped up the last of the chips. "I'm a winner."

She was all flushed as she huffed and lightly gave his shoulder a bat. He was stunned. She liked him. *Liked* liked him. He had never guessed.

"Want to make it interesting?" she said.

He halted, the chips halfway to his mouth. "Sure."

"Loser buys the winner coffee."

He smiled. Another surprise. She was pretty much asking him on a date.

"You're on."

He held the chips out to her. He always had an image of what these hunts would be like, and it hadn't accounted for the presence of an innocent like Robin Brissett.

I guess we all started out innocent, he thought, and figured he should warn her.

"These people," he said, then hesitated. He had to be careful. For years and years, he had kept his low opinions of these friends to himself. There was absolutely no point in dissing them now, when they were all so close to the end. "They feel entitled. They get bored easily, and if something's too hard, they'll cheat. Cage has been known to hire smart kids to do his homework. Larson just screws—"

He broke off. Larson's typical solution for raising his GPA was to hook up with some smart nerd, get her to do his homework, and then break it off with her.

"Look at how much August has to bribe them to play his game," he said. "They'll never have to work a day in their lives, not really. They'll just coast along and get everything while you and I will have to work our butts off just to make it."

Her eyes widened, and Kyle wondered if he had said too much. No one knew he was this bitter. He was suddenly nervous.

"Anyway," he began, and she smiled gently at him.

"Actually, I agree with you," she murmured. "Sometimes it pisses me off, too."

He blinked. "Whoa, Robin. I—"

Then August jumped back on the stage with his arms wide. "Okay, scavengers, finish up. The countdown has begun."

"Ten!" Stacy cried, and everyone looked at her with amusement.

"Hold on a sec there, Stacy," August said amiably. He pointed at Robin. "For the newbies, even though they did *not* realize that we run in pairs, not threesomes, there is a penalty."

"Kill! Kill!" Cage bellowed with Larson and Heather joining in. Kyle whispered it, and Robin mock-glared at him. Pretty soon everyone was clapping and calling for the demise of the newbs.

"Beth says we *will* die horribly," Robin told Kyle.

He exhaled soberly. The moment for confessions had passed. "There is always that chance at a party of August's."

"Fifteen-minute penalty!" August said as the hooting died down.

"What?" Beth shrieked. "That's not fair!"

"I have spoken," August said grandly. "Ladies, keep your envelopes sealed until fifteen minutes has passed. The rest of you, begin!"

"Well, good luck," Robin said, moving away. Kyle had a crazy impulse to ask for a good-luck kiss, but that was all it was, an impulse, and he ripped open his envelope.

```
Tonight's the night!
Do or die!
In the fields of _ _ _ _ _ _ _
You will never lie.
```

Your prize: I know you got accepted at Cal
State Long Beach. My family has connections
with the athletic dept. and if you win, you
will get a general athletic scholarship—full
ride, my friend.

Kyle's heart sank. He read and reread the lines about the prize. Then he moved on, mentally and physically, going in search of Heather and her untouchable fields.

Cage and Morgan were together—the jock and the cheerleader, a matching set of athletes. That left Larson and Praveen. Weird combo.

He glanced over at Robin, who was standing with her two girlfriends. Beth must have told August he'd been accepted to Long Beach, the result being the scholarship prize. Beth was nearly as pale and sweaty as that girl singer in Maximum Volume. August had pretty much crushed her in front of all their friends. He wondered what had gone wrong between them. In the blink of an eye, your whole life could change.

He was proof of that.

The band ended their set just as he and Heather found each other, putting the pieces of their clue together:

Nine o'clock from Lacrosse's car,
when it comes to real, Kyle raises the bar.
Mirror, mirror on the wall,
who stole away the curtain call?

"What does that even mean?" Heather said nervously. "'Stole away the curtain call'?"

"Well, you do always get the leads in all the plays," Kyle said bluntly. Maybe he would like her more if she didn't *try* to be so ignorant.

She gave her blond mane a shake. "Because I deserve them."

Kyle just shrugged. That was what these friends were all about—lying even to themselves to get what they wanted.

"I do deserve them!" she cried.

As she sputtered and protested, he walked over to where he'd left his stuff and picked up a flashlight. The others scattered to the wind, the band taking a break. Stacy waved and laughed and wished them all happy hunting as Hiro, the drummer, gave himself a solo. Mick, the one who had almost been electrocuted, played along. But Drew the bassist stomped off by himself, using the same silk hankie he'd dabbed Stacy's forehead with to wipe the sweat off his own face.

Kyle led the way along the seawall to the parking lot. Everyone on the hunt had parked there—he knew all the cars. Fog spilled over his ankles like freshly poured milk. It seemed to crawl up the building hand over hand, an excellent cover if you wanted to hide and then jump out and scare the hell out of someone. August had never mounted a hunt at such a sprawling, remote location.

As they moved away from the warehouse, Kyle turned

on the flashlight, trying to ignore Heather, who couldn't seem to stop talking. She was driving him crazy.

If he traced a straight line to the left from his car, it stopped at the wooden dock on the other side of the warehouse. The dock looked like it was sliding down into the ocean. In the center, the rusted remains of a twelve-foot-wide conveyer belt lay in chunks inside two large grooves in the dock. He supposed the fishing boats had tied up alongside it, and then the fish had been taken off the boat and loaded onto the conveyer belt. From there, they must have gone straight into the warehouse.

"I'm cold," Heather said. "Can't we do this faster?"

"*We'll* try," he replied.

Toward the back of the warehouse, a spiral of weathered cement stairs was attached to the dock. They led down the side of a chalky cliff, then onto more gently sloping ground. The remains of a red-and-white parking barrier tilted at the head of a narrow, twisting road pointing like an arrow to the water's edge. Moonlight spilled onto a pitted cement ramp, a boat landing, he assumed, that sloped down and disappeared into the ocean waves.

"Do you see anything?"

He turned around impatiently and glanced up at Heather, who had been trailing behind him.

"Not yet. You can sit on the stairs and wait for me if you want to."

"Okay." She said it without a jot of apology.

So entitled.

As he was heading away from the buildings down toward the beach, the silvery tide splashing into inlets and cubbyholes of rock, he thought he heard someone calling his name. He paused and cautiously turned about, examining his surroundings. It definitely wasn't Heather, who was up on the stairs, busy examining her nails. Frowning, he stopped walking and listened.

On second thought, he didn't think it was his name after all.

It sounded like someone whispering *"Help."*

9

CANNERY ROW

Soap on a
row your

Robin blinked. That didn't seem like much of a clue.
Beth's envelope contained a piece of paper with the first
line and Thea's envelope had the second.

"That's *it*?" Thea shrieked as she took the envelope
from Beth and looked inside, tipping it upside down as
she shook it. They had run out of the warehouse as soon
as August told them their penalty was over, and now

they were brought up short. "Are they all going to be this hard?"

"We're already behind," Beth groaned. "I have no idea what this is supposed to mean."

"Row your *boat*," Robin suggested. "Maybe we're supposed to go down to the beach and find a boat or an oar or something like that."

"I think there's a path over that way," Beth said, gesturing ahead and to the right.

They walked shoulder to shoulder, listening to other kids hooting and hollering. The ground was too uneven to risk moving any faster. Robin could hear the sound of glass breaking somewhere out in the darkness.

"These people party pretty hard," she said. She'd seen the rows of glittering wine and liquor bottles in the factory, the large tub of ice and bottles of beer. If Beth was to be believed, Cage was on a steroid diet and the bass player in Maximum Volume was a major addict.

Kyle had stuck to water. That was pretty cool. Her dad had always called Kyle a straight shooter. He liked Kyle a lot. So did her mom. Whenever the team had come over for dinner, Kyle would help clean up. She imagined herself inviting him over next weekend for chicken enchiladas. Did he have a girlfriend? If he did, she wasn't at the party.

Beth was scanning everywhere, searching for clues, although Robin wasn't sure exactly what she was looking for. Robin didn't expect to find a boat up here. Beth was serious about winning this hunt, and Robin wondered what her prize would be should they win. She was a bit surprised at what Beth would win; apparently she wanted to get a letter of recommendation for Oberlin from August's dad, which was the prize listed on her clue paper. Robin had had no idea that Beth had picked out a college.

Thea was mostly studying her own feet, as if she was afraid she would step on a land mine or something. There was sufficient broken glass and debris on the ground to necessitate shuffling along with intense care. Tripping up here could mean a tetanus shot.

They reached the edge of the cliff and aimed their flashlights downward. Watery light pierced through the swirling fog, revealing patches of ice plant and the outlines of a tile roof. Beyond that was forest; below, the Pacific rushed and retreated in a syncopated rhythm.

"This path is practically vertical," Thea muttered. "This must be a false lead. August wouldn't make us go down there."

"Soap on a *rope*," Robin said triumphantly.

"Oh, yeah, duh, huh. You're right," Beth said happily. "So, we're looking for rope or a boat or something they have in common."

Thea moved back from the edge of the cliff and shifted her weight. "They both have four letters and an *O* for the second letter."

"And when we're playing Scrabble . . . ," Beth began.

"Be nice." Thea sounded hurt. She gave Robin her full attention. "What do *you* think?"

"Well, you tie a boat to a dock using a rope, don't you?" Robin said.

Thea brightened while Beth seemed to ponder this.

"So maybe we have to find a piece of rope that's tying up a boat, or at least by a boat. And boats are by the water. And the water is at the bottom of this vertical drop."

"And there you have the fine mind of Robin Brissett!" Beth cried.

"Which is down there in the depths of watery death," Robin added. "Thea does have a point."

"Oh my God, are you channeling Edgar Allan Poe or what? It will be fine." Beth took the first step off the cliff and down the path. "See, no slipping. No monsters. None at all."

Thea crossed her arms. "I'll wait up here."

"We all have to go," Beth insisted. "Or we'll be disqualified."

"He never said that." Thea hesitated. "He didn't, right, Robin?"

"He has spies," Beth countered.

"Who? What if we run into some stranger and we don't know if they're one of the spies or some child molester?"

"Oh my God, Thea," Beth said. "This is the real world, not some cheesy horror movie."

Thea frowned. "Or Jackson. What if Jackson shows?"

"He has no idea where you are," Beth said.

"But—"

"I have two words for you: *test answers.*" Beth turned to Robin with a devilish grin. "I mean, Thea dearest, *your* specific prize is a loaded credit card, and of course you and I will choose the limo for our team prize because the test answers are immoral. So, Mick Jagger's butt on the same leather as your butt."

Robin smiled to herself. Her prize would be coffee with Kyle. Kyle au lait.

"Your smile is freaky," Beth said. "Is it because you're fangirling on Mick Jagger?"

Robin smiled some more.

"*Robin,* stop it. You're acting all weird," Thea said.

"Ladies, we're wasting time," Beth said. "Thea, no one is going to try to kill us."

"Okay, *okay!*" Thea cried. "But if we die, don't say I didn't warn you."

"I'll go first," Robin volunteered. "We can put Thea in the middle so if someone attacks us from behind, they'll get Beth."

Beth made kissy noises at Robin. "I love you, too."

The loud wail of an electric guitar bounced off the buildings and arced overhead like a comet as they formed a line. Robin heard the distant *popa-popa-popa* of the generators.

This night is already pretty crazy, she thought. *I wonder how far these people will go to win this game.*

And then she began her descent.

CAGE'S RULE #1:

Winning is good; working for it is bad.

Morgan's clue card read:

> Taking someone else's measure
> Gives you such sadistic pleasure

Cage's page was a series of pictures:

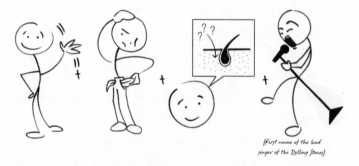

(First name of the lead singer of the Rolling Stones)

Cage took Morgan's clue—the poem—and held it below his. He considered various possible solutions, none of which made any sense. Then he swapped the two halves.

"I got nothing," he confessed.

"Me neither. I'm not sadistic. What's *that* about?"

It didn't make a whole lot of sense. This hunt was *hard*. He had half a mind to blow it off, get wasted, and see if Morgan wanted to hook up. He wasn't going to win—he was stumped by the first clue, and Morgan wasn't exactly a rocket scientist, either. But she was looking hot tonight.

Sizzling. He and Morgan had gone a couple of rounds at parties, but it had been a while.

They had wandered all over the cannery and were now lumbering across the parking lot. August's Porsche was so sick. Cage's family was well off, but they weren't rich like the DeYoungs. Cage drove a used Honda Accord. Not exactly a sexmobile, but he did okay.

Above the steep, weedy embankment ran the road they'd all taken to get here. They both saw the mouth of the cave at the same time, and as they approached, neon red lights shaped into capital Cs and Ms flashed on and off on either side of the entrance. Morgan stumbled backward and then they both started laughing.

"Guess this is our first stop," Morgan said.

"And our last," Cage said in a creepy stage whisper.

She batted his arm. "You're not funny."

The arrows went dark. Cautiously, Cage stared into the cave, then shined his flashlight into it. The maw of deep, black velvet devoured the light but shadows were moving around. August's holographs, the bodies in the coffins, and the bats in the factory all came to mind and he braced himself for something to jump out at them.

Morgan brushed up against him. He felt her body heat, smelled her recently applied perfume, and grinned to himself. Fear was an aphrodisiac, right? That was why teenagers liked to watch scary movies.

"Something is going to jump out at us," she said. "I just know it."

"Guaranteed." He waggled his eyebrows at her and moved closer, waiting for August's jack-in-the-box to scare her right into his waiting arms. "Something really horrifying and gross."

She pouted like a baby. "I can't believe August said I'm into sadistic pleasure or whatever. I am *so* going to kick his ass."

"Before or after you win an audition to become a Laker Girl?" Her prize for the win.

"After," she said dreamily.

Shapes came into view as they entered the cave. It was packed with stacks of wooden pallets, steel buckets, and random piles of junk. A lit camping lantern had been hidden behind a battered piece of metal adorned with a skull and crossbones.

There.

He hid a smile as he visually traced the outline of a figure propped against the cave wall to his right. It was about the same height as the writhing bodies in the coffins. He subtly eased her toward it so it could jerk or moan or whatever it was programmed to do. He could barely make it out in the dark but its head was hooded and it was wearing something long, like a duster. As he watched it, he was sure that it began to move, and he herded Morgan even closer to it, unable to hide his grin.

She was oblivious. Her attention was focused on the swaths of light her flashlight painted on their surroundings.

She ran the light against the back of the cave, then swept it upward.

At once, a dozen or so Barbie-style dolls dropped from the ceiling on spirals of red lights in clear plastic tubing. They were dressed like Callabrese High cheerleaders in green-and-yellow sweaters and pleated minis, and they chattered in high-pitched childlike voices. It was Alexa DeYoung's voice, and the words were spoken through racking sobs.

"I'm too fat, I'm too fat, I'm too fat."

Yodeling with terror, Morgan climbed up his body and clung to him. He grabbed one of the dolls and yanked it free of the tubing.

"I'm too fat I'm too fat I'm too fat—"

Morgan dug the doll out of his hand and threw it onto the ground.

"Okay, August! Whatever!" she shouted. She pulled two more dolls free and stomped on them. They kept yammering; Morgan wrapped her hands around another dangling doll body and pulled the head off. She ran forward, grabbing them and pulling them down as if they were tiny piñatas.

"What the hell?" Cage said, following her, stepping on fist-sized torsos and heads.

Then he came upon a small wooden table with a black velvet cushion on top. On the cushion was a very familiar cardboard box tied up like a present with a green measuring tape. And a small ceramic sea lion.

Cage's stomach clenched. His jaw tightened as his heart went into overdrive. His anger was nearly overpowering—a side effect, he had been warned, of what was in the box: it contained the same brand of anabolic steroids in the same dosage that he was using. He had never told anyone, not one person, that he was on steroids. Not even his coach.

But somehow Alexa DeYoung had found out. And she had threatened to tell the world unless he got her something to help her lose weight, fast. He had been shocked. Her wrists were sticklike, and her face gaunt. She sure as hell didn't need to drop any pounds.

She was trying to lose weight so she could become a cheerleader, he realized, looking from the box of steroids to the doll bodies to Morgan. That's why she was freaking out, too.

"So what did he leave for you?" Morgan snapped as she picked up the box. He grabbed it away from her. "Hey. What is it?"

"Nothing," he mumbled.

If his coach found out he was using, he'd kick him off the team. Coach always said that the players at Callabrese High played clean or they didn't play at all. Cage had told himself he'd take them for just one more game, then just for the season, but what about the college scouts?

He'd heard that collegiate coaches would look the other way, sure, but not if someone publicly denounced him before he even got accepted to a university. He'd be blackballed before he even got his chance to make his mark, hopefully go pro. He was a superstar at Callabrese, but high school was almost over. Who would he be without football?

I have to talk to August, he thought desperately. *Alone.*

He could feel the vein in his forehead throbbing in time with his accelerated heartbeat. At school they laughed and called him Hulk on the field, but they had no idea how accurate that nickname was. His strength and speed came from rage. It was a side effect that he usually kept under control.

Alexa must have told August that he got her some speed to help her lose weight. And now August was making him sweat.

All I did was get it for her, he thought, ripping the dangling measuring tape off the box and stuffing the steroids into the pocket of his letter jacket.

Morgan let go of him and picked up the sea lion. "Alexa collected sea lions," she said. "This is weird."

Then she crossed her arms over her chest and stomped on the nearest chattering doll.

Obviously he wasn't the only one standing there with a guilty secret.

"Oh my God, she was so uncoordinated," Morgan said in a rush. "I don't know why she even tried out for the squad. She had to *see* what a klutz she was."

"Shit, Morgan," he said as they gave each other a long, hard look.

Confessing.

"What was I supposed to say to her? 'Alexa, you're too short and too weird to be a cheerleader'? So I told her what we always tell girls we don't want. What's he going to do about it? He can't do anything. Because I didn't *do* anything."

Cage was rooted to the spot. "Morgan," he said thickly, feeling both dizzy and sick, the blood roaring in his ears. It sounded like the world was crashing down around him. "I have to talk to August."

"What a crummy trick," she said. "Lure us all here for one last major party, fool us into playing for big prizes, and then dis us. I didn't do anything illegal."

But I did. He was reeling. They say sometimes you just *know* things. And he had a funny feeling that his life was over.

From out of the dark, the figure in the hood and duster shot toward them, a baseball bat in his gloved hand. He slammed it against the back of Cage's skull. The impact spun Cage around just as his attacker swung it again, hard, against his face. His nose broke and he grunted as he staggered backward.

Morgan tried to run, but the figure grabbed her, yanking her head back by her hair and forcing her into an arch, but finally he let go. She went sprawling.

The bat came across Cage's knees, then his face again. All Cage was, was pain. The force kept coming down and down and down.

August, he immediately thought. *God, stop.* He couldn't speak.

The bat came down again.

Why? he thought. But he knew why. He knew several reasons why:

His last image was of Alexa at the party. Of her crying and saying, "I need to go home. Can you take me home?"

And he hadn't. Not just blowing her off, but laughing at her, too. Saying, "C'mon, Alexa, just call your private helicopter or whatever. Or your brother. That's why you don't get invited to our parties. Because you can't even get from point A to point B in a shitty little town like this."

He never saw her alive again.

I didn't even really know her, he tried to tell the person in the ski mask. The person he assumed was August.

I'm sorry. I'm so sorry.

Then he wasn't sorry anymore.

He was dead.

MORGAN'S RULE #1:

Do what it takes to stay on top.

The masked figure turned on Morgan. Pain skittered through her body as she tried to move. He pried her mouth open and stuffed something into it that was thin and pliant and tasted like plastic.

He picked her up and flung her over his shoulder, trapping her arms against her sides. She tried to spit out the plastic but it was stuck. She moved her head from side to side, fighting to catch the plastic on his coat and work it loose from her mouth. It remained lodged in her throat.

He carried her deep into the cave, skirting piles of junk. He seemed to know exactly where he was going, where he was taking her: away from Cage, and escape.

Cage, be alive, she pleaded. *Save me.*

They went down at an angle, descending a spiral of cement stairs surrounded by rock. She felt like she was doing cartwheels as she spun dizzily, gagging and sucking air through her nose.

They ended up in some kind of room. Dusty crates and barrels were stacked, broken alcohol bottles strewn all over the place. He carried her through the room and into a small, narrow tunnel. It twisted and turned as she drifted in and out of consciousness.

When she came to, she heard crashing waves, the smell of the sea, blood, and an odor that reminded her of cars. He flopped her down in the darkness. A light flared on and all she saw was a coat, a hood, and gloves.

Morgan could only manage a dry, husky retch. The ski mask loomed over her. The gloved hand reached into her mouth, pulling out the plastic and automatically clamping his hand over it, hard. She got out one ragged, hoarse shriek, but the hand muffled it. A fist slammed against the left side of her head and her skull clanged like a gong.

Everything went black, and then yellow dots bubbled and popped behind her eyelids.

The hand moved away.

"Help," she ground out. Her voice sounded like she had eaten broken glass. "Help me!"

"Tell me you know why," a voice whispered gruffly over the roar of the ocean, as if he were trying to disguise who he was. But wasn't it too late for that?

"I'm sorry." Tears ran down her face. "I *did* say she was too fat. And . . . and I *did* lie about the vote."

The blank black hood moved closer, the fabric brushing against her nose. She could smell something sweet. She began to panic. What was that smell?

What did it matter? It didn't matter. She had to concentrate on things that mattered. On getting out of this alive.

He stayed where he was, and her mind darted back to what she had been saying. Her confession. He must already know, but maybe he wanted her to admit everything and ask for his forgiveness. If she begged him, promised him she would make up for it, then maybe all this would stop.

He tapped the other side of her head and she sobbed, a jolt of pain coursing through her as a painful reminder of how hard he had hit her.

"The vote," her attacker whispered.

"Okay," she said, gasping. "Okay, whatever you want."

"Tell me."

"Alexa . . . ," Morgan sobbed, "tried out for j-junior varsity cheer when she came to Callabrese."

The masked head nodded. So far, so good.

Morgan cried harder. He raised his fist and a shudder went through her entire body. "I got everyone to say that she was too fat but that she could try again in the fall. She came back." She spoke in a rush, almost babbling. She would tell him anything he wanted to know. She would tell him what she knew about Heather and her teacher if he wanted that, too.

"She was pretty g-good. I didn't expect it."

Her attacker waited for her to go on. When she heaved and panted, he hit her again. Her entire body convulsed.

He waited.

"Then w-we voted on all the girls who tried out." She tasted blood. Oh God, blood was streaming all over her face. Her left ear was still ringing. She could barely hear herself speaking. "I counted the votes alone. The other cheerleaders had voted Alexa in. But I lied and told them she didn't make it."

The hood nodded encouragingly. She burst into tears and began to hiccup with fresh sobs.

"We all had a terrible fight. But then she stopped coming to Callabrese, and it didn't matter."

"It didn't matter?" he whispered.

"You can't be a cheerleader for a school you don't go to!" she cried desperately. Snot ran down her face. "Oh, please, August, please let me go. I won't tell anyone you did this. I'll never tell."

The hood moved out of her field of vision. Receding

footfalls echoed in the tunnel, and tears and blood and mucus made her gag as she prayed that he was leaving, letting her live.

"She didn't die because she didn't get to be a cheerleader," she said. Then she shut her eyes. That was a terrible thing to say.

The wrong thing to say.

The footfalls stopped abruptly. She sucked in her breath, held it. She heard him walking back toward her.

Coming closer.

He jerked her head sideways, exposing her right ear, and bent down low.

"You're a liar. All you do is lie. This time, you won't get away with it."

He clamped her nostrils shut with his other hand and pushed down hard on her mouth.

The roar of the waves.

The roar in her head.

The roar of the crowd in the stands at her last football game washed over her as Morgan drifted far, far away.

10

ROLLING THE DICE

THEA'S RULE #2:

If you aren't strong,

find someone who is.

"You guys, something touched me!" Thea cried, twisting right. Her elbow collided with something hard.

"Thea, Thea, Thea, *ow,*" Beth said, rubbing her chin. She waved her flashlight at the sky and a white-winged moth circled it. Probably the same moth that had tickled Thea's cheek. "Good Lord, have you considered medication? Is this post-traumatic Jackson disorder?"

Thea clamped her jaw shut so she wouldn't yell at Beth for making jokes at her expense when she was so scared. They were only halfway down the stupid cliff, and it was steep and dark. It was Jackson plus this whole creepy night.

She didn't like being trapped out here in the middle of no-where with no car and no cell.

They inched down the rest of the way. As they reached the bottom of the trail, Thea felt her ankle turn and sucked in her breath. She abruptly stopped, causing Beth to bump right into her.

"What's wrong *now*?" Beth asked.

"Are you okay?" said Robin, turning around to face her.

"Perfecta." Thea flashed them a very weak half smile, even though she didn't want to. Robin was always so nice. But Beth had turned into such a major bitch.

"Well, let's start looking," Beth said.

Robin and Beth took off toward the breakers, leaving Thea alone in the dark, their flashlight beams bobbing up and down farther and farther away. She waved her flash-light back up at the trail. If Thea knew she could make it back by herself, she would already be gone. But it was so steep she was afraid she'd get dizzy and fall.

"Wait!" she croaked as she chased after the two girls. She wrenched her ankle again but forced herself to keep going.

Robin and Beth stood beside a couple of beached row-boats riddled with rusty holes. It looked as if someone had shot at them with a machine gun.

"Look at what someone's written on this one," Robin said, playing her light over some spray-painted words:

"'Rub-a-dub-dub, three men in a tub,'" Beth read.

"And what better place to have soap than in a tub?" Robin asked triumphantly. "Check *this* out."

She and Beth focused their flashlight beams on the rope that was resting in the bottom of the boat. It was thick, long, and coiled like a snake ready to strike, and for some reason Thea shivered when she saw it.

"Don't touch it," she murmured.

Neither of the others seemed to hear her, or if they did, they didn't care. They hauled the rope out.

"The envelope!" Beth shrieked, jabbing both forefingers machine-gun style at the white rectangle. It was so white it nearly glowed.

"Remember, we can't open it until we take this back to the party," Robin cautioned.

"Gross. It's wet." Beth turned and wiped her hands on Robin's jeans.

"Not on the bomber jacket, please. You should have worn scavenger-hunt clothes," Robin teased, clearly in a better mood now that they'd found their object.

"How did you know?" Thea blurted.

"Know what?" Robin asked as Beth bundled the rope in her arms. "Blech, you're right. It is wet."

"Told you," Beth said.

"How did you know there'd be boats? You couldn't have seen them from where we were. But you came straight here."

Robin shrugged. "Lucky hunch. Now help us carry this thing. We've got to get it back to August so we can move on to our next clue."

Thea gathered up a section of the slimy rope, still trying to parse how Robin had zoomed in on it so fast. What she didn't want to say was that she hadn't made any of the connections Robin had. She was the one flunking physics. *And* trig. Maybe she was just stupid. She tried to imagine going through life as a stupid person and all her anxiety flooded back over her. Her ankle hurt. Not only did she have to climb up that narrow trail, but she also had to do it lugging this rope.

But there was no way Beth and Robin could be convinced to give up now. Even she could see that.

"Okay, let's do this!" Robin said, and Thea trudged through the sand, keeping her fingers crossed that they could barrel through all the other clues just as fast and get this dumb hunt over with. She still had hopes that a certain guy might be into sneaking off. Except if Beth found out, and it got around . . .

"If you ever cheat on me, I will kill you," Jackson had once promised her. He wasn't in one of his bad moods when he said it, either. He had stared her right in the eyes and said it as though he was saying something sweet.

And right there was proof that she was very, very stupid indeed.

AUGUST'S RULE #2:

No one is worthy of trust.

The band's lead singer was falling-down drunk.

"I'm sick," she moaned, her voice echoing around the room. August pressed a button on his black box sound mixer and the little robot bats in the rafters squeed in response. She just stared upward as though mesmerized. It was so pathetic it slightly took him aback.

Larson and Praveen arrived, Praveen carrying a black sweater decorated with little white picture-frame shapes. By the looks of Larson's wrinkled brow and faint smile, it was obvious that he was pleased they had found their object but was confused by Praveen's skittishness. She was scratching her arms and chest the way she did whenever she was nervous. Beth had told him that Praveen was rumored to have some icky skin condition, but that she had never seen any blotches, bumps, or anything else on Praveen's smooth, dark brown skin. Beth said Praveen was a neurotic hypochondriac.

August didn't know for certain but was absolutely positive that she was a neurotic kleptomaniac. She stole things just for the thrill, or for some other whacked-out need her twisted psyche required.

How far will they go? August wondered. *How much will they put up with to get what they have coming?*

Praveen held out the sweater and he gestured to one of the coffins containing an undulating corpse. Over the coffin read TEAM PRAVEEN AND LARSON. He had put the signs up after the teams had formed and run off into the night. He was going to ask the band to help, but they'd scattered during the break he'd given them. You'd think for the money he was paying they'd offer to pitch in. But no, they were rock stars. Or so they thought. August predicted an extremely short career trajectory for Maximum Volume.

Praveen laid the sweater down in front of the coffin like an offering to the gods, and Larson's arm brushed against hers as he detached the white envelope.

Larson usually got what he wanted, but not tonight. August had seen to that. Larson was as horny as usual, and for Larson, any girl would do. There was no way Praveen was going to hook up with him, not if Beth's intel that she was secretly dating someone was correct. And August would thwart Beth every way he could to keep her from having her heart's desire.

"Before you read your next clue, you have to decide Truth or Dare," August reminded them.

"Dare," they both said, and August smirked. He'd expected that. They had a lot to hide. He reached into his trench coat pocket and held out a black envelope. Larson took it and ripped it open as Praveen stood on tiptoe to read over his shoulder.

"What the hell is this?" Larson asked.

August shrugged. "What does it say?"

"It says we need to stand on either side of the pipe on the north wall, hold hands around it, and close our eyes for a spellbinding surprise."

"Then I suggest you do that," August said, before sipping his beer.

"How are we supposed to know which wall is north?" Praveen asked.

August jerked a thumb toward the door. "The ocean's right outside there. So that's west."

Without a word the two of them walked over to the north wall where a massive pipe extended from the ceiling and disappeared into the cement ground. There was barely enough clearance between it and the wall for Larson to slip his hand around it so he could grasp Praveen's.

"This is ridiculous," she hissed.

"Yeah, but the sooner we do it, the sooner we can win the hunt," Larson said.

"Close your eyes," August told them. "And don't open them until I tell you to."

Once he was sure they had their eyes closed, he moved soundlessly toward them, pausing at a box of props. He would have to be fast, but that wasn't a problem.

"Okay, guys, you're doing great," he said, distracting them with the sound of his voice.

"How long do we have to stay like this?" Praveen asked.

"That depends on you." August lifted a pair of hand-cuffs. He took careful aim and then slapped one on each of their wrists resting on the far side of the pipe.

He leaped backward out of reach as they both opened their eyes, shouting and jerking their arms away from the pipe.

With their hands cuffed together between the pipe and the wall, they were going nowhere.

"What the hell, August?" Praveen said.

August pulled the key to the handcuffs from his pocket. "You can get out any time you want and continue your hunt. If one of you will admit to why you deserve to be hand-cuffed for real, I'll give you this key and you can carry on."

Praveen flailed for the key, but all she succeeded in doing was pulling Larson's arm farther through the narrow space between the pipe and the wall.

"Praveen, stop," Larson barked at her. "You're about to wrench my arm out of the socket."

"Shut up, Larson," she said. "August, this isn't funny."

August heard the worry in her voice. He loved it.

"Not really meant to be, Praveen," he said.

"What are you *doing*?" She clenched her jaw and tried to scratch the arm behind the pipe. Then her chest. She couldn't reach. He couldn't help his grin. He hadn't planned on thwarting her loony-tunes tic, but it was great to see her squirm, *literally*.

"Just admit to something you've done that would get you arrested and I'll let you go."

"I've never done anything like that," she said, the guilt on her face so obvious that he had to laugh. Her brows shot up.

And then she looked scared, and his insides churned.

Do you have any idea how scared she was that night at the party? And then she went to find her sweater on the bed in the guest room? And it wasn't there?

The door flew open and Kyle came in with one arm

around Heather's shoulders, the other cradling a massive crowbar against his chest. Heather was hunched over, the fingers of her right hand wrapped with a couple of tissues. August could see blood seeping through and felt a glimmer of satisfaction. In her other hand she was holding a cute felt sea lion.

"There," August said, pointing to the coffin next to Praveen and Larson's. TEAM KYLE AND HEATHER, read their sign. Kyle set the crowbar down with a clunk and yanked free the bright white envelope. Then he noticed the little drama in progress and froze.

"Are we interrupting?" Kyle asked.

August shook his head. "One of them has to confess to committing a crime. You're just in time to watch them bare their souls."

Kyle looked askance at August as he checked Heather's finger. "Okay, that sounds a bit . . . extreme."

"Oh my God. What did you two do?" Heather asked excitedly. She sucked on her bleeding fingertips.

"Nothing!" Praveen jerked her arm again.

"Ow!" Larson bellowed. "Shit, Praveen, stop it!"

August could see the panic in Praveen's eyes. Her big secret would come out. One of them, anyway. The one that mattered to him.

The one that had mattered to Alexa.

Then Larson let out a surprised guffaw. "Hey, wait. Praveen, it's okay. I've got this."

August was ready to call his bluff. "Oh, ready to confess your sins so soon?"

Larson gave his glossy brown hair a shake. "Sure, this one's easy. I deserve to be arrested because I'm underage and yet I brought alcohol to this party, I'm drinking it, and I'm corrupting my fellow youth. So call the cops on me."

August blinked, stunned at his own stupidity that he hadn't thought of that. It was so obvious. Not humiliating or degrading at all.

"Well played," he grumbled, tossing him the keys. Larson snatched them out of the air. Moments later he and Praveen were free. Larson tore open the white envelope and unfolded the piece of paper inside. Praveen rubbed her wrists and gave her left forearm a good, long scratch as she read along with him. August wondered if she wore long sleeves because she had scratched herself to shreds.

"What does this even mean?" Praveen said, frowning at August as she finished reading the clue.

August remained impassive. "I guess you'll have to find out."

"What I should do is quit," she said. "Go home."

"Or maybe you should just play along," he said. "Confession is good for the soul. Test answers are good for college. By the way," he added, "there are some things in the pockets of that sweater."

Praveen gave him a look, then picked up the sweater,

stuffing her hand first in one pocket, and then the other. She pulled out a wadded-up piece of paper and a pair of earrings.

Sea lion earrings.

He waited. So did she. Alexa must not have shared her sea lion fetish with these people. He'd have to elaborate later, once the hunt was over, about why he had parceled them out to everyone.

"Just put them back for now," he said. "But give Larson the piece of paper and keep looking."

She did. Larson worked at the scrap of notebook paper like he was unfolding an origami Yoda. August knew that printed on the paper were the area code and first three digits of Alexa's cell phone number.

"I don't know what this is," Larson said, turning it over, then frowning in puzzlement as he gazed expectantly at August. August wasn't going to help him out.

Figures, August thought.

And Praveen didn't even recognize the sweater.

He could feel the fury pulsing through his bloodstream, pounding in his heart. These thickheaded morons. They didn't even get it. He'd been more blunt with Cage and Morgan.

"We already did the dare," Larson said. "We should get to move on."

"Oh yes, it's always about what you should get," August said. *And you will definitely get what's coming to you.* He waved toward the door. "Be my guest."

Flashing him dirty looks, Larson and Praveen left the

room, slamming the door shut behind them. August turned his attention to Kyle.

"I'm assuming since there's an envelope, this thing is what you meant?" Kyle asked, indicating the crowbar. "We wouldn't want to be accused of cheating."

"That's your first object. No cheating on *your* part, Kyle. Not ever," August said with a sigh. He picked up his clipboard and opened his spreadsheet. It was okay. He had lost that round, but he would eventually have his revenge.

"There was a mirror, too, right?" he said.

"Yes," Heather said. "It scared me half to death when Kyle's flashlight hit it. I made him break it. Then I found this little plushie behind it."

"That's seven years bad luck," August said.

"I've already had my bad luck," said Kyle, "so I guess it's on you, Heather."

August didn't know what Kyle was referring to. What bad luck had Kyle Thomas possibly endured? Getting paired up with Heather? He gestured to Heather's fingers.

"You have blood on your hands," he said.

"Yeah, no kidding," Heather snapped.

"So, Truth or Dare?"

Kyle said truth at the same time that Heather said dare. Kyle deferred to Heather, and August handed her a black envelope.

"We're supposed to act out a brief Shakespeare-inspired scene," she announced. "Now?" She frowned. "There's no audience."

"Do you ever really need one?" August asked her. "Isn't all the world a stage?"

"Whatever." She handed a page to Kyle and kept one for herself. "You have the first line."

Kyle cleared his throat and began.

"But soft! What light through yonder window breaks? It is the East, and Juliet is the sun! Arise, fair sun, and kill the envious moon, who is already sick and pale with grief that thou her maid art far more fair than she."

"Ay me," Heather said with zero inflection.

This is for you, Lex, August thought.

In the beginning of sophomore year, Alexa had decided to try out for a part in the school play. It was *The Tempest.* The drama teacher, Mr. Riker, had told her she'd nailed her first audition for the part of Ariel, the island sprite who made all the magic happen. She'd basked in his praise, chattering to August about costumes and rehearsals.

But in the second round of tryouts, she suddenly wasn't good enough for anything, not even as an extra. She had been crushed, bewildered. She'd cried all night.

It was not until after she'd died that August got the 411 on what had happened:

Heather. Just a freshman, like August, she was also up for the role of Ariel. Heather had gone to Mr. Riker and flirted and teased and gotten exactly what she wanted. She also convinced Mr. Riker that tiny little Alexa would be a distraction in any other part, and so Alexa was out.

Alexa had never tried out for anything again.

"She speaks. O, speak again, bright angel!"

August was so angry that he wasn't really even enjoying his revenge. It wasn't enough. It would never be enough.

"O, Romeo, Romeo! Wherefore art thou Romeo? Deny thy . . . boss?" Heather said, stumbling over the change to the text. She shook her head and continued. *"And refuse thy . . . profession! Or, if thou wilt not, be but sworn my love, and I'll no longer be your student."*

Heather put down the page, rage and fear warring across her features.

Kyle hesitated, glancing at her, but then gamely continued. *"Shall I hear more, or shall I speak at this?"*

Heather stood as still as a statue.

"You have to finish your scene," August said. "Or . . . no casting agent. No ingénue role. And that's what you live for, isn't it?"

"We're almost done," Kyle said softly.

For a moment August didn't think she would finish. Maybe a shred of decency lurked inside that vapid blond head. He didn't want her to have any decency. It would be much harder to hate her then.

" 'Tis but thy profession that is my enemy. Thou art thyself, though not a teacher. O, be some other name! What's in a name? That which we call a rose by any other name would smell as sweet."

"Whoa," Kyle said as she tore up her page and threw the pieces to the floor.

"Happy? Happy now, August?" Her voice cracked.

He had no idea why he felt a pang of remorse. He really, truly hated her. *She's an actress,* he reminded himself. *She goes for emotion. She knows how to play people as well as Beth.*

"Bravo!" August cried, clapping his hands.

"Moving right along," Kyle said, clearly trying to smooth things over. He ripped open their next envelope and read the clue. When he was finished, he tsked. "You outsmarted yourself this time. I know what this is."

"Don't count on it," August said.

Then Beth, Thea, and Robin burst into the warehouse. Flirtatious energy zinged between Kyle and party-crasher Robin as they caught sight of each other. August's heart constricted. He didn't want to see nice people being happy. He needed to keep his rage hot so he could follow through with his plans.

"You know what, Kyle?" Heather said. "I'm done. This party sucks." Her big baby blues glittered. That was more like it.

"No, wait, Heather. I've already figured out our next object. It's a gas can," Kyle said.

August hid his surprise. Kyle was on the nose. Larson had slipped through his dare, and it had taken Kyle all of ten seconds to decipher his clue. He had underestimated these people. Again.

"A gas can that we will try to find first," Beth declared.

"That's cheating," Robin reminded her.

"Well, I'm not looking for it," Heather said.

She stomped over to where the girls had set their purses down and grabbed one. Unzipping it, she began to dig inside her bag for something, stopped, and exhaled loudly. August figured she was looking for her keys and that she just remembered she'd driven there with Morgan. It was difficult to make a grand exit when your ride was nowhere to be seen. Swearing under her breath, she rezipped her purse, grabbed a bottle of red wine and a lantern off one of the tables, and disappeared down the hall stage right.

"Nice rope," Kyle said. "I love what you've done with it."

August registered the surprise on the faces of the three penalty babes as they looked to where Kyle was pointing. The end of the rope was fashioned into a hangman's noose. A nice detail, if he did say so himself.

"Morbid," Robin said.

"All the better to lasso a gas can with, my pretty," Beth said.

"Or hang it high," Kyle shot back, smiling again at Robin before he left.

11

HANGMAN

HEATHER'S RULE #1:

Do as Mother says.

Halfway down the hall, Heather took a slug of wine and reconsidered her decision to bail out of the scavenger hunt. The TV pilot she had said she was in? A total lie. She had nothing going on career-wise. Everything she auditioned for wound up a dead end. Her mother was pissed and pushing her harder than ever. She *would* make Heather famous, and Heather *would* do whatever she said. Or else.

Heather wasn't eager to find out what "or else" actually meant. At the moment, though, it weighed heavily on her mind as she pondered her mother's reaction if she discovered the truth.

Heather was in trouble. Big trouble.

I shouldn't be drinking this, she thought. Clutching the

wine bottle to her chest, she turned off the lantern so that they wouldn't see her coming and hung a U-turn back down the hall. From the safety of the shadows, she searched for Kyle and realized with a pang that he had left.

The three girls were still dragging the very long, heavy rope across the floor. They reminded her of sailors on a pirate ship. August pointed to a sign he had placed over one of the coffins that read PENALTY BABES. Heather noted the hangman's knot at the end of the rope and blew air out of her cheeks. August's hunts were always edgy, but tonight that edge was *sharp*.

She was a jittery mess, all her emotions about to spill out over her barely maintained surface tension. She hadn't realized that so many people knew about Mr. Riker. But they didn't know the worst part—her deepest darkest secret.

She hung back as August approached the trio of girls, admiring their handiwork. He was holding a little black box in his hand and as he waggled a joystick, the moldering corpse in the girls' coffin shifted around like it was trying to get comfortable.

"August, you need to make us do our Truth or Dare so we can go get our next thing," Thea prodded him sharply as she stepped away from the coffin and glanced fearfully upward at the screeching bats.

From her vantage point, Heather could see an expression of vicious glee sweep across August's face, the light from the lanterns lending him a positively demonic cast.

She took another swallow of wine. He was freaking her out. He'd teased hard at these hunts before, but he'd never been mean. This was a new August. Or was she finally just now seeing the real one?

"Okay, so decide, Truth or Dare," August challenged the girls.

Beth looked petrified. Then Robin Brissett stepped forward. "I'll do it. Truth."

"Sorry, Robin, but you're just along for the ride." August waved her off dismissively. "It's up to Thea and Beth."

"Dare," Thea and Beth said simultaneously.

August nodded. "As I expected." He held out a black envelope. "Here you go."

Thea took it while Beth sucked in a deep breath. Heather shot daggers at Beth Breckenridge Bitch the First. She had no idea how Beth had learned about Mr. Riker, but she had no doubt that Beth was the one who had spread it around.

"We're the third ones back with an item?" Robin asked, studying the coffins.

"Yes, and it's amazing how fast you're catching up. That fifteen-minute delay in your start clearly wasn't long enough," August told her.

Robin was still busy taking inventory, though.

"Rope, crowbar, a gas can on the way. Except for the sweater, aren't these all very . . . I don't know, Colonel Mustard–like?" she asked.

"Like Clue," Beth said with false brightness. Thea

struggled to rip open the envelope. Beth reached out to take it from her but Thea frowned and shook her head, giving it another go. "You know, August, Robin is a killer gamer."

Robin looked shocked and frowned at Beth, who ignored her and kept smiling at August.

"Really," August said, inclining his head in Robin's direction. "You have hidden depths, Ms. Brissett."

Robin flashed Beth a dirty look. "Not so much. But I do play Clue."

Thea smiled at a satisfying rip and pulled out a page from the envelope.

"Welcome to the Second Act of Cheater Theater," Thea read. *"You'll feel ever so much better if you get things off your chest. So your choice: take off your tops or your bottoms, and then tell us the person you've most recently cheated out of something, and how."*

Beth paled. *"August."* Her voice was strangled.

Heather shrugged. That wasn't so mean. It was vintage scavenger hunt. And she herself had stripped down to less than that on dares.

"That's not a dare," Robin said. "That's a truth."

"Excuse me?" August cocked his head.

Robin crossed her arms. "You're asking them to tell you something, not do something." She gestured dismissively with her hand. "Taking off their clothes isn't the main point. Confessing is."

"It's my hunt," he said.

"You're breaking your own rules," she shot back. "*You're* cheating."

Heather snorted as August flushed. Look at that— Albino Man was *pink*. And *pissed*.

"Fine," he snapped. "Then strip down to your underwear and run a lap around the warehouse." His look included Robin, and she shook her head.

"I'm just along for the ride," she said firmly.

Heather almost whooped. *Robin, you have got a pair on you!*

She wished she could stand up to her mother like Robin was standing up to August but that was unthinkable.

August locked gazes with Robin. Neither blinked. In spite of everything, Heather giggled. Robin turned her head in Heather's direction and Heather backed a few steps down the hall. At this point she was feeling a little stalkerish; she did not need to watch other girls strip to their undies. She spared a couple drops of pity for Thea because it was so cold and wet outside, but none for Beth. If there was any justice, Beth would fall off the cliffs, hit every rock with her face on the way down, and drown in the ocean, where sharks would devour her conniving flesh.

With Kyle gone, she didn't see much point in letting August know she had started to weaken in her resolve not to play. She defiantly carried her wine bottle back down the hall and flicked her lantern back on. Maybe there were objects hidden back here that she could snag and hide to screw up the other players. Maybe that would help Kyle out. He was a nice guy. He'd do better in the hunt on his own. And if he won, maybe she'd still win, too.

There were rooms upon rooms of junk—piles of old ledger books, chains, hooks, and serrated knives. A rectangular room was crammed with bed frames on wheels, metal cabinets, and mirrors covered with jade-green mold. Why did they need a hospital at a cannery? Gross.

She heard Hiro Yamamoto drumming, and she smiled faintly. Maximum Volume was a great band. They were going all the way to the top. Just like her.

At least, just like she should be.

Her stomach shifted uneasily and she pressed a hand over it. She was four weeks pregnant and desperately trying to figure out what to do about it. The simplest thing would be to have an abortion, but she knew there were risks involved with those, and she wasn't sure she wanted to do that to her body. The thought of it made her queasy. Then again, giving the baby up for adoption meant actually having to carry it nearly a whole year and getting fat in the process. She couldn't afford the time or the pounds. Plus, she could get stretch marks.

And could she really do either of those things? Get rid of it with an operation? Give it to someone else? Wouldn't Mr. Riker have to know if she did that?

She sniffled a little, scared, and as mad at herself as she was with Mr. Riker. They'd flirted for *years*. The looks, the sighs, the occasional brush of his hand against hers.

All his promises to help her make it in Hollywood.

The people he claimed to know. The auditions he'd set up for her. For three years, he had kept telling her it was only a matter of time. Freshman year, he'd said she was at an awkward age, too old for the little-kid parts, a little too young for the ingénue roles. She'd reminded him that Miley Cyrus had been fourteen when she'd booked *Hannah Montana*, but he had countered that Miley Cyrus's dad was famous. Then sophomore year he said she had such a unique look that casting directors were having trouble deciding how to "position her." He said he wished he'd known "back then" that the DeYoungs were rich. That could have been "a big help." *For who?* she wanted to ask him, but she was afraid to.

Then this year, junior year, he'd started talking about her going to college and majoring in theater. Just in case Hollywood "didn't click right away."

But she didn't want to go to college. She wanted to go to L.A. She wanted to have a movie deal that she had to skip high school graduation for, like a real kid actor.

Her mother was always on her. She said Heather needed more voice lessons. Needed more coaching. She kept telling Heather that she had refinanced the house to give her only child everything she needed to become a star. So what was Heather doing to make that happen?

"I want a return on my investment," her mom said over and over. "I mean, honey, really, are you serious about this?"

Heather tried to defend herself, but it was hard when

everything her mom said was what she was thinking herself. *Was* she serious?

Then they had a huge fight and she'd slammed into Mr. Riker's office and informed him that she was quitting acting. No more auditions, no more plays, nothing. But the moment she said it, she started breaking down. That wasn't really what she had planned to tell him at all. She didn't want to quit. It was like she was speaking lines written by someone else. She kept crying and trembling and she really, really wanted him to shut her up and tell her that he'd just gotten a call from one of his director friends and she was now able to audition for a big-budget movie. To know that all the wishing was over.

And he did stop her. With a kiss, their first *ever*, even though she had fantasized about kissing him for years. He was as handsome as any movie star; when he led her drama class through their creative movement exercises, all the straight girls and the gay guys fanned themselves because he was so hot.

His kiss burned her alive. It immolated her world.

And when it was over, he had folded her in his arms and called her his angel, explaining that while he would always love her and support her career, it would be bad for her image to have a boyfriend as old as he was. He would be thrown in jail. They had a real love, yes, but it could never be more than it was now. This one time.

Except for the second time. And the third. And all the

others. She was irresistible, he told her. He couldn't stay away. He loved her so much.

For a while she had bought it. She had actually believed him.

Until she'd seen him with his real girlfriend at the Starbucks on Vineland. Holding hands. Gazing into each other's eyes. Feeding each other pieces of a flakey, buttery croissant.

All the softness inside her turned to stone. She thought of all the things she'd done to make her mark that had hardened her, sharpening her ambition with a diamondlike precision: getting rid of the competition, talking him into choosing the plays that her mom said worked for her . . .

In the filthy warehouse out in the middle of nowhere, Heather wanted to throw up. Her mother was going to kill her once Heather told her she was pregnant. She could never know it was Mr. Riker. Being knocked up by her drama teacher was not the kind of fame Heather's mother was looking for. Besides, scandal was fleeting.

Stardom was forever.

Heather hadn't told Mr. Riker, either. But *God,* what if someone else knew? What if Beth knew and he found out from her?

How could she know? Heather reminded herself. But Beth knew everything.

She heard someone run into something behind her and curse quietly.

"Hello?" she called, lifting her lantern.

Hiro Yamamoto blinked in the sudden light. A white T-shirt was stretched across a molded set of pecs, and tight jeans accentuated narrow hips. Hiro had the makings of a rock god. He was even hotter than Mr. Riker.

"Hey," he said, coming up short.

"I was listening to you drumming," she said. "You're really good."

He gave her a little bow. "The drummer never gets the love. It's always the lead guitar."

"You're a lot cuter than Mick," she said.

"Don't let Mick hear you say that." He laced his fingers, stretching his arms. "August said we won't be playing again for a while yet. This is a weird gig, even for us. Everyone taking off all the time."

She remembered that he'd been on the stage when she'd thrown her tantrum. "I hope you got paid up front," she said, even though she had no reason to believe that August would cheat them. He was so into his integrity tonight. Jerk.

Hiro got a funny look on his face and rolled his shoulders. "I'm sure he's good for it." He stepped into the room. "I was just looking around."

She looked more closely at him and felt a familiar heat at the base of her spine. Six-pack, and a drummer, on his way to the top. Getting together was half the reason everyone came to these parties. It wasn't like it *mattered* anymore. She could do it if she felt like it. The heat fanned outward, and she smoothed her hair with her free hand.

121

"So, what are *you* doing back here?" he asked. "Hiding?"

She set her lantern down so that the light bounced off the ceiling, wrapping them both in a muted, flattering glow. "I needed to take a moment away from everyone. I have this neck ache," she said, stealing the idea from the way he cricked his own neck and rolled his shoulders. "I've had it all night and I can't even think straight. I pulled something."

"Oh? I get a lot of those," he said. "Drumming." He held out his hands, an offer, and she turned around. Lifting waves of blond hair off her neck for him, she licked her lips and took a slow breath. His hands dipped lightly against her skin as he began kneading her neck and upper back.

"That's so nice," she said, rolling her head, daydreaming about being in Hollywood together, the actress and the rock star. The classic story. It could happen. People who weren't on her career path had no idea of how likely it actually was.

Hiro moved in closer, his body heat bathing her in toasty goodness. Then he kissed the flare of her jaw beneath her left earlobe, his breath tickling the inside of her ear.

I'm going to do this, she thought, turning around to face him. As his lips met hers, a new thought suddenly occurred to her. She could claim he was the father. Young, impassioned artists in love, rocketing to the top together in Los Angeles sounded much better than the truth.

As his kiss deepened and his arms tightened around her, she realized that this could work out really well for her.

"Hey," he murmured, "so . . ."

"It's okay," she whispered in his ear.

They kept kissing. Hands began to move. It only took a minute for bells to ring and his breathing went completely ragged.

"How old are you?" he asked her.

"I'm fine." Her mom had initiated the process of emancipating Heather so that she would legally be an adult. Mr. Riker had suggested it, saying that it would make things easier for her in Hollywood. Heather wasn't sure why, but she hadn't argued because she had nursed another crazy dream that Mr. Riker would marry her.

That was before Starbucks. Before she'd seen him all cozy with that woman.

"I need to get a condom," Hiro said.

"I won't tell if you won't," she murmured, pushing farther.

He slid her arms from around his neck and kissed her knuckles. "I've got some in my bag. I'll be right back."

"You really don't need to do that."

She pressed herself against his chest before he finally took a step away and she realized she couldn't protest too hard for fear of him guessing why she wasn't so concerned.

"Right back," he repeated, trailing his finger down the side of her face.

"I'll be waiting," she purred.

"Don't you dare move," he said.

He trotted into the darkness.

His persistence put a minor crimp in her plan, but condoms weren't a hundred percent effective. She could always say it was defective.

A few seconds ticked by. Maybe half a minute. She stood in the dim light and looked at all the crap in the room, the cobwebs, the dust. It was gross.

"God," she whispered. "What am I doing?"

She fanned her hands across her abdomen. This was pathetic, and it was wrong. She couldn't do this to this guy. She didn't even know him.

A footfall on cement echoed behind her and she spun around.

"Listen," she began.

Then she staggered backward.

And screamed.

12.

PRIME SUSPECT

LARSON'S RULE #1:

Don't work if you can cheat instead.

"What was that?" Larson said as he stepped across the threshold of a shed about fifty feet away from the warehouse.

It had sounded like someone in trouble.

"Praveen?" he called, ducking back outside. "Did you hear that?"

The fog levitated in layers of bundled cotton and the beam from his flashlight bounced off the billowing white. No Praveen. Maybe she'd bailed. Gone home. Scratched herself to death.

Weirdo.

"Hello? Praveen?"

Was she trying to scare him? Have some fun?

This whole thing was anything but fun. She wouldn't

tell him what the deal with the sweater was, but he was sure it meant something big. Larson didn't like August tonight. Not a bit. Albino Man was acting like a total a-hole.

Finally he shrugged and entered the shed. Everybody was letting loose tonight. It was the nature of the game.

August had installed some fun house mirrors and Larson grunted at the image of himself with no head, then super fat, and then skinny. Praveen had the paper with their clue on it but he remembered the lines:

```
GoIng thRough life
NicKing what you choose
But Believe it or not
Eye C u
```

That had to be the clue: **Eye C u**.

"Hi," Larson drawled, waving. Maybe there was a camera or something. He tried to peer around the mirrors but they'd been bolted firmly to the walls. He waggled his flashlight all over the room for something to take. A pair of glasses? A telescope?

He'd realized what the numbers in the sweater had been: part of Alexa DeYoung's phone number. Larson figured he'd better set the record straight with August. Yes, he had given Alexa a ride to Jacob's party. And yes, he had slow-danced with her. She'd stepped on his toes and sprayed him with spit while she'd talked so fast he had no idea what she was saying. His friends had made gagging gestures behind her back and Cage laughed so hard he fell down.

So yeah, he blew her off after that. He didn't even know she'd left the party until she had called him in tears and told him that she needed him to come get her out and then they got disconnected. He'd tried to call her back but his call had gone straight to voice mail. She was too wacko to deal with. She was dead, and that was sad and freaky, but it hadn't been his job to babysit her.

"Praveen, shit," he said irritably, poking his head back outside. "Where are you?"

This hunt was too hard. They had always been a fun excuse to party, not some kind of reality show audition. If he got to vote anyone off the island, it was going to be August. The test answers would be nice, but he knew he'd be going to Yale unless he really blew it. And as for his own prize, a getaway on *Guilty Pleasure* for two would also be nice, but nothing he couldn't live without.

Maybe she'd gone back into the warehouse. He crunched over the fifty or so feet of shells to the back door, moving mostly by memory because he couldn't see a damn thing. His hand brushed against the door handle and he yanked. It squealed open just like in a horror movie.

Oooh, I'm so scared.

This room had not been decorated; it was just a bunch of crap that had been stashed for a million years. He ran the flashlight beam along the floor. Something glittered and he bent down to get a closer look. Nestled among some

127

rodent turds and scraps of filthy cardboard lay a shiny diamond hoop earring. It looked familiar and he ran down the list of girls at the party, trying to figure out who had lost it.

He dropped the earring into his pocket and turned his head at a noise. A cough? A chuckle? Someone trying to get dressed?

"Hey?" he said.

The noise stopped, and Larson laughed. *Busted.* He said, "Did you lose something?"

No response. Maybe it was one of August's winged monkeys. His *spies.*

He heard the sound again. Not a cough or a chuckle this time. Like someone dragging something?

"Hello?" he called again. He cupped his ears, trying to pinpoint the location of the noise, crossing the room and walking into a hall on the opposite side. Go left? He took a few steps before he paused and listened again, then continued down and tried the door there, but it was locked.

Suddenly he was sure that someone was standing directly behind him. He could almost feel their eyes burning holes into the back of his skull. Someone in the hallway. Maybe it was a girl looking for her earring or Praveen had caught up.

"Boo!" he cried, whirling around.

To his surprise, there was no one there. He made a slow pan with his flashlight. Not only was the hall empty, but also there weren't any doors along the walls that a stalker could have darted into to escape detection.

It had to have been his imagination. But it had felt so *real*.

"Good one, August," he said casually.

Then he ran-walked back outside as fast as he could.

PRAVEEN'S RULE #1:

Only trust Drew.

Praveen was running her flashlight along the wall of the warehouse, batting at the fog as it rolled in. She'd been hoping Drew would come see her on his break but it seemed he was keeping up the façade that they meant nothing to each other. Praveen was more disappointed than she should be, she supposed. But half the reason she had shown up tonight was to see him.

She stopped and readjusted her top, which wasn't nearly as comfortable as it looked. It was so unfair. Seeing the green wrap on the hanger in the boutique, it looked like the softest thing in the entire world. She knew she needed it. It would complement her skin perfectly, move like a dream, and drive Drew absolutely wild.

So she had slipped it into her purse and casually headed for the front door. She didn't even see the antitheft device tag clipped into the armpit. The boutique had never used them before, which was one of the reasons she "shopped" there.

When the alarms went off, she'd panicked. She'd had

the hood on her sweatshirt up so she was reasonably sure they wouldn't be able to identify her on the security cameras, but a guard had given her the run of her life.

She had met Drew in the Callabrese music store. Her cousin Sudeep wanted a harmonica for his birthday, and she was casually going through the sheet music, which was organized in bins close to the harmonica display, preparing to make her move. Once she'd accounted for all the clerks, making sure their attentions were occupied, she had sidled over to the display and wrapped her hand around the nicest one.

Suddenly there was a clatter across the store. She jerked and glanced in the direction of the noise. At the same time a clerk who had been squatting undetected behind the harmonica display had popped up like a Whac-A-Mole and she had pulled back her hand just in time.

A shaggy-haired guy in a Death Cab for Cutie T-shirt and jeans said, "Whoops," and picked a pair of cymbals off the floor. As he straightened, he gave Praveen a wink. She caught her breath. *He knew.* And not only did he know she'd been about to take the harmonica, but he'd also saved her from getting caught.

"We all have our things, man," he'd told her, and then she'd recognized him and realized he was Drew from Maximum Volume. She was breathless. He was famous.

They went for coffee—she was dizzy with amazement— and she was just about to ask him for his autograph when he'd invited her to a practice and then a concert and then she was, like, his girlfriend. But they had to keep it quiet because of his image. It had been exciting at first to be together in secret. It was like they had a world all their own, where everything could be perfect for a few precious stolen moments.

Praveen went to as many of Drew's gigs as she could, but she had to pretend to be a fan, a pathetic groupie. She did it for love, but she did not have a song in her heart when she joined the other girls at the foot of the stage, gushing over him and talking about his hotness and his great butt. *Mine, mine, mine!* she wanted to shout at them. Drew said it wouldn't be like this forever. And she knew that, but it already felt like forever.

He'd been super moody lately, but she had chalked that up to his responsibilities to the band. He was under a tremendous amount of pressure. Maximum Volume had been signed by a record label, and their first album had to be perfect or they'd be back on the street. Drew had worked so hard for so long. She wasn't sure the others fully appreciated what he had done for them. But she'd found strange bottles in his underwear drawer—she had *not* been snooping, just looking for a pen—filled with little blue and white capsules. She was afraid to ask him about them because it *had* been a little odd to think she could find a pen mixed in with his boxers and she didn't want him to think she was checking up on him.

"Praveen!" someone shouted, and she winced. It was Larson.

She waved her flashlight back and forth, watching it

bounce off the fog, until a dark shape approached and her scavenger hunt partner materialized through the mist as if he were moving curtains aside. She wondered, not for the first time, what crime he had committed that August had tried to humiliate him with.

"Where have you been?" he demanded, scowling at her.

"Where have *I* been? Where did *you* go?" she countered.

"Never mind." He waved a hand. "I got nothing. I don't even get what we're supposed to be looking for."

"A brick," she said.

"What? How did you get that?" he asked.

She handed him their clue.

```
GoIng thRough life
NicKing what you choose
But Believe it or not
Eye C u
```

Larson studied it, then looked at her.

"Well, *genius,* he capitalized the letters *I, R, K, B,* and *C* when they shouldn't have been. Unscrambled they form the word *brick.*" She sighed and ran her beam along the wall. "But I haven't found anything yet."

"It'd have to be a loose brick," Larson said. "We have to take it back to him."

She winced. She hadn't thought of that. Maybe Larson wasn't a total idiot who deserved to be lobotomized.

"There's a pile of bricks in the parking lot," he said.

She nodded, and they began to walk over the noisy shells, then around the tall wall made of abalone shells, rocks, and cement.

"So what's he got on you?" he asked. "What did you do wrong, Miss Demeanor?"

It took her a moment to realize he was making a pun. "I could ask you the same thing."

"Underage drinking," he replied smugly. "But you've got another story—am I right?"

He should mind his own business. She imagined his head exploding like a giant watermelon dropped from a thirteen-story building. It made a satisfying *pop* as his brains sprayed everywhere.

Drew's groupies? There were so many things she'd do to them. In her mind's eye she armed herself with ice picks, knives, matches. The girls who pushed in front of her, that girl who had flashed her boobs at him two weekends ago at Petrol, the local coffeehouse—

They came to a pile of blackened bricks, pieces of trash, and beer cans. Gross.

Eye C u. He'd used texting abbreviations for *see* and *you,* but he'd spelled out *Eye* for *I.* So an eye must be significant to the brick they were looking for. Or else he was being a perv, or reminding her that he had spies or whatever. This was all so annoying.

She crouched down and passed her flashlight over the blackened brick. "Not fun, August," she muttered as she inspected each mottled surface.

"What are you looking for?" Larson asked, crouching down beside her.

"A picture of an eye on one of them. At least, I think that's what we need to find."

"You're shivering," he said. "Let me rub your arms."

"No!" She jerked away from him.

"God, Praveen, what's your deal?" he said. "I only—"

"I *know* what you *only*." She got to her feet. She wished she could pick up a brick and hit him with it. "Go away!"

"But we have to—"

Then she bent down and picked up a brick. Larson stared at her openmouthed. "Oh my God, did you get arrested for assault?"

Her arm spasmed as if it had a will of its own; he held up his hands and backed away. "No problem. I'm gone. See you, Praveen." He turned and muttered, "Psych ward."

Once he was gone and she had calmed down, she resumed her search. Her prize was a shopping spree in San Francisco and she was all for that. She'd get some black leather pants and a corset for when she went to live with Drew. And black satin sheets for their bed.

Finally something white caught her eye and she trained the flashlight on the bottom set of bricks. The rough chalk outline of an eye was drawn on the brick closest to her left knee.

She heard a footstep behind her. Rising, she turned, expecting to see Larson. There was no one there. Not too surprising: with all the hard surfaces, sound bounced and ricocheted.

She swept her flashlight across the jumble of parked cars; fog drifted lazily along the ground, but nothing else.

She turned back to the bricks to collect her so-called object. A moment later she could swear she heard a muffled laugh much closer than the footstep.

She spun around fast, light slashing through the darkness.

Cold, empty space.

"Okay, August, very funny," she said.

Silence answered her.

Praveen waited a few seconds, then shoved the top bricks off with her feet. They fell with dull clunking noises, and she had nearly worked her way to the bottom when something scratchy touched the back of her calf.

She bulleted into the air and landed, wrenching her knee and nearly falling.

"That's not funny!" she shouted.

A laugh skated on the wind.

"S-s-s-teal it." An amplified whisper in her ear. *"Thief."*

Fury rushed through her, blocking out most of the fear. People did *not* mess with her.

"You suck! You're dead!" she shouted, kicking aside the last two bricks and then grabbing up hers.

Running footsteps echoed against the bricks, the shells, the cliffs.

"You better run or I'll use this to bash your head in!" she yelled.

There was an envelope taped to the side of the brick, proving that it was indeed the one she was supposed to get. Now she was sure that August knew about her little habit of taking things. So what? It had nothing to do with him. Who died and made *him* her judge?

Hefting her spoils, she angrily marched back toward the main building. Maybe she would bash his head in with this brick.

That would shut him up.

13

THE WALKING DEAD

STACY'S RULE #1:

Drugs don't kill people. People do.

"It's so hot in here," Stacy muttered from the table where Drew had parked her.

No one else was there. August had disappeared. He was always running off. Hiro had charged into the room, taken something out of his bag, and disappeared again. He didn't even ask her how she was feeling. They used to be so close.

She wiped the sweat off her face, caking her fingers with eyeliner and mascara, and guzzled down the rest of a water bottle. Then she caught sight of her travel tumbler on the chair beside her. Maybe she *was* kind of careless with her drinks. She really hadn't been trying to kill Mick.

But he was being such a butthole now that she kind of wished she had.

"Not nice," she murmured.

But she was feeling not nice. Maybe they were planning to go to Los Angeles without her. With a sob, she lurched sideways, plucking up the tumbler and cradling it against her chest. She tottered outside on her heels, sucking in the cold air. Her lungs were aching. The moon gleamed on the topmost layer of fog, making it almost shine; she could smell and hear the ocean but not see it, and she staggered left and right. Maybe she'd go crawl into the van and go to sleep.

Did someone scream?

Her eyes were tearing up; she held a hand to her face and her fingers blurred and stretched. Her hand was like a foreign object, or someone else's hand. She peered through the fingers and saw—

"Hello?" she whispered at a figure standing a few feet away. It was a fuzzy outline, human-shaped, but who it was she couldn't tell. She turned her hand around and contracted her fingers in a sort of clawlike greeting.

It still didn't move. It just stood there and then, as she stared at it, a hazy glow bounced around and she saw two black holes where its eyes should be. *It has no eyes.* It was a white-faced monster, and it took a step toward her.

"Don't hurt me," she blurted, and her ankles gave way. She crashed to the ground, palms slamming into crushed shells, the sting of it shooting up both arms and slapping her cheeks. She let out a terrified sob.

The figure approached. Huge black half-moons took up her field of vision. Somehow she understood that they were the toes of a pair of boots.

"No, no," she bleated. "Stay away from me."

A hand wrapped around her upper arm and pulled her to her feet. She dangled like a string puppet, struggling to find her footing. The figure's face swam before her and she batted at it.

"Stacy. What the hell?" It was Hiro. He sounded angry. She pressed her face into his shirt as silent tears dampened the cloth.

"I think someone screamed," she told him.

"They're all playing their games," Hiro said. His voice lowered. "Lots of games. She's probably laughing right now."

"She," Stacy repeated. "She who?"

"Never mind."

"You hate me. You want me to quit and go away. You're afraid I'll mess things up in L.A." She waited for him to deny it. "You do!" she cried.

He kept his gaze fixed on her and she moved cautiously, feeling totally detested. She lost track of time, and then her boots echoed on wood, and she knew they were at the dock. She heard the ocean; the fog was thinner here, and she saw sharp stars above and sharper rocks below.

Leaning over the railing, she closed her eyes and tried

to let herself throw up. But she'd never been able to do that; she hated vomiting. Hiro rested his hand on her back and the weight of it made her lean farther over.

He's going to push me, she thought in a flash of terror. *He's going to kill me. He hates me that much.*

"Hiro, stop! Stop!" she begged. She tried to turn around but she couldn't do it. The world was whirling. The deck rocked back and forth.

And then there was pain.

ROBIN'S RULE #4:

Believe the best of people until they prove otherwise.

```
Beth may bluster and Thea may rave
But when you give in, girls, you . . .
Tonight someone will change your life.
The  tension's  so  thick  you  could  cut  it
with a . . .
```

When you give in, you *cave.*

Robin led the search for a cave on the property. There was a ginormous one in the cliff beneath the highway. Thea, Beth, and Robin trooped across the parking lot to search it, Thea whimpering dramatically as they passed Beth's Beemer. Beth was getting very touchy and seemed to be taking every expression of less-than-loving the scavenger hunt as a personal insult. Robin was suffering from cognitive dissonance: she wasn't particularly enjoying the hunt, but once it was over, there would be real partying. She and Kyle were definitely connecting, and she couldn't wait to hang out. Maybe make out; for sure crow over the Penalty Babes' victory.

But the large cave was completely trashed, and the coppery tang of blood permeated the darkness. Thea retreated, Beth loping behind her. Robin didn't argue her case very hard that they should give it a more thorough search for their next object, which was obviously a knife. More with the theme of murder weapons. It didn't smell good and she was afraid they would find a dead animal, which then got her to worrying about the presence of coyotes or even mountain lions, which were more aggressive. It simply wasn't true that wildlife stayed away from people, at least not in wine country. Coyotes were actually welcome in Callabrese because rats loved to nibble on the wine grapes, and the coyotes took care of the rats. Mountain lion sightings were not unusual, either. If animals were lurking around the cannery, the smell of food might encourage them to be bold.

The other hunters were busy: hair-raising screeches were followed by raucous laughter echoing over brick and stone; the fog paced and shifted, alternately obliterating the cannery and then focusing the moonlight on new sets of details. Robin stared up at the bell tower and jerked; she was pretty sure someone was up there, and she squinted hard to see if she could tell who it was. One of August's spies, she supposed. She gave the figure a wave. It didn't wave back, and with the next roll of fog, there was no one there.

"I hate this," Thea muttered.

"Grand prize," Beth said. Robin tried not to react and Beth chuckled. "Test answers." She grinned at Robin. "Or limo."

"Test answers," Thea said. "I'm only in it for that."

"But the Rolling Stones are so cool," Beth said. It was obvious to Robin that Beth was just messing with Thea. She wanted the test answers, too.

"I don't think we should go in there," Robin said, studying the mouth of the large cave.

"Maybe there's another cave?" Beth suggested.

"Like a sea cave?" Robin asked.

"Yeah."

It could be. Of course, if they were wrong and this really was the cave they were supposed to go into, they'd just be delaying the inevitable and wasting precious minutes. She took another step and the smell of blood hit her hard. She backed away. "Let's check just to be sure. We can come back if we have to."

They made it to the beach quickly, and as they walked toward the redwood pylons of the dock, half a dozen *things* burst from beneath the sand and stood fully upright. They moaned and gyrated as Thea shrieked, running smack into Beth and falling on her butt. Beth grabbed on to Robin and Robin's flashlight panned across their clump of attackers.

Their rotted faces glowed in the dark, their eyes shining with crimson light. They began to groan and claw at the fog with their arms.

"Help! Help!" Thea hollered, crabwalking away from them, and Robin and Beth doubled over with laughter.

"They're zombie robots," Beth said. "Halloween zombies."

The zombies stopped moving. They were truly hideous, with hacked-up plastic fingers and eyeballs dangling from beneath matted gray hair. Their clothes were tattered, "bloody," and covered with dirt and cobwebs. Bones protruded from shoulders and legs. One zombie was dressed like a bride. A shriveled bouquet was laced through skeletal fingers.

Robin darted forward and waved a hand in front of the bride zombie's face. The zombie's eyes lit up and her jaw clacked open. She swayed from side to side and moaned.

Robin took several steps back and the zombie stopped moving.

"Motion-controlled," she confirmed. "I don't see any cords. They must be battery-operated."

"Oh my God!" Thea cried in disgust. "That's it! I'm going!"

"Wait! Look!" Beth shouted. She darted forward, weaving in and out of the cluster of undead to the figure farthest away from Beth. Human-shaped, it was standing just inside a large hole in the cliff. Another cave. A faint light shone behind the figure, impossible to notice except at a precise angle.

A dummy was wearing a tattered khaki jacket and pants and a big-game hunter-style pith helmet. It was aiming what appeared to be a real rifle straight at them. Robin reflexively put her hands on Thea's shoulders and moved her out of the line of fire.

"That's not a real person," Thea said uncertainly, and Beth laughed.

"Are you *kidding*? Does that look real?" She looked expectantly at Robin, and Robin trotted around the zombies, joining Beth in front of the thing. It didn't move and somehow that made it creepier.

It wasn't as real-looking as the other zombies. It appeared to be made out of some kind of rubber, its decaying features dotted with tiny mushrooms and velvety blotches. One eye was blank; a brown iris and ebony pupil were chipped and fading in the other. As Robin cocked her head at it, a spider crawled up the side of its face.

Robin spotted the black hilt of a knife positioned behind the upraised hands that were holding the rifle.

"When you give in, you *cave*. You can cut the tension with a *knife*," Beth whooped, rising on tiptoe and patting the mannequin on the head. "Sorry about that, old chap."

"Gasoline, rope, knife . . . okay, this is completely deviant," Robin grumped.

"So where's the clue?" Thea asked, hugging herself and staying well away. "Let's just get the envelope and get out of here!"

"We have to take the knife to August," Robin reminded her. "So we have to pull it out of his chest."

"Yucko." Beth made a face. "You do it, Rob."

"It's going to move or something," Thea warned. "Or something else behind it will leap out at you." She took two steps back.

Robin raised her brows questioningly at Beth, who moved her shoulders and gave her head a shake.

"Don't touch it!" Thea said. "Something bad will happen!"

"The Penalty Babes are not big babies," Beth said.

Kyle, whispered Robin's inner voice. *Coffee with Kyle. With a red velvet cupcake and a make-out session on the side. Kyle and his adorable dimples.*

Then she clamped both her hands possessively around the knife. Taking a deep breath, she slowly drew out the blade.

There was a sucking noise as blood gushed down the statue's chest. Robin steered clear of the spray, almost landing on her own butt. Thea let out a shriek and Beth swore.

The knife dripped bright red liquid onto the sand, barely missing the toe of Robin's boot. Of course, it wasn't blood, but she had no desire to find out what it actually was. Instead, she wiped the blade on the dummy's filthy clothing. The sleek shank was maybe eight inches long and very shiny—in other words, new. August must have bought it and planted it just for tonight.

Then she peered at the mannequin's chest. A clear plastic bag had been taped such that when she had pulled out the knife, the sharp edge had sliced open the bag, allowing the contents—the fake blood—to spill out.

"He should have at least put this thing in a sheath so we wouldn't hurt ourselves when we found it. I could have cut myself," Robin said, gingerly clutching the knife as if it might bite her.

"Or cut one of us," Thea whined. "Are all the hunts this violent?"

Beth didn't reply as she tugged at the dummy's khaki shirt. Slashed nearly in two by the knife, an envelope was taped to the chest. She grunted with satisfaction and dislodged it, coating her fingertips with "blood" in the process. "I think this is colored corn syrup. That's how they make fake blood in the movies. I read about it."

Robin reached into the pocket of her bomber jacket and pulled out a couple of paper napkins from McDonald's. She handed one to Beth, who began to wipe her fingers. Robin wrapped the other napkin around the hilt of the knife.

"Sticky. Corn syrup," Beth confirmed. "It's all in fun, Thea. C'mon." She dropped the dirty napkin in the sand. "Let's go inside while we're here."

"Are you nuts?" Thea said. "Do you *want* me to die of a heart attack?"

"We have what we came for," Robin pointed out. "We should hustle back to August as fast as we can."

Beth crept forward and peered into the cave. "Hell-loooo?" she called in a singsong voice. "Anybody in there? Oh my God!"

"What? What?" Thea covered her eyes.

"Nothing, you big baby."

Beth dissolved into helpless laughter. Thea crossed her arms, whirled around, and started heading in the direction they had come, toward the path.

Robin sighed. "Must you?" she said to Beth. "Hey, it's okay, Thea," she called after her.

"Stop laughing at me!" Thea yelled.

"I'm not laughing at you," Robin yelled back.

"Hey, wait," Beth called. "Wait, I think someone really is in . . . Hey . . . what's this?"

The zombies began to moan and clank and whirr. Robin rolled her eyes and bounded after Thea as she picked up speed. Beth stayed behind.

"You can't fool us anymore!" Thea said. She started up the path.

"Robin. Oh my God, Robin," Beth said. Her voice was strained; she sounded genuinely frightened.

Fool me once, shame on you. Fool me twice, shame on me, Robin thought, and she kept going.

"Robin!" Beth shrieked.

Robin slowed. Then she turned around. Beth was cowering beside a boy zombie that was wearing a do-rag, a basketball jersey, and enormous polyester shorts. There was something in his mouth, and when Robin's flashlight passed over it, a reflection glinted off something small and metallic.

Beth was staring at the object; then she shifted her gaze to Robin. She was silent, wild-eyed. As Robin drew near, the boy zombie writhed and moaned, the object in his mouth tumbling to the ground.

Robin bent over and shined her flashlight. The yellow cone of light caught the glitter of a ring whose rhinestones spelled *MVP*, and below the *V*, a shiny enamel *C* gleamed.

It was Cage Preston's ring.

Firmly lodged on the pinky finger of a bloody, severed hand.

14

NEW RULES

BETH'S RULE #2:

Make people feel special and you'll gain the upper hand.

"Robin!" Beth shouted. They had bolted together but after a few steps Beth had stopped running. Within seconds, Robin and Thea both were scrabbling up the path to the top of the cliff like a pair of mountain goats.

And in those seconds, Beth had time to process. To think about what she had really seen. A prop. A fake. Just one of the many melodramatic pranks. A typical August prank, actually. She and he used to pore through special effects catalogs the way some people drooled over fashion magazines. A corner of August's bedroom was piled with computer parts, servos, soldering equipment, bottles of corn syrup and red food coloring, rubber shrunken heads, tarantulas, and snakes.

"Thea! Robin! It's a joke!" she yelled.

Beth heard the crash of a wave and then frigid water swirled around her ankles. She squeaked, running toward the big-game hunter and the cave. The foamy surf bubbled around her.

Robin had the flashlight, but by the dim light positioned inside the cave, Beth could watch the water recede into the ocean. One or two of the zombies jerked their heads and arms, but then they tipped over, clattering facedown into the water and the moans died out.

She tried to see if the hand had washed away as well, but the light was too weak. Even now, accepting that it had been a planted joke, she shuddered. It had looked so real.

A chuckle bounced inside the cave and she turned around. Larson was leaning against a stack of wooden crates, mischief twinkling in his eyes.

"Boo!" he said.

Her heart skipped a beat. She darted a quick glance around for Praveen but didn't see her. She crossed her fingers mentally that Larson was alone.

He ambled toward her, lanky and broad-shouldered, and her knees turned to rubber. She was so glad to see him that she couldn't hide a genuine smile, and he grinned at her in return.

"I scared the crap out of you," he preened.

She gave her head an imperious toss. Time to turn on

the hard-to-get vibe. She hadn't forgotten the way he'd pushed past her on the way into the party. Larson had to know he couldn't take her for granted.

"Sorry to disappoint you, but it was August's zombies that scared us. More like they scared Robin and Thea and just startled me."

He bent down and picked up a piece of seaweed, shaking it at her. He snickered when she wrinkled her nose and let it fall to the ground.

"Actually, the hand scared them," she said.

He waited a beat, then shrugged. "What hand?"

"August keeps leaving us these gory presents," she said, debating the wisdom of revealing anything more. She didn't want to give him an advantage in the hunt.

Unless he fully appreciated such generosity and reciprocated his knowledge.

He raised his brows. "Like what?"

"Why should I tell you?" she challenged.

"Because I'm nice?" he asked, walking closer, and she made a show of snorting with derision. In reality, though, little tingles of excitement were practically electrocuting her as she stood there. Larson was so hot. She knew he was a player, but there had to be one special girl who could tame him. Where chicks were concerned, Larson had a little ADHD problem. The trick was in getting him to focus.

"You are not nice," she said flatly.

"Oh, Beth, Beth, you know me too well." His smile was slow and sly. "Okay, how about this? We could form an alliance. I'm pretty much on my own at this point. Praveen is a complete psycho and I think she decided to go home. I'm hoping, anyway. She threw a brick at me."

Beth's lips parted as she filed this choice bit of gossip under *usable*. "No way."

"Okay, she didn't throw it, but I think the only reason she didn't was because I was out of range. Seriously, Beth, I always knew she was wound pretty tight but *damn*. If we ever have another hunt, don't even invite her, okay?"

We. It was her new favorite word. The tingles became sparklers of joy that skittered over her nerve endings. Larson obviously assumed she had helped to organize this hunt just like all the other ones. He didn't realize that August had broken the Pact. But she knew she needed to maintain her advantage in the eternal battle of the sexes. Playing hard to get was the only way to convince Larson to focus.

"That settles it," she said. "August and I were discussing her last night. We almost didn't invite her this time." She mimicked drawing a line through a name. "Next year when I run the hunts by myself, she's deleted."

"You don't need to do this one by yourself," he said.

"An alliance." She tapped her chin thoughtfully. "I believe that would be cheating." She put a challenge in her voice.

She knew from the other hunts that Larson lived for cheating. He really shouldn't have won first prize last time, but August told Beth privately that Larson had cheated the least. Except for Kyle. He and his little-miss-whoever date hadn't cheated one jot.

Which is why they hadn't completed the hunt when August called time three hours later than scheduled.

Now Larson tsk-tsked and rose to the bait. "No one would have to know that we cheated."

"But if August's spies see us together, we'll be busted," she argued, but then Larson wove his arms around her waist, making her unable to think straight.

"We can make them think we're hooking up." He moved a step closer. "There's nothing in the rules about that. Just no maiming."

Maiming. An image of the hand flashed through her mind. August had truly outdone himself with the realism. And the ring had looked exactly like Cage's. A tour de force. She should have been there when he'd had it made. Shared in the accomplishment. The gloating.

"Are you okay?" Larson asked, and she caught herself.

She thrust out her lower lip, giving him her cutest pouty face, and said, "I was just thinking about the hand. It was *freaky*."

He let go and moved past her toward the mouth of the cave. "Cool. I want to see."

"No," she said breathlessly. *Not* in her game plan. "It got washed away by the tide." She looked back over her shoulder; the light in the cave glowed from one of the portable lanterns, which Larson must have brought with him from the warehouse. There were splotches of something dark around the lantern's base. Probably more candy blood.

"If we go back via the beach, we'll get washed away, too," she said. "Where does this tunnel go?"

He lingered just inside the mouth of the cave, framed in the soft light as if he were a model in a photograph for some sexy men's fragrance. "There's more than one tunnel, and they go all over the place. One of them was really nasty. The other one . . ." He made a face. "I'm wondering if someone's using it to smuggle drugs or something. There are boxes from floor to ceiling. Did you guys check this place out? I mean, what if the cannery is being used by a Mexican drug cartel or something? And they find us all here?"

"What?"

"Yeah," he said. "I mean, they might shoot us or something, you know? Or hang us. They're totally into that. I saw it on the news the other night. They hung some American undercover guys from a bridge in Tijuana. You *did* check it out, right?"

Are you kidding? Beth thought. Check out a scavenger hunt location to make sure there weren't any *drug lords?* Was he just trying to scare her?

"I want to see the boxes," she said. "The ones you think mean there are smugglers."

Shaking his head, he moved into her way. "The tunnels are way too gross. And I got lost at least three times. It's like a big maze."

He was actually blocking her. Was there something he didn't want her to see? Her stomach knotted. Was some other girl down here with him already? Not Praveen. Praveen was too weird and too prissy. But Heather maybe.

He laced his nice strong fingers through hers. "Let's go out this way." He looked down at her feet. "The water doesn't matter. Your shoes are already soaked."

That was true. Not only soaked, but her feet were also freezing. *Why* had she worn her good boots? Because she was used to orchestrating the hunt, not playing in it. She'd wanted to look fabulous. The last hunt. The last chance to make a fantastic impression.

Larson was wearing sneakers that were already fairly trashed. He extended one long, muscular leg out of the mouth of the cave and onto the sopping beach, then the other, sucking his breath between his teeth as the breakers splashed his jeans. He hunkered down and stretched his arms behind himself, like a diver about to bounce off the board.

"Here, I'll carry you. Take the lantern and climb on," he told her.

She didn't need to be asked twice. Her face went hot and then she was hot all over as she put her hands on his shoulders and he bent lower, catching her around the thighs as she saddled up piggyback style. His fingers gripped her for balance while she maneuvered the heavy lantern so that it rested at an angle against his shoulder, casting light downward like a desk lamp. She wanted to feel his skin against hers; she was sorry she was wearing tights, especially since they were soaking wet from the backs of her calves on down.

His curly chestnut hair was silky and she inhaled the smell of tobacco. It was so Larson. She just couldn't believe this was happening. This was the beginning of something wonderful. She just knew it.

He straightened his knees as a larger wave crashed against the beach and lapped at his shins. The water was rising.

"Tide's coming in fast," he said. "You guys must have forgotten about that."

I wouldn't have, she thought, but she didn't say anything. She spared one more moment to wonder why doing this was better than going through the tunnels—the water was *cold*—but she didn't figure he would have carried her if they'd gone that route, so she forgot about it.

"Look out for the zom-bots," she said, giving them a name, an implication that she had had a hand in putting them in the hunt. "They might float back to shore."

"And since they don't have to breathe, they won't drown, wahahaha," he said. "Okay. Here goes."

Seagulls wheeled and called to the moon as he slogged down the beach. Larson was walking like a zombie himself, and she didn't know if it was on purpose or because she was too heavy for him. The idea mortified her.

She monitored the light and looked up the hill for the two cowards Robin and Thea. She wouldn't put it past Thea to abandon her, but Robin was a different story. Robin was the goody-goody. The nice girl. It surprised her that Robin hadn't doubled back to check on her.

"Hey, I think . . . ," Larson said. "Is that the hand you're talking about?"

She tried to look around his shoulder but couldn't see. He rocked forward, staggering a little under her weight, and she was suddenly very anxious.

"Don't," she said, but he was already fishing around in the water.

"Got it." There was a beat as he lifted it up and she could see it. "Oh God."

Everything in her froze. Her heartbeat blared like a siren in her head. The hand was fleshy and bloody, with bones and tendons trailing out of the wrist.

It is real.

LARSON'S RULE #2:

Know who your friends are.

"Beth," Larson ground out. "Beth."

Larson knew Cage Preston well. Knew that he had given himself a homemade tattoo of the letter *U* at the base of his middle finger. Most people missed it, but Larson had been at his house the night Cage had done it.

This hand bore the same tattoo.

He dropped it and began to lurch sideways. Beth was

bellowing in his ear and the lantern splashed into the water. He backed away. Beth kept howling. With no light but the moon, he looked everywhere. For whoever had done this.

For more of Cage.

It's just a joke. A joke. He staggered around. *Pick it up. Take it with you.*

Shrieking, Beth leaped off his back and sloshed past him. He caught up to her and they ran together for a couple of steps before he passed her easily. He saw a path and angled for it as she screeched at him to wait for her. But he couldn't slow down. He was on autopilot as he charged up, reaching the top of the cliff and barreling over crushed shell as he threw himself at the warehouse door and flung it open.

"Hey!" he bellowed.

Robin and Thea were with August. Mick the bassist was there. And Praveen. They all looked at him as he staggered to a halt, dripping seawater on the floor, shaking and trembling, wiping his hand over and over on his jeans.

Larson pointed at Thea and Robin. "I saw it," he said to them. His voice shook. "I saw the hand." He wiped his face with his arm. "That was Cage's hand!"

Robin paled and Thea whirled on August. "I *told* you!" she bellowed at him.

"And I told *you*," August said, his attention fixed on Larson as he staggered over to the wall and leaned against it, panting. "I didn't plant a fake hand in the zombie graveyard.

Someone else did. Probably Cage." He looked around as if he expected Cage to make a grand entrance.

"Where's Beth?" Robin asked.

Larson felt a flash of guilt. "I kind of bailed on her. I freaked out. She'll be here in a sec."

"You left her out there?" Robin said incredulously. She ran across the floor and leaned out through the doorway. "Beth!"

"You left her out there, too, Robin," Larson said.

"Oh my God, people. It's not a real hand." August rolled his eyes. "Please."

"It looked real," Larson said. "And if you didn't put it there, how can you know anything about it?"

"Yeah." Mick gave his guitar a strum. He looked massively unimpressed.

"Have you seen Cage since the hunt began?" Praveen asked.

"No, I'm sure he and Morgan found a nice quiet spot and are doing . . . their own thing," August said with a smirk.

"Maybe they're both dead," said Thea.

"And maybe someone's pranking you. People *are* allowed to do that," August rejoined.

"What's going on?" Kyle said from the doorway. He was carrying a big red metal can with GAS written on the side in yellow letters. As he set it down in front of his coffin, he grinned at Robin and then smoothed back his hair. His cheeks were flushed.

August huffed. "Someone planted a fake hand and scared the newbies."

"Are you all *insane*?" Thea cried. "Aren't you listening? It was a hand! A real hand!"

Kyle chuckled. "Guys, really? This is how these hunts go."

From the doorway, Robin gave her head a shake. "Beth isn't answering me," she said. "Something's wrong."

"I'm sure she's *fine*," said the Maximum Volume lead guitarist, Mick, who had been strumming some melody onstage.

"We don't know that! We don't know *anything*!" Thea shrieked.

She was right, except Larson did know one thing: that really had been Cage's hand.

"I'm done! I want my phone and I want to leave!" Thea cried.

She spied the tarps bunched up in the corners and ran to the nearest one. "I want my phone *now*!" she yelled, ripping the tarp away. Two cardboard boxes were stacked onto a wooden crate.

"Thea, *stop*," August said, starting to sound irritated. "You need to talk this over with Beth. She drove. And she's your partner. Really, it's just for fun."

"Where did you hide the phones?"

Thea ran over to the coffin that said PENALTY BABES and started rooting through the black wrappings of the

160

"corpse" August placed inside it. "I put my purse here. Where the hell is my purse?"

"Hey," August began, and then he let out a horrible scream.

Praveen and Robin shrieked. Thea, too.

The figure in the coffin was not a robot corpse that could writhe on command. Cage Preston was swathed in black velvet, his face a pulpy, bruised mess. His nose was broken, his skin the color of eggplant and cold ashes. His swollen lips were purple, white, and blue.

As Thea backed away, she dragged the black velvet with her, exposing Cage's body.

Where his left hand should have been was nothing but a bloody, mangled stump.

15

REST IN PIECES

KYLE'S RULE #2:

Always follow the rules.

In the frenzy, Kyle dashed toward Cage's body and collided with Larson, hard. The force spun him half around.

"Hold on, man! Hold on!" Larson yelled, grabbing Kyle, righting him.

Together, Larson and Kyle pried Cage out of the coffin and laid him on his back on the concrete floor. Larson kept shouting Cage's name and pounding on his shoulder. Cage was completely limp and the back of his head was bashed in. Cage's face was a mess. Kyle leaned down and snaked his hand against Cage's neck to look for a pulse. His skin was clammy and cold, and his artery was not pumping blood.

There was no air blowing from his ruined nose.

Someone was tugging on Kyle's sleeve. It was Robin; he didn't want her to see, so he jumped up and threw his arms around her, dragging her away. Robin jerked around in his arms and pounded his chest. He kept her shielded as she socked him, hard; it finally registered that she wanted him to let go but he couldn't make himself do it. She wasn't even supposed to be here. She hadn't been invited.

"Kyle! We have to find Beth!" she yelled.

"No, I will," he said. "I'll look for her. You get out of here. Go for help. *Now.*"

August and Mick were wildly pawing through the boxes that had been concealed under the other tarp. As Kyle watched, Thea ran to the pile of clues for PENALTY BABES and grabbed a wicked-looking knife with a long, bloody blade. She raced back toward August, and Kyle sprinted to intercept her.

"Whoa," Kyle said as he planted himself between her and the two guys. "Hey, Thea, stop."

"Get out of my way!" She tried to get around him but he stuck to her like a guard in basketball. "August! He bashed in Cage's face and he cut—"

Her eyes widened; she dropped the knife and brought her hand against her chest. She stared down at the floor and then at August and Mick. Kyle made the connection that she just had: maybe that was the knife that had been used to hack off Cage's hand.

Yellowed papers seesawed to the floor from the boxes Mick and August were tipping upside down, shaking them as hard as they could, and discarding them on the floor. Larson was still kneeling beside Cage, completely losing his mind.

"Damn it, Thea, help us," August yelled at her. He looked at Kyle. "The phones are missing."

"Even yours?" Thea flung at him. "You didn't put your own phone in that basket, you bastard! You should have yours!"

"I set it down right here," August shouted, moving to the coffin-shaped table where his headset and clipboard rested beside the two purple skulls. He turned them upside down. Black envelopes slid to the floor like oversized playing cards. "And it's gone!"

"Hell with this. I'm getting out of here." Mick threw the box down and ran toward the door.

"I'm going with you," Thea cried.

"We have to get a phone. Cage needs an ambulance," Larson said from his position beside Cage, and Kyle winced.

"No, man, no, he doesn't," Kyle said softly. He looked at Robin, who hadn't left. "Go with Mick and Thea," he said to her. "Go. I'll find Beth." He looked around the room. "And . . . everybody else."

Her face was ashen. "Morgan. Stacy. Hiro. Drew." Her eyes widened. "Where's Praveen? She was just here!"

"Maybe *she* did it!" Thea trotted back toward the knife, but Larson threw himself across the floor and grabbed it. "Hey, that's mine."

Larson cradled it against his chest. "No, it's not."

Thea opened and closed her mouth. Then she glommed on to Mick, and together they crossed the room. August hurried after them but Kyle reached out and grabbed his forearm.

"Hey, we have to find the others," Kyle said. "We can't just bail on them."

August shook him off. "Cage is *dead*. Someone *killed* him." He started to catch up to Thea and Mick.

"Don't you take one step near me," she said, baring her teeth at him like a wild animal. "Don't try *anything*. My boyfriend will *kill* you, August. He'll effing kill you!"

"I didn't do this!" August yelled.

"You sent us to the zombie graveyard to find his hand!" She whirled on her heel and she was out the door. Mick bounded after her.

Kyle heard Larson throwing up. He turned back to him as Larson straightened, wiping his mouth.

"Let's go," Larson said. "I left Beth down at the beach. Tide was coming in."

"I'm going, too," Robin said. She looked close to fainting, but she stayed on her feet.

"Okay." Larson quickly looked around. "Hey, Heather's not here, either. She's been gone *forever*."

Robin sucked in her breath. Kyle grimaced. "Heather. Right."

"Okay"—Robin began counting on her trembling fingers—"Heather, Praveen, Morgan, Beth, Hiro, Drew, Stacy. We have seven people to find."

Larson nodded. "And one of them might be the killer. So we go armed." He gestured with the knife.

August ran to where the band had been playing and picked up his head mike. He tapped it to make sure it was on.

"Beth, Stacy, Hiro, Drew, Praveen, Heather, Morgan, this is an emergency. Go to the parking lot. Immediately. I repeat, go to the parking lot. Don't screw around."

He found the volume control and turned it as high as it would go. He repeated what he'd said. He kept saying the words over and over as Kyle, Robin, and Larson walked toward the door. "What are we going to do if we can't find anybody?" Larson asked.

"We're going to find them," Robin retorted.

Or die trying, Kyle almost said.

But he kept that thought to himself.

ROBIN'S RULE #5:

Be brave when it counts.

Kyle, Larson, and Robin headed back toward the path leading down to the water. Kyle held a large, police-style flashlight high so that the light would create a pie shape before them in the murk.

Robin froze and stared down as she watched the sea rush over the beach and smash against the bluffs. The shore had become fully submerged.

"I went down the other side of the dock," Kyle said. "There's a road with an old traffic barrier. That's where I found my crowbar."

"That'll be underwater, too," Robin said. "Oh my God. Beth . . ."

Kyle squeezed her against his hip and she wrapped both of her hands around his forearm. She remembered one of her mother's sayings: *We are strong.* But someone was stronger. He—or she—had beaten a boy to death and cut off his hand. And Robin may have abandoned Beth to him.

"There's an alternate way to the beach." Larson was panting. He leaned forward on his thighs to catch his breath. "You have to go through a cave across the parking lot. I went in that way and I wound up down there. It's really gross. . . ."

"I saw that cave. It's the one over there, right?" Kyle pointed toward the upper cliff, where the highway led to the gate with *ZUL* written in wrought-iron letters, and Larson nodded.

"We found it, but we didn't go inside," Robin said. "Let's go."

"Grab your crowbar first," Larson said.

"It's too heavy. Let's just go," said Kyle.

They broke into a run. Kyle had her hand in his but she had gone numb. She couldn't feel his fingers or the ground beneath her boots. Her heart was pounding so hard it was scaring her.

About thirty feet to her right, August was raising the hood of his Porsche. She didn't know what was up but she didn't stop to ask.

They reached the cave and barreled inside. She smelled the blood. Kyle panned his flashlight over the vast landscape of discarded odds and ends as he, Robin, and Larson slowed to a halt.

"Dude," Larson blurted, grabbing the flashlight and lowering it. At least two feet tall, the letters AEDY had been painted on the floor in what appeared to be dark brown paint.

"Holy shit, that wasn't there before," Larson said. He bent over the graffiti. "This could be a gang tag. I told Beth I thought a drug cartel might be using the cannery as a drop point."

"*What?*" Robin cried.

An owl hooted and she flinched, half expecting some guy with a machine gun to attack them. She thought about her family, who had no idea where she was or what had happened. The owl hooted again, almost as if it were trying to warn them.

"I'll go on alone," Kyle said. He took a step forward but Robin clamped on to his wrist, shaking her head.

"No way," she said. "We'll all go."

His face softened and he reached up, running his fingers through her hair. They didn't say anything. But Robin knew they had both said a lot:

We're going to get through this. Together.

Footsteps crunched on the shell gravel just outside the mouth of the cave and the three of them whirled around, Larson raising his knife over his head. It was August, huffing and puffing. Robin had no idea how anyone could look even more freaked out, but August did.

"Guys," August said, "we found Hiro, Drew, Stacy, and Praveen. They're in the Maximum Volume van." He got the funniest look on his face. "Our batteries have been stolen."

"Batteries?" Robin said slowly, not understanding.

"Out of our cars. Our cars won't start."

There was a beat, and Larson moved past Kyle to stand nose to nose with August. He pushed August's shoulder.

"What the hell, August?"

"Me?" August said.

Larson pushed him again. "Did your 'spies' take the batteries? Before or after they killed Cage for you?"

"Hey." August hunched his shoulders and took a step away from Larson. The pale-faced guy glanced over at Robin, who glared back at him, and then he tried to stare Larson down. "I didn't do any of this. And I *don't* have any spies. I made that up, okay? So I could try to get you guys to follow the rules for once."

"Game's over, asshat!" Kyle yelled.

August took a deep, ragged breath and his bravado blew out of him like the last bit of air out of a party balloon. Then he looked at the letters on the floor and pointed.

"Who did that?" he asked in a flat, nervous voice.

"You didn't?" Robin asked. He shook his head. "Does it mean anything to you?"

He nodded. "Those are my sister's initials. Alexa Emily DeYoung."

"Oh? More of your *I know that you screwed my sister last summer* crap?" Larson said. "Is that what this is about? Some revenge trip?"

"What are you talking about?" Robin said. She looked at August, who was shaking his head.

"I swear it. I didn't do any of this," August said.

Robin didn't understand what Larson was driving at, but she didn't have time to care. She turned to Kyle. "I'm going to look for Beth. *Now.*"

"With you," he said.

"Give me your keys. I'll check your cars," August insisted.

"I came with Beth," Robin reminded him.

"I'll check my own car after we find the other guys," Larson said while Kyle handed over his keys.

"But—"

"Don't touch my car. Don't touch any of my stuff, or I'll kill you," Larson snapped at August.

"Larson," Robin said. "Easy."

He narrowed his eyes at her. "Stay out of this, Robin. You really don't want to piss me off."

Her brows rose as she tried to stare him down. But he was scaring her, and she broke contact first.

"Fine," she murmured. "I'm backing off."

Larson huffed. "Hey, sorry, it's just—"

"Backing off and staying well away," she said emphatically.

Then hand in hand, she and Kyle jogged into the cave, Larson trailing after.

THEA'S RULE #3:

No one ever comes to save you.

Since Thea didn't have Beth's keys, she had bolted for the Maximum Volume van with Mick. It turned out that Hiro, Drew, Stacy, and Praveen were huddled inside. When they heard August on the mike, they did exactly what he said and stayed there.

That meant four of the people Robin and Kyle were looking for didn't need to be found. Someone should tell them, but Thea totally wanted it to be someone *else*. They had to get out of there *now*. Stacy had a huge goose egg on her head from falling on the dock, and she was sick to her stomach.

Then August came back and told them the cars weren't working because someone had taken the batteries. *Stolen* them. Everyone completely freaked out. He kept telling them that he didn't do it. How could he have? Thea was afraid they were going to murder him then and there.

August said that they'd better go back inside the warehouse. That caused more arguments. Stacy was barely able to walk two steps without throwing up. When they reached the warehouse door, Drew balked.

"No. I'm not going back in there. It's *insane*," Drew said, crossing his arms. He was jittering and sizzling, and if Thea *ever* needed a reminder that drugs were evil, she had only to recall how he looked right now. They were all terrified, but Drew was on another planet.

"We have to all stick together," August said, confronting Drew, totally in his face. "We should just go inside and wait for our parents to send out a search party or something."

No one knows where we are, Thea thought. *No one, anywhere. Except whoever is doing this to us.*

"No frickin' way," Drew said. "We'll be in there with the killer."

"Hey, we don't know who it is or where he is," August said. "It could be someone lurking around out here right now, watching us."

"Try 'she.' Morgan, you bitch!" Drew shouted. "Give us back our frickin' batteries!"

"We don't know that she killed Cage," Praveen said.

"The hell we don't. She was his partner. No one's found *her* body," Drew said.

"I'm done," Stacy said to Thea in her gravelly voice, "with the hurling." Raising her head, she wiped her mouth with the back of her hand. "Get out of the way," she said dully to Drew before pushing into the warehouse.

Reluctantly Thea followed.

Cage.

Thea's stomach lurched as she caught sight of the tarp that had been draped over his body. August had come in alone to search Cage's pockets for his car keys while everyone waited in the lot. After August had opened Cage's car to release the hood, he'd shown everyone a small cache of steroids he'd found in the glove compartment. It was almost as if August had known exactly where to look for them.

After that, August had decreed that they would search each person's car for "anything suspicious," but other than drugs and more drugs, they were left empty-handed.

Lacking Beth's keys, Mick had suggested holding off on inspecting her car, but August smashed in her window. He found the release, and Mick popped the hood. Her battery was missing, too. Mick drew the line at breaking into Larson's car, and this time August backed down.

Her life was becoming a terrifying horror movie, the kind she hated with all her heart. Beth had talked her into breaking up with Jackson because he was in a *gang*? She'd be safer with him. The Free Souls had Jackson's back.

Shaking, she held on to Stacy as the tattooed singer staggered toward the stage. Thea couldn't stop looking at the tarp. The floor tilted and she covered her mouth with both hands. She had to find a phone. She had to call the police.

Stacy let go of her, wafting past Hiro like a ghost. Turning her back on him, she grabbed a water bottle from the table still loaded with food. Hiro didn't look at either of them. Thea slid down the wall, then remembered a slasher movie she'd seen where the killer knifed a girl through a wall and scooted away. She draped her hands over her knees and lowered her head so she could hide her tears.

She heard Drew yelling some more: "How are you going to stop me, August, stab me? Shoot me? Do you have a gun?"

"You can't leave!" August shouted. "We have to stay here, together!"

"Like Beth, Morgan, and Heather or Kyle and Robin?" Drew said. "They're probably off planning their next move. I'm going out the gate, and I'm walking up the road, and I'm sticking out my thumb, man."

"You're drugged up. You'll probably fall and kill yourself first," Mick countered.

"You'd hate that, wouldn't you," Drew snapped.

Mick didn't reply.

"I picked this place because no one ever comes down that road," August argued. "I didn't want us to be disturbed. So we could have a blowout. Remember that one time when Cage had the party and it was so loud that . . . that . . ."

That the police came, Thea filled in. She had heard all about it. Rumor had it that Cage's father had paid the cops off. They left and the party kept going.

Oh my God, she thought suddenly. *That was the night Robin's dad got hit in the fog. What if one of these people hit him?*

"Drew, no!" August yelled. "Damn it, no!"

Thea wiped her eyes and saw Drew stride out the door and slam it behind him. August was looking at them all; then he dragged a chair over to the door and positioned it beneath the knob. She heard someone crying. It was Praveen.

"You shouldn't have let him do that," Stacy slurred. She was nearly lying on the food table with an unopened water bottle in her hand. "He's going to die." She hefted the bottle toward August. It thudded onto the cement floor and rolled a couple of inches.

"Or he's the killer and he'll mow us down with an Uzi or something," Hiro said. "Nice work, August."

"*Drew*? An Uzi? Are you for real?" Mick walked over to the glittering assortment of booze, picked up a bottle of bourbon, and tipped it back. Hiro joined him and grabbed a bottle of tequila.

"This is totally screwed, man," Hiro said. "We have to get the hell out of here."

"No shit," said Mick.

Thea pulled in her arms and legs. One minute she was about to have a meltdown, another she wanted to run outside after Drew. She looked at the other people in the room. Had one of them killed Cage? Would she be next?

She had no idea how much time had passed when August, who had been standing beside the door, jumped back.

"There's someone outside."

The door rattled hard. The chair under the knob skittered to the floor, and the door burst open.

16

REVENGE TRIP

HIRO'S RULE #1:
*Don't get pulled into
other people's drama.*

About to chugalug the tequila, Hiro nearly dropped the bottle when the door flew open. Kyle, Robin, Larson, and August's chick Beth stagger-walked into the warehouse. Beth was soaking wet, hunched over and crying with Robin's arms protectively slung around her. Kyle was holding a baseball bat covered with what looked like dried blood, and Larson had a firm grip on his knife.

"Oh my God, Beth!" Thea leaped to her feet and jetted across the room. She threw her arms around Beth and Robin. She hadn't so much as glanced at Hiro in hours. Last Monday had only been a hookup for him, too, but he could use a hug right now.

And a gun.

He was seriously terrified and he knew Mick was, too. Maximum Volume was freaked out to the max.

"I saw someone down there," Beth told the group as she limped into the room like she was a million years old. Thea was attempting to wipe the sand off Beth's clothes, but it was hopeless. "He was wearing a coat. I climbed into the cave and then I started trying to find my way out and I couldn't. I thought I was going to die in there!"

"A coat," Hiro repeated. He pointed in August's direction. "Hey, nice trench coat, August. That you aren't wearing anymore."

"What the hell?" August cried. "I took it off and I put it . . . right here." He stomped over to the coffin-shaped table by the door and lifted up his coat. "Does it look wet and sandy? Does it look like I've been wearing it? Haven't I been in here with you?"

"Oh, stop it!" Beth shouted. "August, we *know*!"

August jerked. "Know what?"

"That you're doing this! That you killed Cage. *With this bat.*"

"*What?*" He stared at her as if she were speaking in a foreign language.

She pointed at the bat that Kyle was holding. "It's covered with blood. Cage's blood."

August stood with the coat in his hands. "That bat isn't mine," he said.

"Don't even. You *wanted* us to know. You left all those

sick clues to taunt us that you were going to kill all of us!" She was shaking her fists at him. Shaking all over. She lunged at him; she would have attacked him except Robin and Thea grabbed her arms and held her. Mick swore under his breath and moved back toward the stage. Hiro followed.

"Oh shit," August said, shutting his eyes tightly and grimacing. "Yeah, I know it looks that way, but—"

"Looks that way?" She struggled hard to get free, teeth clenched, eyes wild. "Get him. Kyle! He's the killer!"

"I'm not!" August shouted.

"Beth's right." Praveen glared at August. "He's been acting so crazy all night. Like it's all a big joke and now Cage is *dead.*"

"I didn't kill him!" August said.

Larson took a step forward with the knife in his hand, and Hiro's hair rose on the back of his neck. Drew really did have the right idea earlier. It was time to get the hell out of here.

"You guys seriously need to chill a second before someone else gets . . . hurt," Hiro said.

"Yeah," said Mick. He looked at Hiro as if to say, *We can take a couple of them if we have to.*

"Then break it down for us, August. What have you been playing at all night?" Beth yelled at him.

"You don't know?" Larson asked her, looking surprised. "I thought you two were so tight."

"This time he didn't share," Beth said. Then her mouth

dropped open. She blinked several times before she sucked in a breath. "Oh my God. It's about Alexa. She died about this time last year."

They all fell silent. The room itself was holding its breath, beyond tense, minds racing, tempers in the stratosphere.

"Exactly this time," August ground out, his voice hoarse.

More silence. Consternation. The monster, unmasked. The motive, explained.

"It's her anniversary, isn't it," Beth said. It was not a question. "Oh, *August*."

August gave his head a hard shake but the tears came anyway. "No one even remembered."

"I didn't even *know*," Beth said. "It was before my time."

"You did. I told you. You just *forgot*. You were too busy texting about Albino Man."

Beth sucked in her breath again. "Oh crap. I'm sorr—"

"Don't. You're not sorry."

"So . . . you decided to make *us* sorry," Praveen flung at him, and the tension rose again. It was as if a moment of silence had been observed for August's loss, but the pressure was back on. "By butchering us?"

August stared hard at Praveen. His crystalline eyes lasered in on her. This was one seriously pissed-off, messed-up, heartbroken brother.

"You want to talk about butchering? You stole her sweater right off the pile at that party," August said. "And it had my new cell phone number in it. On a piece of paper. I *told* her to create a new contact on her phone and she said she'd get around to it. But *you* took it and she couldn't call me when she got locked in at the country club."

Praveen paled. "I . . . I didn't do that."

"You *did*. She had her phone and she tried to text me. But she couldn't remember my new number. I would never have known *anything* but the cops found it under a deck chair. You just used her. You broke her. You *all* killed her!" He broke down. "Lex. Oh God, Lex!"

Beth stepped forward but August recoiled, backing up from her as if she had a gun in her hands. His white face was even whiter; he looked like he had seen a ghost. Then he dissolved, sinking to the floor like he had no bones.

"Morgan told her she was fat and Cage hooked her on speed and Heather, that *bitch*, got her blackballed from all the school plays." He raised his head and stared somewhere far away, somewhere terrible.

"She wanted friends. She wanted love. And she tried everything and none of it worked. She went to that party and then she went swimming with Jacob. He left her and then one of you locked the gate on purpose. I know that for a fact."

"Did she say that in the text?" Larson said. "The one she didn't send you?"

August went silent. He looked utterly defeated.

"She didn't say, did she?" Praveen said. "It wasn't me."

"That's what I wanted to find out tonight," August said.

"Jacob made sure it was unlocked before he left her there. He told me that much."

"So you lured all your friends here tonight," Thea said. "With prizes. So you could find out who to blame."

"For revenge," Beth said.

"Yes," August said, and everyone stiffened, even Hiro and Mick. "Yes to both. But not by killing you. I knew if I gave you the test answers, you'd share them. You'd sell them to each other for weed, or sex, because that's what you do. You're all so lazy and greedy. I hacked the system to make sure the next one to go into the dropbox would get caught. They would expel you. All of you."

"But the winners could have picked the limo instead," Robin said. "They wouldn't get expelled for that."

"I was going to pay the chauffeur to make them miss prom." He smiled bitterly. "Because it was so damned important to all of you. Because Lex will never go to prom. She'll never graduate. Because of what you *did*."

"Hey, that's not fair," Larson said. "Okay, I should have kept calling, but people don't die from a guy acting like a bastard. August, I hate to break it to you, man, but Alexa was already broken. She was seriously messed up. It wasn't just us or one locked gate. Dude, *a locked gate*. I mean, really?"

Robin whirled on Larson. "Really, Larson? You have to say that right now?" She walked toward August. Kyle reached for her hand but she kept going and crouched down beside him. She almost put a hand on his shoulder

181

but held back. *Right move,* Hiro thought. This guy was on the edge. Still, Hiro was not convinced that August was the innocent he was claiming to be.

"She was locked in," August said between clenched teeth. He balled his fists. "She had no clothes. *Someone took her clothes on purpose.*"

"Jacob," Larson said impatiently.

August was seething. "He said he didn't."

"Like he'd tell *you,*" Larson huffed.

"Please, tell *us,*" Robin said to August. "Did you do that to Cage?"

August shook his head. Shutting down, withdrawing. These kids should give this guy some space before they got hit by the blowback.

"I don't believe you," Praveen said. "You've always been so . . . so *weird.*"

"I don't believe him, either." Wow, you could cut steel with Beth's hard fury. "All those hours we spent trashing your *friends.* You despise every person you invited to this hunt."

August didn't react. Not a good sign.

"You didn't despise me," Robin said. "You didn't even invite me."

"But he had this all planned out," Beth cut in. "That's why he was so upset that I brought you."

"I *did* have it all planned out," August said. "But only to get back at the guilty ones. I did normal hunts for your

182

team, Beth. Because even though you are a two-faced, backbiting bitch, you didn't have anything to do with Lex's death. And Kyle, too. I knew people would ask questions if I didn't have you both here at the party."

"So, no tricks or humiliation planned, but you had us gather the murder weapons. Like the baseball bat," Kyle said angrily. "We found it in the tunnel."

"No," August argued. "I didn't have a bat on the list. I didn't bring a bat."

"We'll see." Kyle crossed to the coffin-shaped table where August had placed his clipboard. He picked it up and started paging through it. Frowning, he flipped the pages backward. Hiro could read his expression easily: no baseball bat on August's lists.

"Was there an envelope attached to the bat?" August said.

Kyle didn't answer.

"No," Robin admitted.

"Because it's not mine," August said desperately. "If I killed Cage with it, why would I leave it lying around?"

"Because if you killed us all, it wouldn't matter what you left lying around," Larson said. "You could get rid of all the evidence later."

"You think I'm going to kill the band, too?" August demanded.

"Hey, what?" Stacy slurred, making Hiro jump. He'd forgotten she was even there.

Beth took a deep breath, as if what she planned to say

next was painful. "Larson, you told me that you thought there were drug dealers here." She nodded at Hiro's incredulous look. "He said there are boxes in the tunnel."

"Boxes," August deadpanned. "Holy crap, Larson, there are boxes *everywhere*. But what do I know? There's also a murderer on the loose, and I sure as hell didn't expect that."

"What about Drew?" Praveen piped up nervously. She looked at Robin. "You must have seen him."

"At the beach?" Robin asked, confused, and Praveen shook her head. "Seen him where?"

Praveen licked her lips. "In the parking lot. When he left."

"Left?" Robin echoed. She looked excited. "Did you guys get one of the cars to start?"

"No, he walked." Praveen pointed to the door. "He said he was going to the road to get help."

Kyle shook his head. "We didn't see him."

"Oh no." Praveen scratched the backs of her hands. Her nails were leaving angry red lines. "What if the killer . . . Oh my God, please go look for him!"

Beth narrowed her eyes. "Or he's the killer and he just *walked* out of here."

Quivering, Praveen ran to Kyle and latched on to both of his hands. "Please, *please,* Kyle. Go look for him. He was going up to the road. You can find him. Maybe if both of you wait for a car to go by . . ."

In spite of everything that was so massively more important, Hiro felt sorry for Praveen. Drew might be nothing but an unreliable doper who stole songs, but he did pull in the ladies, and it was just so ironic that he had gotten stuck with Praveen. Just more proof that Drew had no common sense. Everyone had been teasing Drew mercilessly about his jailbait, and he had sworn he'd dump her once they got to L.A. Hiro and Mick firmly believed they had to get rid of *Drew* before they got to L.A. Once Samurai Records realized what a buffoon Drew was, they'd dump "his" band.

Maybe fate had just taken a hand in that.

"The fog's really bad," Kyle said, and Robin nodded. "Who's going to see him and stop?"

"All the more reason to bring him back," Praveen said. "Please."

Kyle and Larson traded looks as Robin got up and stood beside Kyle. Hiro glanced at Mick and they both smiled grimly. Mick shook his head. He was staying put. Hiro would rather be with the search party than with the rest of the Breakfast Club. He was also still suspicious of August, and frankly he wanted to get as far away from Cage's body as he could.

"I'll help," he announced, putting his tequila bottle on the table. "Safety in numbers, right?"

"Cool," said Larson.

"And we can check your car," Hiro told Larson. "Maybe we'll get lucky."

Larson nodded and fished in his pocket. "That'd rock."

"Wait. Stop." August made a circle with his hand. "We should stick together."

"We can all look for Drew," Robin said, and Thea shook her head.

"No way," she replied, bursting into tears. Beth slung an arm over her shoulders. "*Why* did you invite me to this f'ing thing?"

"We're staying here," Beth announced. "Me and Thea. And Robin. Until Larson checks his car."

"And me," Stacy muttered. "I can't even walk."

"Yeah, guys, go check the car and come back," August insisted.

"*And look for Drew,*" Praveen pleaded.

"Watch him," Stacy said. "Watch Hiro. Don't turn your back."

Hiro scowled at her. "God, Stacy, I didn't do anything to you."

"What's she talking about?" Mick asked, narrowing his eyes at him.

"No idea," Hiro bit off. He didn't like the way Mick was looking at him. This was getting way too crazy.

"Please stop arguing and go look for him," Praveen said.

"*Check the car,*" August said.

"Okay," Robin said. "Let's do this."

"Stay here," Kyle said gently to Robin. When she began to argue, he said, "We'll be right back."

All eyes were on Larson, Kyle, and Hiro. Getting out of this death trap.

Going into the fog. And the unknown.

17.

THINNING OUT

ROBIN'S RULE #6:

When things are bad,
they can always get worse.

"He'll push him," Stacy murmured.

Robin's forehead wrinkled. She felt sorry for Stacy, who was now sprawled on the floor beside Praveen. Robin walked over and squatted beside them. Stacy's head lolled as she looked up at Robin.

"Hiro pushed me," Stacy enunciated carefully, her head lolling as she looked up at Robin. Her lids were fluttering. "He *says* I fell but I didn't . . . *not.*"

"Well, it's possible that you . . . ," Praveen began, then trailed off. "Oh my God, could it be *Hiro*?" She stared at Robin and jostled Stacy's shoulder. "Stacy? Is Hiro the killer?"

"Hiro pushed me," she said again. "He tried to kill me. He used to love me."

"She's just high," Mick said dismissively.

"How do you know?" Robin asked. "Why don't you believe her?"

"Well, just think about it. If he really tried to kill her, would he bring her back here?"

"I don't know," Robin said. "I don't think like that."

"I'm sick. Robin, I need help," Stacy whispered.

"I'm so scared," Praveen said to Robin, and she pressed a fist against her mouth.

"We're all scared," Robin said. "We just need to stay calm and stick together. Because otherwise—"

A horrible wail pierced Robin's eardrums. It was Drew.

Robin leaped to her feet as Praveen started shrieking. August ran to the stage, picked up his cordless mike, and tried to put it on, dropped it, tried again.

"Drew!" he shouted. "Drew, people are out there looking for you! Try to let them know where you are!"

"No! No!" Praveen yelled. "The killer will know where he is, too!"

"He already knows," Robin said. Her heart was thundering; she tried to force herself to stay calm. Kyle, where was Kyle?

Stacy raised a hand. "Maybe he fell down or something."

"Then he could be hurt and the killer can get to him!" Praveen shouted.

August ignored her. "Drew, make noise! They're out there for you. Let them find you!"

"Not Hiro," Stacy pleaded. "Tell him not to go to Hiro."

Praveen buried her face in Stacy's chest, shaking, crying. "Drew, baby, oh, please, *please,*" Praveen said.

Robin flew to the door, hands around the knob, and Thea and Beth ran up behind her, pulling on her and shouting at her not to turn it.

"Get off me!" she shouted. "Let me go!"

She pushed them away with all her strength; then she was out the door.

August was back on the mike, yelling, "Whoever you are, tell us what you want!"

Robin shut the warehouse door behind herself. The fog was thicker than ever, and her flashlight was useless. She turned it off and minced her way carefully, arms out in front of her. She honestly didn't know which way to turn, and her heartbeat drowned out the crash of the water far below.

"Kyle?" she whispered once, just once.

"Robin," he shouted, and then his arms were around her. He was wet from head to toe and his momentum carried her back to the warehouse.

He was holding on to her, hugging her; he lowered his head and kissed her, hard. Need and energy; she held on as seawater sluiced all over her. They clung to each other; now he was something she could have lost. Someone she had a claim to.

"Where's Drew? What happened?" Praveen demanded from the doorway.

The spell was broken, and Robin pulled away. Kyle kept his hand cupped around the back of her head, trailing it down her back to her waist. Together they trooped inside, past Praveen, with Larson following them.

Robin kept looking at Kyle, fixing her attention on him only. Willing him to look at her because if he didn't, if he looked away . . .

"Oh God," Larson murmured, covering his eyes with his hand. The bat and knife, which he'd been holding, clattered to the ground. "Oh my God."

"No," Praveen cried, scratching her forehead, her cheeks. "Stop!"

"We split up," Larson said. "Kyle and I went to check my car first. Hiro went the other direction."

"Where is Drew?" Praveen shrieked. "Where is he? Did you leave him somewhere? Why isn't he with you?"

"Shut up," Larson snapped. "He's dead." He blinked and his mouth formed an O, as if he hadn't believed it until that moment. He said, far more gently, "Drew's dead."

"No!" Praveen screamed. "No!"

Shivering, Kyle looked away, and Robin began to quake inside. Her heart raced.

No. Not happening, said a little voice in her head. *Not more.*

All eyes fastened on Larson. Robin could hear Praveen screeching like a madwoman.

"We were looking everywhere. Larson and I were going to go down the road but we thought we saw something on the trail," Kyle said. "Then I saw something on the cliff, above the road." Larson's eyes were practically spinning. "It looked like a person, standing. We figured, Drew. Maybe Heather. I cupped my hands to call out to him. And then . . . he . . . he *fell*. Into the ocean."

Praveen was still screaming. Robin pivoted, the room spinning around her. Things were stretching sideways. She was going to faint.

"You don't know that it was Drew," Thea said. "It could have been Heather. Or Morgan."

"I ran down, jumped into the water. I tried to swim out to him," Kyle said. His voice broke. "There was definitely someone in the water."

"You don't *know* that it was Drew!" Praveen shrieked.

"Don't you get it? Hiro pushed him off the cliff!" Stacy said.

Then Beth let out a high-pitched wail and Kyle was yelling and covering Robin, people were running and shouting. Robin was baffled; then she looked up and followed the line of Beth's hand, extended toward the dead skull lights, toward the loft—

—toward the loft—

—where Heather seemed perched as if she was going to jump. Her face was bloody, her eyes bloodshot, and the terror in them made Robin scream, too.

Then Heather jumped out of the loft—

—or was pushed—

She fell straight down. There was a rope around her neck, a hangman's noose. Robin shrieked, running with her arms out, as if she could catch her. But the rope went taut.

Above all the fury, Robin heard a crack like a gunshot.

Heather's feet swung out of reach. She was wearing just one shoe; the other foot was bare and bleeding; then the lone shoe fell off and smacked the floor.

Heather swung back and forth,

back and forth,

like a bell.

18

HELL BREAKS LOOSE

ROBIN'S RULE #7:

Help others whenever you can.

Screaming.

Nonstop screaming.

Hands grabbed and dragged Robin backward. Larson leaped at Heather's feet, but they swayed above him.

He finally grabbed a knife and dragged a table over, yelling, "Damn it, help me!" Beth and Thea, confused, picked up a second table. Larson shook his head and put a chair on the table, then climbed up.

"Heather!" Robin cried. Wildly, she struggled against whoever was holding her. August led Mick around the stage, disappearing. Stacy pointed up at the loft. She tried to get away. Had to get to Heather. The whole room tilted and blurred. Someone ran past her; someone was still holding her, putting their hand over her eyes, forcing her not to look.

She heard a sickening thud as the floor took an impact. They had cut Heather down.

She pried the fingers away as Larson flung himself down to his knees trying to loosen the noose from around her neck. Bloodshot eyes as big as plums were pressing outward from their sockets.

"Shit!" Larson bellowed. "Shit! She's dead!"

Larson got up and staggered away from Heather. He looked around with huge eyes, shell-shocked; Beth ran toward him but he turned away. She threw her arms around him from behind, sobbing.

Robin's throat was raw and her scream finally croaked to an end with bile searing her vocal cords. She buried her head in Kyle's chest. He was the one who had been grabbing at her. He wrapped his arms around her and held her so tightly she could barely breathe.

August and Mick ran back into the room. "I had a ladder to get up there," August said, pointing at the loft. "For the lights. But it's gone. I don't know how she got up there. I don't know . . ."

"That's the rope you made us bring here!" Beth shrieked at him.

Robin shook harder as the words sank in. The rope August had sent them to find had a hangman's noose at the end.

"Kyle, I found that rope. *I* found it," Robin said, gasping.

He tightened his arms even more until she was afraid he was going to crack her ribs.

"No. Don't go there."

"Who did this? Who would want this?" she whispered.

"It's August's party. His rules. His sick collection of stuff," Kyle said.

For one insane moment she felt like she was back home, sitting at her kitchen table, playing Clue with her brother. *I suspect Mr. August in the warehouse with the rope.*

She didn't know which was worse—that three people were dead or that she was trying to parse who had killed them as though it were just another puzzle to solve, just another game. One thing was for sure. This wasn't going to end. She'd thought earlier that maybe someone with a grudge had followed Cage. But this was someone who had it out for more of them, maybe *all* of them.

That was when she realized that she *had* to solve it. No cars, no phones. She couldn't let anything happen to Kyle. Or Thea. Or Beth. Or . . . everyone.

Heather lay crumpled on the ground. August, Mick, and Larson gathered in a half circle behind her. Mick and Larson were staring with open hostility at August, and Robin tensed, certain that they were going to attack him.

Praveen staggered over to a crate, put her head between her knees, and unceremoniously vomited. Stacy was across the room on another crate doing the same. Thea and Beth stood well away from the body, arms around each other as if they were holding each other up.

The door flew open. It was Hiro, eyes wide.

"I heard . . . *Shit*," Hiro said. He stared at Heather's body.

Praveen ran toward him and threw her arms around him. He stumbled from the impact. "Tell me Drew's alive!"

He held on to her as his gaze fixed on the rope around Heather's neck. "Who did this?"

"Well, *you* weren't here," August ground out. "Were you?"

"No, man. No way." He looked at Praveen and cautiously began to disengage. "I'm sorry. Yeah, I saw it. He fell, Praveen."

"No. It wasn't him. It was someone else," she insisted, grabbing at him. She hit his chest with both her fists. "You're lying!"

Mick came over to Praveen and gathered her up. His gaze flickered over to Hiro as he forced Praveen to walk back across the room with him.

"Wish I was," Hiro said. He staggered over to the drink table, grabbed his bottle of tequila, and threw it back. He looked up at the ceiling, then around the room. "What the hell happened?"

"We don't know," Kyle said.

"Yet," Robin added.

She made herself look at Heather. Everyone was turning away from her. Soon she would be covered, like Cage. She leaned her head against Kyle's trembling arm.

From that angle, she noticed something white beneath the coil of rope around her neck. It was one of August's damned envelopes.

"Look," she said, forcing herself to squat down and pluck it up with her thumb and forefinger so that she could read what was written on the front.

"*You killed them, you sick bastard,*" she read to the group.

August was obviously meant to be the sick bastard. He was clever; he would have known all eyes would turn to him as the sadistic jerk in charge of this whole nightmare. So staging a note from someone else was a fairly useless attempt to deflect his guilt, if he was guilty. But with all the adrenaline and the emotions charging around the room, Robin wouldn't be surprised if someone snapped and beat up August before he could prove his innocence.

If he could.

Maybe that was exactly what the real killer wanted.

"Okay, but what's inside the envelope?" Mick asked.

The envelope was secured to the rope around Heather's neck, and a tug failed to free it. Robin looked hard at August, who blanched and backed away, hands lifted. "You do it. No way am I touching a dead girl to find out."

A *dead girl*. Robin forced herself to take a deep breath. She didn't want to touch the dead girl, either. More sharp acid flooded her mouth as she bent down again and reached for the envelope. Heather's arm slid sideways and thudded gently onto the floor.

Robin hesitated. Then she grasped the envelope. It was stuck.

"It's taped onto her . . . her skin," Kyle said, looking sick.

Robin's lip curled back and she heard her own breaths

197

through her clenched teeth as she worked her fingers beneath the noose and picked at a strip of clear packing tape on Heather's chest. Kyle put a steadying hand on Robin's shoulder. She bit down hard on her lip and tugged. Heather's chin bounced.

She pulled it free and started to stand, but soon froze, staring at Heather's face. There was a beat and when she still didn't move, Kyle took the envelope. His hand was shaking so badly it was nearly impossible for him to pull out the single white sheet of paper inside.

"Well? What does it say?" Mick said.

Kyle licked his lips. "*Play by my rules or be the next to die.*'"

A wail tore out of Thea. Beth struggled to quiet her as she collapsed onto the floor. As stealthily as she could, Robin picked up the knife and slid it into the pocket of her bomber jacket.

"There's more," Kyle said, speaking over Thea's meltdown, Praveen's wails.

"I didn't do it, okay?" August said, before anyone could even accuse him.

Kyle read.

```
"Water, water everywhere but not a drop to
drink.
If you ever want to leave here, now's the
time to think.
On my words now you must dwell.
For your sins fetch from the well."
```

"*What?*" Hiro set down his bottle.

"Sins? Like sins committed against Alexa?" Larson said.

Robin's mind went into puzzle mode, watching as if from afar as Kyle seemed to realize he would get sick if he didn't change and stripped out of his wet clothes, turning away from the group as Larson offered up his hoodie. Mick gave him a pair of sweats, socks, and sneakers from a gear bag at the back of the stage.

Larson lowered himself into a half crouch, looming over Heather. He swayed, his face a pasty gray. Robin gently touched his shoulder.

He jumped so hard that she recoiled in fear.

"Hey," Kyle said, putting his hand in the pocket of the hoodie. "There's something . . ."

He pulled out his hand to reveal a pair of earbuds.

And a large hoop studded with sparkly stones—the mate of the one Heather was still wearing.

"Larson!" Hiro shouted.

LARSON'S RULE #3:

Never admit anything.

Hiro charged Larson and threw him to the ground. He pulled back a fist and slammed it into Larson's side as Larson scrabbled out from underneath him. Hiro caught Larson around the thighs and pummeled him, fists smashing into Larson's rib cage. A sharp pain swallowed Larson up and he gagged, grabbing at his side. More blows rained down on him and he covered his head.

A second later, powerful arms dragged Hiro off. Larson coughed and heaved. The pain was unbearable. Robin reached out her hands to him, while behind her, Kyle slammed Hiro against the wall.

"What the hell is wrong with you?" Kyle shouted.

"It's him!" Hiro said. "He's the killer!"

Larson coughed again, and a clanging, rolling, throbbing shot through his rib cage. He shut his eyes until he could speak. "I think he broke one of my ribs."

"Why do you have her earring?" Robin asked him.

"I found it," he managed to say. "On the floor."

"Where?" she pressed.

Larson struggled to remember. Pain fuzzed him out; the whole hideous night was an exhausting, chaotic haze.

"Back there somewhere," he said, pointing in what he thought was the right direction. "I was hunting. I saw it."

"You mean after you bailed on me?" Praveen accused.

Beth took the earring from Robin and examined it. She turned it over and then held it up to the light.

"Why didn't you say anything? All this time everyone's been looking for her and you had this?"

"Yeah, and?" Larson retorted, grunting. "Does it mean anything? Change anything? Girls lose earrings all the time. I figured if I said anything, people would treat me exactly like you guys are doing now. I didn't know it was definitely Heather's."

"But you didn't see or hear anything else?" Robin asked.

"No, *Sherlock*," he said, and Robin flinched. He wasn't sorry. He was hurt and he hadn't done anything to anyone. Okay, except for running faster up the cliff than Beth. That was the sum total of his crimes.

"You saw nothing that would have told you that Heather was in trouble?" Kyle chimed in.

Larson started to shake his head, then stopped. Kyle cocked a brow and Larson decided he might as well share, since keeping silent hadn't worked out too well.

"Well," he said, "I thought someone was watching me."

Robin blinked. "Like how?"

There was no way he was going to tell her what he thought had really happened. It sounded ridiculous, like he was making it up on the spot. He'd rather take his chances with the killer than this overamped mob.

"People hook up at these parties all the time. You'd know that if you belonged here, Robin. You'd learn not to look too hard in dark corners, you know?" He touched his right side and sucked in air between his teeth.

"You're *lying*," Hiro said, and everyone looked over at him.

Larson struggled to sit up and despite his petulant dis of her, Robin helped him. A little ashamed, he glared over at Hiro. "What's *your* deal? You took off from Kyle and me. For all we know, you did push Drew and then you killed Heather."

He couldn't tell if Hiro looked more scared or angry.

"No way, man. I was just trying to find him and then I saw him fall, so I was on my way back when I heard everyone yelling. Besides, I wouldn't have hurt Heather," he said, his voice more aggressive.

"Who was the last person to see Heather?" Robin asked.

"She bailed on me after we found our first clue and had to read August's revised Shakespeare," Kyle said.

"We saw." Robin pointed. "She went down that hall."

"Yeah, that's where we ran into each other," Hiro said.

"What were you doing?" Larson asked. "Something that would make her lose her earring? Like knocking her out?"

"No! She wanted to hook up," Hiro said. "I went to get a condom and when I came back, she was gone. Whoever grabbed her must have done it then."

Larson coughed again, the agony causing him to pound his fist on his thigh.

"You didn't puncture a lung, did you?" Beth asked. She was worried but her voice was cold. The love was gone. She was still mad at him for leaving her on the beach.

"What? No, what?" Larson asked.

"If Hiro broke your rib, it could have punctured your lung. Are you coughing up blood?"

"Oh my God," Hiro blurted. "Hey, man. I don't know what came over me. I swear it."

He ignored Hiro. He didn't know why Hiro was pretty much getting away with pounding on him.

"No," he said to Beth. "How do you know that, anyway?"

"I watch a lot of TV. A punctured lung can kill you."

A jolt of panic zapped him. He wasn't coughing up blood, right? He didn't taste blood in his mouth or anything. He wiped his hand across his lips. No blood there. "If you did that to me . . . ," he said, raising a fist in Hiro's direction.

"Newsflash, August. It's *not* safer in here," Beth said.

"Well, it would be if we booted Hiro," said Larson. "Push him out the door and lock it."

Hiro ran his hands through his black hair. It stood straight up from his skull. Larson still couldn't wrap his head around the fact that the drummer had attacked him. The guy was seriously messed up.

Beth took the paper from Robin and waved it in the air. "If we don't play by the killer's rules and follow the clues, we're all dead."

"That's bull," Robin blurted.

Beth raised a brow. "And you know this because . . . ?"

Robin opened her mouth, then closed it. She clearly didn't know.

"He's already killed three people. Do you really think he'd hesitate to kill someone else?" Beth asked.

"If it even is a *he,*" Larson said pointedly as he stared back at her.

"I think we should do it," Thea said, half raising her hand, as if she had to ask for permission to speak. Her face was blotchy and swollen. "We should follow the clues and maybe if we play by his rules long enough, he'll let us live."

"Or we'll find a way to escape," Beth replied.

"What about us?" Mick asked. "We're just the band."

"Drew is dead," Hiro snapped.

Mick closed his eyes and lowered his head. "Let's get the hell out of here."

"He's at large," Kyle said. "I say we don't piss him off until we can figure out a way to take him out."

"No, we shouldn't play this psycho's game. His rules keep him in control," Robin argued. "If we all stick together, there's nothing he can do to us."

"Hey, guys, my gas can's gone," Kyle said suddenly.

Everyone turned and looked. Sure enough, no gas can.

"It was full," August said. "The killer could have already doused the outside of this place with it and be waiting, watching us, ready to light a match and kill us all right now if we don't do what he wants."

Beth sniffed the air. Thea started to cry again. Praveen hadn't stopped. Stacy rested her forehead in her hands.

"That's assuming the killer isn't someone in this room," Kyle said, still pinning Hiro.

"How could that be?" Hiro insisted. "People have died right in front of us."

"Cage was beaten," Kyle said.

"Hey, I was here. In this room," Hiro said.

"You guys have had breaks," Kyle said. "Lots of time to wander around. You could have done it. Look what you did to Larson."

"Okay, I lost it," Hiro said. "I'm sorry. We're all losing it. We're a rock band. We didn't sign on for any of this!"

August looked a little lost without his clipboard and headset. Just one of the pawns, no longer the dungeon master. "I say we play his game. I don't think we can afford not to. He—or she—is holding all the cards now and we just have to play along, hope for a lucky break."

"Nice try, August," Beth said. "But it's over."

"I wish to God it was!" August yelled at her. "I am not doing this!"

"Does anyone even know where we are?" Thea wailed. "I sure didn't tell my parents."

August's defeated huff was the worst possible response. The clues about the party's location had been doled out one at a time.

They were completely on their own.

From the corner, Stacy whispered, "I'm dying." A moment later she face-planted onto the floor.

19

THE TOWER

MORGAN'S RULE #2:

Keep playing until the game is over.

Something skittered across her cheek.

There was a growl.

I'm alive.

Morgan's lids fluttered as she forced them open. Shadows, darkness. She was a ball of pain. She heard another growl, low and menacing, and by some miracle she rolled onto her side; from there, very slowly, she forced herself onto her hands and knees. Something dangled from her chest and she sucked in a shriek as she batted at it. Her fingers closed around what felt like paper and her hand spasmed as she yanked it free.

The black world spun. Her ears were ringing. Knuckles

taut as she clenched the paper, she dropped her hand back to the ground and made herself crawl forward.

A sharp nip pierced her jeans leg. She sucked in a cry. Something had just bitten her. She scrabbled faster, swaying from side to side, feeling something wet dripping from her head.

Get out of here. Get away.

She heard the chuffing of a large animal. The padding and shuffling of large feet through the trash. A glass bottle rolled.

"Oh God, please help me," she whispered as her left arm gave way and she tumbled to the floor. Cage, where was he?

She heard more growling. *Mountain lion.*

She crawled on her elbows when her hands gave way, then pushed herself up. Everything hurt. But she was a cheerleader, an athlete, in better shape than most people. She had to save herself. Had to keep going. There was a wild animal after her.

Faster, faster.

A faint light glowed up ahead. She saw that she was in a tunnel and she was clutching a white envelope. The light was a lantern on a large cardboard box. There was something draped beside it. She heaved out a sob and struggled toward it, but as she approached, her blood froze.

It was a long black coat like the one her attacker had worn. She stared hard past the light, wondering if August was lurking in the dark, waiting to finish the job he had started:

Killing her.

She crawled to the side of the tunnel, panting, eyes darting everywhere. The world began to dim and she fought back panic.

On the front of the envelope was printed YOU KILLED THEM, YOU SICK BASTARD. She opened it with badly shaking hands and pulled out a piece of paper.

"Water, water everywhere but not a drop to
drink.
If you ever want to leave here, now's the
time to think.
On my words now you must dwell.
For your sins fetch from the well."

A new clue. Or half of one. Cage would have the other half. She choked back a sob. Maybe that meant he wasn't dead. She closed her eyes and tears spilled. They were going to be okay. They were going to get out of here.

From the direction she had come, she heard another growl. She flattened her shoes on the ground and pushed backward, sliding slowly up the tunnel wall. On unsteady feet, she lurched forward like Kyle's imitation of Frankenstein. She staggered and pitched forward onto the cardboard box. The coat fell off, revealing a black plastic clipboard with envelopes and pages attached. She was about to slide it under her arm to read later when she caught sight of a single word written in black marker with a circle around it:

ROBIN?!

The word was written over a complicated-looking spreadsheet, and there was another note in marker:

CAGE WHY NO ENVELOPE?! MOVE MORGAN? HEATHER NEXT!

She looked fearfully over her shoulder, then examined the other envelopes. On each was printed YOU KILLED THEM, YOU SICK BASTARD. What did "Cage why no envelope" mean?

The growl became a roar and she dropped the clipboard in a panic. Her hand smacked the tunnel wall as she zigzagged drunkenly, losing her balance, about to go down. Faster, careening completely off balance, falling, getting up, falling.

Footpads picked up pace. So did she. She had to get out of there, had to move.

There were stairs, a rotted wooden banister.

She'd never make it.

I have to try.

Sucking in her breath, she grabbed with both hands and began to pull herself up the first step. Her legs weighed a ton each.

Got to the first step.

The second.

"Oh God, oh God," she whispered.

The third.

Something pushed her from behind, hard. She fell onto her hands with a deep grunt.

Excruciating pain. Her upper thigh.

She kicked and tried to yell, but her voice was gone. Kept kicking. Tried to get up another step. She didn't know if she was moving. Didn't know if she was climbing.

More pain. More growling. Something tugged hard at her legs and then her hand came down on *flat ground*. She was all the way up the stairs. She had made it!

She scooted forward, sobbing with relief.

And a hundred tiny skittering things rushed over her face.

ROBIN'S RULE #8:

It's always better to take action
than to sit and worry.

All the yelling around Robin collapsed into the pinpricks of Stacy's glassy eyes. Kyle was doing chest compressions but there was no use. Stacy was dead. She had said she was dying. How had she known? Had she overdosed? She'd been throwing up for what seemed like the entire night.

Kyle stood up, shook his head. Others swooped down on the body with a cloth as he moved toward Robin.

"We're going to do some quick exploring," Kyle said, taking Robin's hand.

"Wait," August said.

Together they bulleted into action, rushing outside to

look for clues, or help; it had dawned on Robin that the killer might have a working car that they could take away from him.

On the side of the warehouse facing the parking lot, a rusted fire escape dangled about six feet above the ground and Kyle gave her a leg up to reach it. Her weight stressed the strip of salt-encrusted stairs and it squealed and shuddered as he hoisted up onto it like a trapeze artist. It groaned and swayed, and Robin gritted her teeth and kept following, bracing herself every step of the way for a violent tumble onto the brittle fragments of shells.

They kept going until they reached the bell tower. A circle of fluted wrought iron protected a brick enclosure from which hung an old encrusted brass bell on a rusted iron chain. AZUL CANNERY was tamped on the rim, but the clapper was missing. They stood panting for a moment, instinctively holding hands as they gazed into the fog. It was like floating in a hot air balloon far above the horizon, and Robin felt weightless. She heard the crash of the surf and her own breathing. The glow from Kyle's flashlight sank into the swirling white upon white. They couldn't see anything except the shapes of a few of the buildings and a sprawl of darkness in the parking lot, where the cars sat as motionless as toads on the alert, and just as useless. She tried to imagine how someone could steal their batteries without getting caught. How they could hide Cage under a tarp in the busy party room and push Heather.

Did someone poison Stacy? Or did she simply OD? What is simple about overdosing on drugs?

She squeezed her eyes shut for a second. Then her boots hit something uneven in the floor and she bent down to feel it.

It was a trapdoor.

She squatted down and together she and Kyle opened it to reveal, by flashlight, a drop of about ten feet into what looked like an attic. Kyle insisted on going in first, and after he made a circle with the cone of light, he lifted his arms to Robin and she snaked down his front. Heat kindled in her tummy and roared to furnace levels by the time her feet touched the dusty, cobwebby floor. They crushed each other, rocking from side to side. She wanted, needed to stay close to him until her shaking stopped. Until forever.

"I feel like I'm going to jitter apart," she whispered.

"Me too," he said.

They held hands as he passed the flashlight over the piles of items, mostly barrels and crates stenciled with AZUL CANNERY, MANTILLA, CALIFORNIA. Everything was coated with thick layers of grime. Nothing appeared to have been disturbed, but it would have been possible for the killer to move a few barrels and boxes to squeeze through and sneak down a set of stairs they had yet to find, then reposition everything to conceal the route.

Still, they tried to clear out enough space to investigate, but the attic was so crammed it proved an impossible task. Robin wiped her sweaty face, then breathed in slowly as Kyle came up behind her, placing his arms around her waist. He kissed her earlobe. He smelled of cinnamon and seawater.

Tingles went through her cheeks and lips and even her eyelids. Kyle was here, so alive. Everything else was dying.

With a shudder, she dropped her head back and he kissed her forehead. If only they could keep kissing until the sun rose, they would be all right. She turned around and molded her body to his. He sucked in his breath, her hands sneaking beneath the hoodie to touch his bare, cold skin. He shivered, and she did, too.

Kyle's hands passed lightly over her shoulders, her arms, her back. Then they pressed together so fully that not even a dust mote could have drifted between them.

But the dark thoughts could.

They were surrounded by death and murder. Stacy had died. Where was Morgan?

Hush, for just one moment, her heart pleaded. *Let me have this.*

"Kyle," she whispered.

They clung to each other. Kyle wrapped a hand around the back of her head and pressed the side of her face against his chest. His supercharged heartbeat betrayed his fear and, as they wrapped around each other, his desire, too.

"I didn't know you liked me," he murmured.

"You're so stupid," she said.

He grunted. "Why didn't you let me know?"

"Because every other girl at school lets you know."

"I thought you were competitive."

"Not over a *guy,*" she said, tapping his chest with a half-formed fist.

"Why not? If it's what you want." He fanned his fingertips beneath her chin and raised her face to his. Then he kissed her again. This was Kyle and they were both okay and it felt like they had gone somewhere else that she had dreamed of going with Kyle Thomas a hundred times, a hundred thousand, and here they were. For one heartbeat only, they had made it.

Reality rushed back in just as fast, and Robin knew it was time to get back to business. The business of survival.

"We need to stop," she said. He kept holding her, and she knew he wanted to do things she had never done.

"Kyle, c'mon," she murmured, and he moaned in frustration.

"For all we know, the killer's in the attic, too," she whispered. "We're already being foolhardy."

"I'm so sorry you came here," Kyle murmured, taking her hand.

"Sames."

"Robin," he began, and then he stopped.

She waited, and when he didn't go on, she waggled his hand to prod him.

"It's just . . ." He blew air out of his cheeks. "We know that someone is trying to kill us. And . . ." He turned his head. She cupped his cheek.

"Kyle, *what?*"

"If we think someone is doing it . . . if we figure out who it is . . ." He bit down on his lower lip. "To protect ourselves, what if we . . . we strike first?"

Silence fell between them. She could hear her heartbeat.

"Oh my God." She covered her mouth with both hands. "You mean *kill* someone?"

He stood wordlessly for a moment, and then he blurted, "No, no. I mean what if we tie them up? Or lock them up someplace? August . . ."

"But what if we guess wrong? And the killer comes after them?"

"Yeah. I know. No, I don't know," he said. "If anyone tried to hurt you . . . if I suspected *any* of them . . ."

"You're scaring me," she told him. "I'm already scared enough."

"Sorry. I'd be happy if someone offered to protect me." He started to run his hands through his hair and wiped them on the hoodie instead. "Let's go back to the group."

She didn't move.

"Hey." He brushed her lips with his. "I won't do anything crazy. Okay?"

"Okay," she said. "And, Kyle? I will protect you."

They kissed again, longingly, tenderly at first and then once again, Robin reluctantly put on the brakes.

They slid some crates to the trapdoor opening and clambered up them. Then they eased cautiously down the fire escape, hanging on when the aged metal threatened to dump them. Kyle reached the ground first. He put his arms around her waist and lowered her carefully to the ground as if she would shatter, and she realized that she wasn't used to anyone fussing over her. After her dad had been hurt, she had stepped up. Tonight was supposed to have been about acting her age and having some fun.

Big mistake.

They walked around to the door into the warehouse and Robin paused.

"I think we should move out of this building," she said. "We should try to find a way out of here. If we can't find a working car, maybe we should just get to the road. Even if Drew . . . didn't make it." She licked her lips and tried not to hear the echo of his final scream in her memory.

"What about the note?" he asked softly. "Around Heather's neck?" He looked at the door. "What if we go back in there and someone else . . ."

"Don't even say it."

She placed her hand over his and together, shoulders squared, they turned the knob. She closed her eyes for one second, and then she walked in first.

Robot corpses and human bodies littered the floor.

The room looked deserted. Then Beth popped up and ran toward them. Her hands were bloody; Robin sucked in her breath and a wave of disorienting panic washed over her.

Someone else has died.

"It's Praveen," Beth said. "She's been scratching herself to shreds."

Kyle swore under his breath and followed Robin and Beth as they clattered across the cavernous space. Thea and Praveen were squeezed into a corner; Praveen was wrapped in a black tablecloth.

"Hey," Robin said, feeling massively awkward because she didn't know Praveen at all. Beth gave her a look and drew back the tablecloth. Praveen's pretty green blouse was streaked with blood.

"Shit," Kyle muttered.

"It itches," Praveen whispered fiercely. "I can't stop it. It feels like there are matches under my skin."

"Do you have some cream or something in your purse?" Robin asked her.

"Nothing will help," Praveen whimpered. "It's a very rare disease. No one else can even see it."

Robin was freaked. She looked at Beth, who rolled her eyes and gave her head a little shake.

"This is new," Beth muttered. "At least, new to me."

Robin said, "You have to try to stop. You're hurting yourself."

"I don't believe Drew is dead," Praveen said frantically. "I think they saw the killer falling into the ocean. I think the killer committed suicide, like Alexa."

"Alexa drowned," Beth said. "By accident."

"So they say." Praveen itched and scratched.

Robin reached out to pat Praveen, then thought the better of it. Maybe it would be painful to her. Instead she gave Praveen a sympathetic smile and got to her feet.

"Listen, Praveen. Beth. Everybody," Robin said. "We couldn't see much of anything up in the tower. No cars we couldn't account for, anyway. And we couldn't figure out if the killer got into the warehouse from there. So we're not going to stay in here anymore."

"We have to start the hunt," Beth said anxiously. "We need to get moving."

"I don't want to." Thea hugged herself, hunched over, despondent, terrified. "I just want to go home."

Kyle dipped his head. "I'm going to get some more flashlights."

As he walked away, Beth wiped her hands on the black tablecloth and crossed to the refreshment table to pluck up a water bottle.

"Don't. It's poisoned," Praveen said in a weird flat voice. She didn't blink. Surrounded by her dark hair, which had come loose from its braid, and the black tablecloth, her face was a small, gaunt mask of catatonia.

"It hasn't been opened," Beth said, showing her. Then she twisted off the cap and doused her hands one at a time. "What if there's more than one killer? What if they figure out what we're doing—that we're searching for the car instead of 'following the rules'—and they come after us?"

Robin shrugged. "They're already after us."

Beth dried her hands on a black cloth napkin. "I'm sorry," she said. "I'm sorry I tricked you into coming and I . . . I didn't look out for you, Rob. I could have been nice to you, done things for you after I made it. Instead I just kind of left you behind because I wanted . . ." She looked down. "I wanted things I wouldn't get out of you. I'm a user."

"You don't have to be," Robin said. "A lot of people liked you just the way you were."

Beth searched Robin's face. "But the way I was . . . wasn't good enough. Robin, I wanted to have an amazing life like these guys."

"What's so amazing about this?" Robin asked, and a sad chuckle bubbled out of Beth's mouth.

"Well, except for this."

"Alexa DeYoung had it all. It didn't make her happy. She didn't think she had an amazing life. And neither do most of the people who came here tonight. They're miserable. They don't know how to get what they want. They just try to bully the universe into giving it to them."

Beth blinked. She thought a moment, and then she said, "God, you're right."

"Look at Praveen. She's completely nuts."

"And a klepto," Beth said. And the tears spilled. "I don't understand how to grow up," she cried, sinking into Robin's arms. "I'm so scared we're going to die here and I'll never figure it out. When we get out of this, I'm going to do something amazing for *you*. I'm going to help you. And your family. I'm going to be a good person again."

Robin put her arms around Beth and squeezed tight. "You're still a good person, Bethie-B. You just lost your way for a little while."

"I did what I had to do to become friends with these people," Beth half whispered. "I tried to bully my way in, like you said. I *did* bully my way in. I'll do whatever I have to so we can leave here. Nothing will stop me. *Nothing*."

"Same here." Robin let go of her and held out her hand. "Let's shake on it."

"It'll be our pact."

They shook. Beth smiled as if she were almost more excited than frightened. Her eyes glittered. They were both tough as nails. No wonder they had been friends in the old days.

"So we have a few different ways we can go," Robin said. She held up her fingers. "Find the killer. Find his car. Win this game."

"Kill him," Beth whispered, and Robin's brows shot up. "Wow, B."

"Didn't know I had it in me, did you?" Beth said soberly. "No. I didn't."

"What about you? Could you kill someone?"

She had just had this conversation with Kyle in the bell tower. Now it didn't seem quite as abstract. Robin pulled in her chin and raised her eyebrows. "Could I be a killer? How can anyone do that?"

"All these things I know about people," Beth said. "Cheating, stealing. Lying. I was so shocked at first. Now"— she shrugged—"it just seems normal. Everyone breaks the rules. I don't know anyone who doesn't." She cocked her head. "Except maybe you."

"Got the flashlights," Kyle announced. "Let's go."

From out of the darkness, Larson said, "I can't."

20

BETH STEPS UP

BETH'S RULE #3:

Your special thing can be a secret.

Larson was in too much pain to scramble all over the cannery, and Praveen was too shell-shocked. The rest of the survivors separated into two groups: those who were leaving and those who were staying. Beth volunteered to remain with Larson and Praveen, her first act of sacrifice in her quest to be a good person again.

Footfalls signaled a mass exodus to the door as Kyle squatted in front of Beth and handed her the knife. Robin bent down beside him. "I'm not sure it's the best thing, you staying here," Kyle said.

"Someone's got to do it." Her voice wobbled and she searched deep inside for that moment when her courage had flamed like a comet. "But I do wish I had a rocket launcher." She chewed her lower lip. "One thing? The faster we get her out of here, the better." She jerked her head at Praveen, who had retreated somewhere very distant and unreachable.

Robin kissed Beth's cheek as the two turned away. "It might be better if we draw out the hunt," Kyle murmured. "Maybe the killer will get tired and make a mistake. Or someone will come. Our parents will start to wonder. A car might come down the road."

Beth hoped they didn't adopt that strategy. She wanted this over with as soon as possible. But only if at the end, they were all alive.

Kyle took the bat. The others trooped out with him.

"Praveen," Beth said, "I'm going to check the door to make sure it's locked. I'm not leaving. I promise."

Praveen made a mewing noise like a kitten. More than anything else that had been said or done thus far, the unnatural little sound scared Beth, as if Praveen was somehow becoming less human. Beth eased away from her and got to her feet so she could check on Larson.

To her surprise, he was sitting up. According to her medical shows, if his rib was broken, that would have been excruciating. Maybe it was just bruised, then. That would be a hundred thousand times better than the alternative.

"Are you leaving?" Larson asked.

"Just locking the door," she promised.

Holding the knife in one hand, she used the other to

drag the same chair August had used underneath the doorknob. She studied the ebony rectangles on either side of the stage. Lots of places to attack from. She had no doubt that there were doors she didn't know about that weren't locked. Punched-out windows to crawl through.

Stop it.

She walked back to Larson and squatted down beside him. "Can I get you something? Some water?"

He was quiet for a moment. "I'm sorry," he said finally. "I didn't mean to bail on you down at the beach."

"Did you actually just apologize to me?" she asked him.

"If you tell anyone, I'll . . . well, I won't kill you," he said. He screwed up his face and she knew he was hurting.

She smiled at Larson and said, "Apology accepted, Lar."

He grimaced again. "Don't call me that. I hate that."

"Oh." She mimed zipping up her mouth and throwing away the key. "Done."

She wanted to kiss him. He was a captive audience, so to speak, and after all, they'd been flirting pretty intensely on the beach. But she decided against it. The timing was all wrong.

Rising, she steadfastly did not look at any of the bodies as she crossed the room. She lifted a lantern off one of the tables and held it up high as she looked for her purse. She finally found it and fished out some ibuprofen for Larson.

People show their true faces when the chips are down.

Once they were assembled outside the warehouse, everyone paused and took stock. In addition to the bat, Kyle was carrying two flashlights and Thea cradled an electric lantern in her arms like a newborn. Mick and Hiro were each hefting an end of Kyle's crowbar and a lantern, and all August had was a lantern and a barbecue lighter. The sum total of their weapons.

"Is Praveen . . . *okay*?" Mick asked Robin. "I mean, well, you know what I mean."

For the record, he hadn't thought she was okay for a long time. She had this habit of saying the scariest things about what she was going to do to people she didn't like. She just threw them out there like it was perfectly normal to discuss burning down a store because they had accused her of shoplifting. Or poisoning the munchies at a gig because the groupies were crowding Drew.

Poisoning? His heart turned over in his chest. Could Praveen have poisoned Stacy?

"I don't know," Robin replied.

"So now we're in it with you people," he said. "We need to play this dirtbag's game."

"Or find him and stop him," Robin said.

They locked gazes and Mick inclined his head. He

had to give this girl her due. She was smart and people listened to her. He wondered if he should say anything about Praveen.

Kyle took Robin's hand as August stood with the door to his back and gestured for everyone to gather around him. "I think this clue is about a well. Like a water well," August said. "That's what we need to look for."

Robin frowned. "They wouldn't dig a well *here*. This is the ocean. All they would get is salt water."

Thea raised her hand. "Maybe there's, like, a wishing well."

August squinted at her, obviously confused and irritated, and Mick cleared his throat.

"I know this sounds like a dangerous idea, but what about forming a couple of hunting parties? And we can also keep looking for the killer's car."

"I agree with Mick. We should split up. We can cover more ground that way. It also gives the douche bag less chance of taking us all out," Kyle said.

"That's easy for you to say when you've got the baseball bat," August snapped. "Where's the knife?"

"Beth has it," said Robin.

Thea turned a stricken face toward Robin. Mick knew how she felt. He couldn't believe he was in a situation where people were talking about how to improve their odds of living through the night, and all they had to protect themselves with was a baseball bat. And this idiotic crowbar, which they would do well to dump.

"We need more protection," Robin said.

"Here are your spreadsheets from my hunt," August said, passing them out like graded homework papers in a class at school. "Beth's and Kyle's teams had more weapons to find: a wrench, a lead pipe, a revolver—"

"A gun? Where did you hide it?" Robin said, shuffling her paper.

"The revolver isn't real," August said. "Sorry."

At least the knife is real, Mick thought. Although in the hands of someone like Beth it could well be more of a liability than anything else. Sometimes the only thing a knife was good for was getting stabbed with it after someone took it away from you.

"We have a better chance of finding *him* if more than one group is looking for him," Mick insisted. "He can't spy on all of us at the same time." He looked at each member of the group in turn. A few hours ago, the only three whose names he'd known had been Praveen, August, and Hiro. But there was now also Kyle, Thea, and Robin. Six people. Then Beth and Larson and he made nine. Whether that other girl Morgan was alive or dead, victim or killer, remained to be seen.

"No. We should stick together," Thea insisted, biting her thumbnail. "If he attacks us, we can protect each other."

"What if *he* has a revolver?" Mick said. "Just because we don't have dangerous weapons doesn't mean he doesn't."

Kyle nodded as he studied his spreadsheet. "We should

try to snag these every chance we can get. He probably already knows about these weapons and might have already taken them. He knows an awful lot about this hunt. It's got to be someone you hang out with, August. Someone who wanted to come, maybe, but didn't get invited. Do you know anyone like that?"

August flashed Kyle the sourest of smiles. "Yes, and so do you. Half of Callabrese High."

Mick figured he was right. These were the "cool" kids, the ones with money and freedom. Hipsters, or so they thought of themselves. The ones who would leave Callabrese in their taillights.

Unless they died first.

"Well, I'm going to start looking for a water well," Mick announced. He looked expectantly at Hiro. Time to suit up and work together. His bandmate couldn't possibly be the killer.

But when Hiro shifted his glance toward Mick, something dark and malevolent flared across his face. Mick was chilled. Where had *that* come from? He thought about Hiro wailing on Larson. Hiro, who hadn't been accounted for when either Drew or Heather had died. He'd been with Stacy most of the night. Maybe he'd put poison in her travel tumbler.

Oh my God, is Hiro a crazy serial killer? They say you never know. There're women who are married to serial killers and don't have the vaguest idea. No. That's crazy. That is totally insane.

Except suddenly, it didn't seem like a given to pair off with his bandmate.

Mick looked at Robin. "What's your plan?"

"Maybe our new clue is about a bucket," she said. "You get well water in a bucket."

He considered that, giving her a speculative shrug. It didn't feel right to him. He let go of the crowbar with one hand and rubbed his forehead, suddenly aware of how worn-out he was.

"Let's go," Hiro said. "Both those ideas are wrong. '*Water, water everywhere, and not a drop to drink.*' That's about the ocean. Let's check it out." He looked at August. "And you're coming with us."

"August has to be with someone or we tie him up and leave him with Beth," Thea said.

Robin and Kyle shared a look that revealed to Mick they'd discussed that very idea. Interesting.

"I'll go with Mick and Hiro," August said.

Mick was glad. Him and Hiro alone was not his favorite plan.

"Okay, two groups," Robin said. Then she looked at Mick and flashed him the sweetest smile. "Good luck," she told him.

"Good luck," he replied.

21.

SOMETHING FISHY

ROBIN'S RULE #9:

Think through your problems.

"The clue has got to be something to do with that sign," Kyle said.

Perched on the cliff on the other side of the compound was a billboard barely visible in the moonlight. But Robin, Thea, and Kyle could make out the luminescent outline of a child's sand pail in the lower right corner. Kyle confirmed that it hadn't been there when he'd first arrived. The killer had used glow-in-the-dark paint to draw both it and an upside-down arrow pointing at the building beneath it. Robin was amazed at the lengths he—or she—had gone to in organizing this alternative hunt. This do-or-die game where he called the shots.

Just like August and his spreadsheets and his zombies and rowboats.

Dozens of windows stared angrily at them. Part of the first floor had collapsed inward, leaving the impression of an opened mouth waiting to swallow up the unwary.

Nothing in Robin wanted to go inside.

"That is so unfair," Thea said nervously. "What if no one saw the little bucket he painted? Would he kill us all?"

"Maybe it's like a magic trick," Kyle said. "You know how magicians ask you to pick a card? And then they tell you to look under a chair, or pick up the envelope on a table, stuff like that, and there's the same card? It works because they put different props in lots of places ahead of time. The deck is marked, so when you give them back the card, they know which one you drew. Then they tell you where to look. Magic."

"I knew that," Thea said quickly.

"So what you're saying is that maybe there's more than one place to look for a bucket," Robin said.

"Or for a well," Kyle replied. "Or whatever he wants us to find."

They continued walking toward the building and Robin wondered if they should turn off their flashlights and the lantern. That way they would be less of a target. Maybe the killer was waiting inside, watching them come closer, closer. Beside her, Kyle was shivering in the borrowed hoodie and sweats. She could even hear his teeth chattering. His flashlight beam skittered like a mosquito.

"Do you want my jacket?" she asked him.

He shook his head, and they kept walking, their feet making a tremendous racket as they crunched on the seemingly endless tract of crushed shell.

Then something made a screeching noise and swooped past Robin's ear. Bat? Owl? It came back, batting the air close to her ears again. It dive-bombed at them a third time and Robin simply ducked, but Thea let out a yell and began running toward the building.

"Thea, wait!" Robin called.

Thea kept going, utterly panicked, and Robin and Kyle hustled after her. Robin heard the screech again, as sharp as a slap against her eardrums.

"Ow!" Kyle said, letting go of her hand. He fell to one knee and she stumbled over her own feet as she slowed.

"Kyle!" she cried.

"Pothole," he said. "Go ahead. I'll catch up."

Robin broke into a trot, raising her lantern high. "Thea!" she called. Then her foot caught on something and she lurched forward. Her lantern burst out of her grasp and crashed to the ground, winking out.

"Kyle?" she said. "Thea?"

No answer.

Tiny pricks of fear stabbed every inch of her body. She turned in a slow circle, and something inside her—some instinct for self-preservation—told her not to make another sound.

The retreating shriek of the night creature made a

reedy, thin noise against the bass thundering of her heart. She didn't hear anyone else. It was as if the fog had spirited everyone away, and she was the only one left on the cannery grounds.

She and the killer.

Then she heard another sound. And it was so unexpected, and so desperately dreamed of, that for a few seconds, she didn't recognize what it was.

But when she did, she began to whoop with joy.

It was a car horn.

"Thea! Kyle!" she shouted, breaking into a run. "A car! There's a car! Thea!"

The sound of the horn seemed to bounce from building to building, and then the echo died. She couldn't tell which direction it had come from—if the driver had entered through the double scrollwork gates or was still blazing down along the road high above the cannery on the upper cliff. She hoped it had navigated the razor-sharp turn and now was in the lot. It could be a coincidence, just someone out for a night drive along the coastline. In this fog, she doubted he would even see the cannery from the road. And unless he—or she—already knew about the party, they'd have no reason to come down here anyway.

So Drew might have had the right idea all along—go up to the road, wait.

"Thea?" she called. "Kyle?"

Neither answered.

She stopped running. Stopped dead in her tracks.

It was too silent.

Robin caught her breath. She was just about to call out to Thea again when a little voice in her head told her to wait.

Footfalls that were not hers crunched along the pulverized shells. But they weren't coming from behind her, which was where Kyle should be, nor from anywhere in front of her, where the billboard and the building stood. They were approaching from her right.

Slow, cautious. Deliberate.

She stilled her panting, almost strangling herself as she held her breath and steadily let it out. The footfalls kept coming, *crunch, crunch, crunch*. Her breath shuddered against her lips as she fought to stay as quiet as she could. Her nerves were jangling; all her senses went on high alert.

Then they stopped.

This person could be just as frightened as she was, wondering if they were gliding through the ghostly fog beside the killer. Who would make the first move?

The mistake?

Robin didn't know what to do. She stood stock-still, struggling not to pant. Not to panic. But it was so hard not to. Cage's ruined face, Heather's eyes bulging as she swung above their heads. It could be her turn. People all around her were dying. No one who had been murdered had awakened this morning wondering if this day would be their last. Old people worried about dying. Not teenagers.

Robin made herself think, strategize. She wished she

still had the lantern. She could bend down and throw shells in their eyes. If she could see their eyes.

Her best defense was running. But the sound would give her away.

Don't move, said the little voice inside her head. *If you move, you will die.*

THEA'S RULE #4:

Do what you have to in order to survive.

Thea barreled into the disintegrating building, sprinting down a maze of corridors, turning left, right, and then so many times she lost track in her full-out terror. Her shoes landed on hard things, soft things, brittle shards of glass. The place smelled of pee and her brain registered that there might be squatters living in here, homeless people.

Her flashlight bounced along cracked walls and graffiti. As she turned a corner, she saw a floating figure staring at her and she screamed, throwing the flashlight at the very same moment that she realized she was staring at a reflection of herself in a mirror. The flashlight smashed the glass in a cascade of splinters and she ducked, slamming against a wall.

The wall cracked, snapping beneath her weight, and she fell right through it into a pitch-dark room. All the air was squeezed out of her lungs as she dropped hard onto a cement floor. Fragments needled up into her outstretched palm and at the same time that she cried out, she heard another sound.

A car horn.

For a moment, she was transfixed. She couldn't believe it. Her mind tried to deny it. It was a *foghorn*. It was one of the electric guitars. But she knew what it was.

"Oh my God," she whispered. "Thank you, God."

She scrabbled to her feet in the ebony nothing and tried to go back into the hall. Then she fell to a squat and groped along the floor for her flashlight. She thought she heard Robin calling her name, but she sounded very far away.

"I'm here," she tried to shout, but the words came out as a papery whisper. That was probably a good thing, since she was in the building that the killer had led them to.

Was it a trick? Some sound effect he had rigged up to make them *think* a car had arrived? So they would run to the parking lot and then—

Thea straightened. Her side and slivered hand both tingled. She put her other hand against her ribs and her hand came back wet. She was bleeding.

In the darkness, something squeaked.

Then it ran over her shoe.

A rat.

Thea stuffed her hand over her mouth in a struggle for silence. Another rat joined the first, tiny feet skittering over her instep. This time a voiceless moan escaped and she wheeled around, running—

—straight into a wall. She hit it so hard that she was

stunned for a few seconds. Her forehead ached dully and she staggered backward, trying to fix in her head the many ways she had turned. Her shoe came down on a slab of glass, breaking it into more pieces.

Something sharp stabbed the back of her heel. It was a rat, biting her. She wanted to let out the loudest shriek on the planet but she panted in fear instead. She had gotten into this mess because she had panicked.

She thought about rabies and infections.

The car would take her and Praveen to the hospital.

Icy sweat beaded on her forehead. She scanned the darkness, seeing blossoms of velvety blackness, tricks her eyes played on her as they tried to compensate for the lack of light.

Something bright blossomed a few feet away to her right, glowing as if from underneath a piece of furniture. She shuffled toward it, colliding with something, and dropped to her haunches. Her entire body thrummed with pain.

Next she let herself fall forward onto her knees, then very cautiously lay on the floor. The beam of the flashlight almost blinded her but she shifted her line of sight and closed her eyes to let them adjust.

She heard rats chittering and swept around herself with her hand, making contact with something that scooted away. Then she stretched a little farther and grabbed the flashlight.

The flashlight revealed a sea of rats between her and the wall. She swayed, and then she began kicking. They cheeped almost like birds as one of them went flying, and then another.

She found the open door that led into the corridor and tried to remember if she'd gone left or right. Nothing looked familiar; everything looked the same. This was the exact nightmare of her entire life: a haunted house.

And then, to her left at the end of the hall, her light shone on a rusted metal *bucket* with a metal half-circle handle.

Her ragged breaths sounded like machine-gun fire as she studied the bucket. It could be a coincidence that it was there. Or a trap. The killer could be watching, waiting to pounce on her if she took the bait. A montage of images flashed through her mind of each person in the group finding a different bucket or even a well, and then the killer taking them out in horrible, sadistic ways.

She didn't have time to waste. And maybe the old Thea would have scooted past, pretending not to see it, or gone back to it later with Robin at her side. But she wasn't a coward anymore. Not if she wanted to stay alive. So she gathered up all her courage and looked inside.

Her face prickled. There was a white envelope just like the others at the bottom. And writing on it: *#2*.

Clue number two.

She grasped the bucket by the handle. The curved metal piece detached at one end and the bucket canted at an angle, nearly clattering to the floor, but she caught it against her stomach and snaked it up against her chest.

A rat scampered across the next passageway. She came across a swarm of rodents gathered around something on the floor, tugging violently at it, chewing. She averted her gaze and kept going.

Dead end.

"Please don't leave without me," she whispered. And then she heard a creak on the floorboards behind her.

She shot forward, bucket clutched against her chest, going left, right, right again. Locked door. Wrong way. And then into a room she didn't recognize. She painted it with her flashlight. Lying on a corroded white metal counter with deep drains on either side was the perfect skeleton of a two-foot-long fish. A cockroach crawled out of its eye socket. Coiled around it were two hoses, like maybe to squirt water into the gutters to clear away fish guts on the floor.

She whipped around and charged back in the other direction. Her wounds were stinging terribly. She had the stupid bucket and the next clue and *why* didn't Robin and Kyle come and get her? Why was it so quiet all of a sudden?

When she finally burst through the doorway, she realized she had been holding her breath, she didn't know for how long, but she was gasping and sweating and bleeding.

Then she heard Robin shout, "Thea? Is that you?"

Thea raced toward Robin's voice. "Yes! Did you hear a car?"

"Be careful! There's someone here," Robin cried.

Then Thea heard two sets of feet, one running toward her and the other, she couldn't tell. She was confused. Of course there was someone out there. Kyle.

Right?

Then arms came around her and Robin said, "It's me! It's me! Is this a bucket? Oh my God, you found it?"

She took it from Thea, who almost grabbed it back—she knew she was going on automatic because she was so scared—and then Robin took her hurt hand and Thea hissed.

"Was there a car horn?" Thea asked her.

"Yes, yes!" Robin said. She sounded ecstatic and terrified at the same time, just like Thea. Robin was half dragging her to the warehouse. A large shape loomed out of the fog; bits of it were glowing, and Thea realized it was the warehouse lit up with lanterns and flashlights.

"Where's the car?" Thea asked.

"I don't know. I'm going to get on the mike," Robin said. "I'm going to tell everyone to get to the warehouse and for the driver to identify himself."

"Oh, Robin, it's got to be someone good," Thea said fervently. "They wouldn't have honked the horn if they were with the killer."

And then she realized something: she didn't hear the generators. She didn't say anything about it, just let Robin hustle her along. Didn't tell her that she had been bitten by a rat. Instead she concentrated on the lights of the warehouse as they approached.

"I've lost Kyle," Robin said anxiously. "I don't know where he is!"

"C'mon, c'mon," Thea pleaded. "Let's get to the mike! He'll come!"

They reached the warehouse door and Robin pounded on it with her fists, yelling, "It's us!"

After a few seconds, the door crashed open and Beth hugged them both, bouncing on the balls of her feet.

"I heard a car," Beth said as they charged back into the warehouse, "and I yelled and I yelled but I don't know if it left and I couldn't go because . . ."

"It's okay," Thea said. "Robin's going to get on the mike and—"

They reached the stage and Robin found the mike on top of the amp. She picked it up, toggling a switch as Thea watched. She glanced at the amp itself. The lights that were usually illuminated on the display panel were dark.

"Hello?" Robin said into the mouthpiece. She stared at Beth and Thea, who both shook their heads at the absence of amplification. "Oh no."

"I think the generators have shut off," Thea said.

There was more pounding on the door, and Thea shrieked, throwing her arms around Beth. It crashed open, and Kyle and Mick rushed in.

"Robin," Kyle said. "What happened? Are you all right?"

"Where did you go?" she asked him. "I looked every-where for you!"

"What do you mean?" he asked her. "I thought you were right in front of me."

"I lost track of August and Hiro," Mick announced. "I was moving fast. I looked back and I realized I'd outpaced them. I don't know where they are."

Then Robin realized that something else was missing. "Kyle, where's the bat?"

He grimaced. "I dropped it when I fell. I felt for it everywhere. I figured we could go back—"

"Later, guys, okay?" Mick cut in. "Did you hear a car horn?"

"Yes," Robin, Thea, and Beth said in unison.

"Let's go!" Mick cried.

"I'm not just running out there," Robin said.

"If we get on the mike—" Kyle said, and Robin shook her head.

"It's not working. The generators are out."

Mick looked up sharply. "Someone turned them off?"

Kyle looked just as shocked.

"Then let's yell," Mick said. "On the count of three."

BETH'S RULE #4:

Don't drink, because alcohol makes you stupid.

"Look!" Larson said, pointing from his place on the floor.

Yellow light glinted above the Anchor Steam beer cake: it was a window Beth hadn't even realized was

241

there. A shape in the fog was lurching toward them. A yellow ball of light—flashlight—accompanied it. Beth stiffened and began to back away, but Thea broke into wild shrieks of what had to be joy. She obviously recognized the figure.

"It's Jackson!" Thea cried. And then she went dead white, and Beth knew why: Jackson was a psycho. And Thea had dumped him.

"It's Thea's ex," she announced, to put him in context for anyone who wouldn't know who Jackson was. Her mind was going on overdrive. She didn't know what to think. Was this good news or bad? She picked up the knife.

"Thea's ex *with a car*," Kyle said pointedly.

"Right, right!" Thea said, regaining her composure. "He's got a car. He'll get us out of here!"

Thea spun to the right, heading for the door, when Beth caught her arm.

"Let's take it a little slow," Beth said. "Make sure it's okay."

"Are you kidding?" said Kyle. "We'll take him down and steal his keys if we have to."

"Jackson! Baby!" Thea called. Her voice was shaking and anyone could see that she was about to leap out of her skin. That she was both petrified and ecstatic at the sight of Jackson White.

Jackson stomped closer to the window. The fog billowed around him like smoke.

"You *slut!*" Jackson roared, his voice thick; he was

weaving, as though he had been drinking. "You bitch! I am going to gut you!"

"Oh my God." Praveen staggered to her feet and climbed onto the stage. "My God, he's the killer!"

She could be right, Beth thought. She swayed and stumbled backward, watching as Jackson yelled at Thea, swearing to cut out her eyes and stab her and kick her to death. She had never heard anyone talk like that. Telling her that if he didn't do those things, his friends would. Her life was his. And it was over.

He stuttered to a halt. Now she was sure he'd been drinking, and that meant anything could happen.

"Thea, get to the other side of the room," she said.

But before she could get out another word, before anyone could do anything, a figure stepped directly behind Jackson. For a minute, Beth was confused because the person seemed to be made of shadow, and then she realized he was wearing a hood down over his face. He had on a long coat and was wearing gloves. A knife poised in his hand. Ready to strike.

He's the figure I saw on the beach.

"Jackson! Look out!" she shouted.

The others were shouting, too. Kyle went flying to the door. Breaking into a run, Mick threw a chair at the window, shattering glass everywhere. Beth jumped backward and covered her face with her arms.

When she lowered them, blood was spraying from Jackson's neck. Thea's ex stood for a moment staring at them all, hovering as if suspended from the sky by a string. The killer stood behind him, then yanked him backward with a flourish. Jackson collapsed onto his back, the blood gushing out of him like a geyser.

The killer bolted.

Kyle was outside; he raced after the figure and both of them disappeared into the fog to a chorus of shouting, Robin pleading for Kyle to come back. Everyone was yelling. Thea struggled in Mick's arms, trying to leap through the window, but he was holding on to her, fighting her, shouting. Adrenaline must have been fueling Thea, because she almost threw Mick off.

Beth watched as Robin ran outside to Jackson and fell down beside him. Robin threw her hands over Jackson's neck and pressed down hard. It was incredible how much blood was spilling out.

Mick let go of Thea and pushed her into Beth's arms; then he raced outside and knelt beside Robin as Beth dragged Thea away from the window.

A minute later, the door slammed open and Mick stumbled in with Robin in his arms. Her body was drenched in blood, and her hands dribbled scarlet droplets all over the floor.

"It's horrible. It's so deep," Mick babbled. "His neck's been cut all the way through."

Beth met Robin's agonized gaze: *And Kyle is out there with the killer.*

22

NO ONE'S COMING

LARSON'S RULE #4:

Pioneers are the ones with the
arrows in their backs.

Robin scrabbled out of Mick's arms. "I'm going back out there," she said.

But as she grabbed the knife, Mick blocked the door. Larson stood beside him, though the effort to get there and stay upright had cost him a world of hurt.

"For all we know, a second guy is standing right outside this door, ready to mow us down if we go outside," Larson said.

"They might have guns, Robin," Mick said.

She seized Mick's arm and tried to yank him aside. Mick stood firm, though he did glance nervously at the knife. Larson took a few cautious sidesteps, trying to keep from being reinjured.

"Robin, listen, we should get Jackson's car keys," Beth said. "And his phone. Now. We should find his car and get the hell out of here."

"Kyle's coming! Here he comes!" Thea shouted as she looked out the window.

Robin left the door and flew to the window and Mick followed after. The thought of moving pained Larson too much and he decided to stay. Kyle waved but then knelt beside Jackson's corpse, quickly going through his pockets, holding up a cell phone and a fat leather wallet attached to a set of car keys with a big, thick chain.

"Oh thank God, thank God," Beth cried.

In a few seconds, Kyle was back in the warehouse. Robin threw herself into his arms and kissed him hard, then took the phone to turn it on.

Nothing happened.

"Battery's dead," Robin said.

Everyone groaned.

"We still have the keys," said Robin, holding them up. "So let's get out of here *now*."

"Did you see him?" Mick asked Kyle as Thea and Beth helped Praveen to her feet. She looked seriously *Carrie* as she stared straight ahead, like she was going to rip them apart with her mind.

Kyle grimaced. "No. I thought I could outrun him with that long coat, but he hauled ass."

"What about Hiro and August?" Beth said.

Interesting. They're missing and someone gets killed right in front of us again, Larson thought. *And no one's even talking about Morgan anymore.*

"Let's hope we run into them," Mick said.

"We could leave them a note." Thea sounded hopeful.

"And say what? 'Dear Killer, if you read this instead of our friends . . .'"

"Larson's right," Robin said. "Grab a flashlight and let's go. We'll take the back way and keep our flashlights off as much as we can."

They scurried down a hallway and left the factory. The sodden air clung to Larson's face as if someone had thrown cold, spoiled milk at him. Robin had taken the lead and Kyle tried scooting around her but she wasn't having it. They were heading for the main parking area first, hoping Jackson had parked where they all had and they could find his car before the killer could disable it, too.

Does this guy know what I did? Does August? Larson wondered. He looked over guiltily at Robin. For so long, he had told himself it wouldn't have changed the outcome if he had turned himself in for hitting her father. But tonight, he was being proven wrong. If he had told the police, the killer would have no reason to punish him.

Hadn't he punished himself enough?

ROBIN'S RULE #10:

Look before you leap.

Robin half ran as they began to cover territory. Larson was limping beside her, barely making it. She grabbed his arm to pull him along as much as she could. He sucked in his breath but kept pace with her. Kyle had moved to the back of the group to make the stragglers go faster. They were just sitting ducks out here. Creeping ducks. It hadn't really sunk in before how large the cannery compound was. And if there was another road in that Jackson had taken, Robin had no idea where it—

Billboard, she thought. The sign with the pail above the building must have been planted along a road. But it wasn't on the main highway; it was slightly lower, indicating a road behind the factory. Which made sense. When this had been a working cannery, they would have needed to transport whatever they made inside that building to the main road.

"Oh my God," Thea whispered loudly. "I swear I just heard somebody calling for help."

Robin stopped walking and the caravan jumbled to a halt. She listened but didn't hear words exactly, maybe a rustling.

"Are you sure that's what it was?" she asked.

"Yes." Thea was firm.

"I didn't hear anything," said Beth.

"It was *help*. Robin, it was," Thea said.

"It could be a trick," Larson said. "Or wishful thinking."

Then she heard a noise, too. Almost tinny, strange. A sharp wind cleared some layers of fog away.

A few feet away from them, a black Chevy lowrider appeared like one of the magic tricks Kyle had been talking about. Robin bit back a squeal and jerked Thea's hand hard as Thea began to bolt toward it.

"Everyone be careful," Robin said. "Let's just take a minute."

"It's Jackson's car," Thea said, trying to shake free of Robin's hold. "It's what we've been looking for."

"A lowrider? Are you kidding?" Mick muttered. He sounded very, very nervous.

"You can see why I made her break up with him," Beth said to Robin.

"Shhh, guys." Robin counted several good reasons to be nervous:

> The killer might be inside it.

> The killer might be waiting for them
> to get near it, and then he would pick them
> off, one by one by one.

> The killer might have done something
> to make it explode or something like that.

Maybe she watched too many movies. But the killer probably watched the same movies. Searched how to do things on the Internet. It wasn't crazy to think that a deranged maniac *other* than Jackson could have wired Jackson's car to blow if they opened the door.

But not in the short time since the car horn had honked.

But maybe the *killer* had honked it, not Jackson. To lure them here. And when they hadn't come, he had led Jackson to them, killed him in front of them. . . .

There was another tinny sound and Robin cocked her head. It sounded like . . . barking.

"What the heck," Kyle muttered beside her. He put a hand in front of her the way Robin's mom did when they were in the car and she had to brake suddenly. Then he took a step toward the car and Robin clutched his hand. "We have to do this," he said. He held out his hand. "Keys."

Robin wanted to be the one to do it. But somehow she was in charge of watching over the group. She nodded, fishing in her pocket and handing the keys to Kyle. When he took them, she wrapped her hand around his and squeezed. She couldn't let go of him.

"Oh God, oh God, oh God," Beth chanted. "Please, please, please, please, please."

Kyle gently eased himself loose. Stepping up to the car, he draped his hand over the old-fashioned door latch and looked at her over his shoulder as if for luck. Then he yanked the door open and the tinny barking grew louder and more frantic.

He sat down and put the key in the ignition. Robin was shaking. They might be saved. They could leave—

There was a click, and then nothing. Kyle shut his eyes and laid his forehead on the steering wheel. He tried again.

"No!" Thea wailed, and she collapsed onto the ground.

At the same time a tiny black dog scrabbled around Kyle's feet and hopped out of the car. It was a Chihuahua, and as it stared up at the line of people, it began to bark wildly, taking mincing steps forward and then skittishly backing up.

"Inky!" Thea whispered. "That's his dog!"

"Shut it up!" Larson said.

Robin bent down and tried to scoop up the little dog, but it hopped out of reach and ran to Thea. Mick strode up to the hood, felt around for the release, and lifted it. Turning on his flashlight, he looked under the hood, then swore and pounded the car with his fist.

"Easy, Inky," Thea said, gently putting her hand around his muzzle as she joined the others crowding around Mick. Inky squirmed and growled.

Robin didn't know very much about cars, but she could see that the battery was gone. Which meant that even if there was a charger in the car, it, too, was useless, just like the phone.

Shocked silence fell over the group. Their killer had thought of everything.

"Okay. Then we have to move on," Robin said as steadily as she could. She was fighting not to lose it. "Put Inky back in the car."

"No," Thea keened. "He's scared."

"We have to leave Inky in the car or wring Inky's neck," Larson said under his breath.

Pale faces, all disbelieving: everyone had pinned their hopes on Jackson's ride. Mick and Kyle had opened up the trunk and were rummaging around. Kyle said, "So Jackson was in a gang, right? There must be a gun in here."

"No," Thea said. "He was on probation. And—and Macho—the leader of the Free Souls—he said that it would be better if he didn't have one anyway, because of his temper. . . ." She winced and trailed off, as if she knew just how bad that sounded. And it did sound bad. Robin was appalled.

Kyle held up a tire iron and Robin nodded. A potential weapon. Yes. A blanket. She shook her head. They had to travel light.

"No, please, *please* don't leave him in there," Thea begged as Robin placed Inky back in the car and closed the door. Tears and snot were running down her face. "He'll run out of air. He'll get too cold. Please don't let him die."

"It's May, Thea," Robin said gently. "It's cold, but it's not that cold. He'll be okay. This is the safest place for him."

"Robin. Look what I found." Mick held up a phone charger. "If we could start one of the generators back up . . ."

"Yes," she said, and then, a bit less emphatically, "Maybe. We'll have to check it out."

"No, Robin," Mick said. "Time to play the game his way. Let there be light. *Now.*"

23

LET THERE BE LIGHT

MICK'S RULE #3:

Do what you know how to do.

"I went out there with August to inspect the generators after I got zapped," Mick reminded the group. "I know how they work. I can get the phone to charge using one of the power strips in the warehouse. And we can turn on the lights and work on his next clue."

"Which would mean going back *into* the warehouse," Beth said.

Everyone stood around Jackson's car. Inside, Inky was going berserk, hopping up and down on the seat and yipping at the interlopers. Thin moonlight trickled through the clouds, the stars twinkling as if nothing were wrong. But Thea brought them right back to reality. She wept with big heavy gulps like a little kid; she was getting scarier than Praveen, who had checked out emotionally and was utterly silent.

"Making the killer happy and getting our butts saved," Mick said slowly, as if he had to lay it out for her. "And we can all go together."

"Yeah," Larson said excitedly. "That works."

"That does *not* work," Beth said.

"Hey, we shouldn't discuss this out here," Larson cut in. "We should move. We're easy targets."

"We're targets anywhere we go," Mick retorted.

"I think you're right about the generators," Kyle said, trying to keep everyone focused. "I think that's what the killers want us to do, but what if it's a trick?"

"The generators might have simply run out of gas," Beth said as they all formed in a huddle next to the car. "August probably didn't think we'd be out here this long."

"August thought we'd never leave," Mick retorted.

"We need gas for this to work," Kyle said.

Mick made a fist and gently pounded on the car. "This baby has gas."

"Right. Good. We need to figure out a siphon," Larson said. "And then we're in business."

There was silence save for Thea's weeping as everyone contemplated taking the next step. Then Thea wiped her nose and said, "Fish guts."

"What?" Mick asked.

"In the . . . the factory. I saw hoses in a room." Her voice was quaking. "I don't want to go in there. I don't know which room they were in. I don't remember anything." Her voice rose to a shrill wail and Mick winced. They had to calm her down. She was making more noise than the dog.

"No problem, Thea," Mick assured her. "Larson and I can go. Or . . . more of us, if we have volunteers."

He looked at Robin. She was doing something in the shells beside her boot, running her finger though them purposefully, but when he glanced at her hand, she stopped and turned off her flashlight.

"I'll go with you, Mick," Beth announced.

Robin nodded. "You guys go do that, and Kyle and I will try to find Morgan and August and Hiro. We need to be ready to go once the phone is charged." She put her hands in the pockets of her jeans and threw back her shoulders, like a video game character getting ready to take it to the next level.

"I want to stay with you, Robin," Praveen said softly.

Thea shook her head. "I don't want to go anywhere. I'm too scared. I want to stay in the car. I can take care of Inky."

She's really losing it, Mick thought. Fine by him if she stayed well away with her noisy crying.

"Not by yourself," Robin said, but then Kyle put his hand on Robin's forearm and smiled at Thea.

"You'd lock the doors, right?" he asked her. "And . . . maybe we can leave the tire iron with you." He looked at Robin. "We need to give Mick the knife so he can cut the hoses off for the siphons."

Robin opened her mouth to protest, then shut it. Mick

could see the wheels turning as she decided that the best course of action was to yield on this one.

"Okay," she said finally. "Thea can stay here. Mick, Larson, and Beth will check on the generator. Kyle, Praveen, and I will try to track down Morgan, August, and Hiro."

"Or whoever the killer may be," Kyle said. He cleared his throat. "Because I hate to say this, but . . . those three might be dead."

Robin nodded wanly, and Kyle put his arm around her.

"Okay," Mick said. "If we get the generator to work, we'll signal you by turning on some lights in the warehouse. If you find the killer . . . kill him. Or them."

Robin handed him the knife and glanced over at Praveen, who stepped over to her. Two teams. Two missions.

"Okay, then, good luck," Mick said to Robin's group.

Beth hugged Robin tightly. "We're going to pull this off," Beth said. "No one else is going to . . . to . . . We're all going home soon. I can just feel it."

"Me too," Robin said. "Get in the car, Thea."

Kyle handed Thea the tire iron and she got into the backseat. "Lock the doors and lie down on the floor."

Mick's back was already turned when he heard the car door click shut. Then he, Beth, and Larson headed toward the building Thea had indicated, and he went in first.

"Every time I walk into a building around here—" Beth began, and Larson mildly shushed her.

They kept looking. And looking, with Mick's flashlight

moving across a wasteland of filth and destruction. He began to wonder if they should have let Thea off so easily. But really, what good would she have been?

He heard Larson exhale. Dude was in pain. This was all so screwed up. He took the rooms on the right side and Larson the left. Beth's job was to quickly recheck each room after each guy gave up. No one spoke much. Everyone was scared.

And then Beth screamed.

Mick ran over with Larson shuffling right behind. She was aiming her flashlight at what appeared to be a moving mound in the corner of one room.

"Dude, what is that?" Larson asked.

"Rats. Lots of them," Mick said, wrinkling his nose. "It looks like they're eating something."

"They're . . . they're . . . oh no." Beth lurched and fell against the wall. The flashlight in her hand made flaring shadows, but Mick could now see what she had seen. Shiny curled hair, splayed out on the floor. Crawling with rats.

Lots of rats. Swarming, tearing, chewing.

They had finally found Morgan.

It took time to pull themselves together and more time to find the room with the fish skeleton and the tubes. The things Mick had to do to clean them out so that he could use them didn't even faze him.

The rats were working on Morgan, cleaning her like

buzzards cleaned a kill. He could hear them. He drifted like a sleepwalker back to the car and got the gas, nodding dully at Thea as she sat up and waved at him. He stared at the faces of people who, after only a few hours, no longer looked recognizable to him. He felt surrounded by a bubble that bobbed him along, keeping out sounds and sight. Everything was becoming a blur.

He handed Larson the knife when they got to the generators. The one closest to him was the one that hadn't blown when Stacy had knocked the contents of her travel tumbler into the amp.

Except maybe she didn't, he thought. *Most likely she didn't.*

He opened the gas cap, then looked around for a stick to measure the generator fuel tank, and saw none. So he dipped one of the hoses into the gas tank and pulled it out. His hands were shaking so badly he could barely keep hold of it. He aimed his flashlight, examining a dark spot about a quarter of an inch from the bottom of the hose. There was hardly any gas left. So the generator really had run out.

Better news, he thought.

"Hold the flashlight," he told Beth.

Very carefully, he angled the bucket over the mouth of the tank and poured the gas in. So far, so good. He wondered about the impurities from the bucket, the hose. But what could happen from pouring the gas in? If something was going to happen, it would be when he turned it on, right?

"Mick?" Larson asked. "Is everything okay?"

Beth reached out a hand to pat him, then pulled it away. Frowning, she got up and stepped back with Larson.

Gee, thanks, guys.

He set down the bucket and grasped the rope to start the generator, giving it a pull. Nothing. He pulled it again.

The generator rumbled to life, and Beth sucked in her breath. Larson stepped forward and clapped Mick on the shoulder.

"Oh my God, yes, yes," Beth said, bursting into tears.

He knew it was great, but he felt nothing. Then he realized he should put the gas cap back on.

Mick picked it up, dropped it. "Here, man," Larson said, handing him the cap. Mick placed it over the threads as Larson tapped the can with the tip of the knife.

Metal touched metal touched metal touched metal.

There was a spark.

ROBIN'S RULE #11:

Don't hurt others.

As Robin, Kyle, and Praveen skirted the "fish guts" building, Robin used her flashlight to examine the bit of fabric she had found beside Jackson's car. It was a shiny green color that looked familiar. She thought it might match Praveen's top, but it would be difficult to be certain by flashlight. It would be very close, though. She didn't know what to think about that. Maybe Praveen had crossed that section of the cannery grounds before Jackson had driven to that exact spot. But the likelihood seemed remote.

Praveen was trudging along like a mummy and Kyle was watching Robin with an expression of curiosity. She held out the fabric and murmured, "I found this by the car."

He looked from it to Praveen and back, and wrinkled his brow. She knew he wasn't making the same connection she had, so she waved her hand, indicating that they should drop the subject.

Robin stepped onto the blacktop. Her heart skipped a beat as she realized they had found the road Jackson must have come down. Despite how exhausted and thirsty she was, Robin broke into a trot, and Kyle did the same. Even Praveen picked up the pace.

The road rose steeply, just like the other road at the opposite end of the property. Robin's calf muscles ached but she kept hiking; then, at the top of the hill, the moonlight drifted down on double gates identical to the ones that read ZUL on the other side of the property.

She burst into a run. She wanted to get to the road, flag someone down—

"Hey, wait," Kyle called after her. "Do you hear that? Wait!"

She didn't hear anything. She wasn't going to wait. She was going to run. She was almost at the gate—

"Keep away from it!" Kyle shouted.

An object flew past her head. It slammed into the

scrollwork of the gates, buzzing before falling to the ground. Startled, she stumbled to a stop.

The gate was electrified, and the thing Kyle had thrown at it was his flashlight. She hadn't heard the hum. When she turned her head to thank him, he grabbed her, wrapping his arms around her body.

"I didn't even hear it," she said against his shoulder,

"Your dad taught us how to listen on the lacrosse field," he said. "So we could hear the coaches and our teammates even when there was cheering going on."

The mention of her father was like a hand clamping around her heart. She wished she'd gone to say good night before she'd left for the party. Wished she was home playing Clue with Carter and that Kyle and Beth were with them, too, and none of this had ever happened.

"Is there a way to turn the gate off?" Praveen asked.

"We probably can turn it off," Kyle said, "but we know two things now. One, no one stopped us. And two . . ." He looked at Robin. She was so relieved that tears spilled down her cheeks.

"There's power. We can charge the phone," she said.

There was a groan in the bushes to Robin's left. She dashed over and parted the branches, to find a figure lying on his back, one arm slung over his head. Kyle's beam revealed August, the side of his face bleeding, his lids fluttering.

"Fence . . . electrified," he managed to say.

"Thanks. We know," Robin said. Clearly, he had found out the hard way.

Robin leaned forward and clutched one of August's arms with both of hers. Kyle was beside her, taking August's other arm, and together they helped him to his feet. He staggered and swayed, hanging on to Kyle.

"Thanks, man," he said. "Oh my God, I thought I was dead. Praveen, don't touch it."

Praveen was staring at the scrollwork on the gate with her hands tucked under her chin. Shock and longing warred on her features as fog curled around her ankles and blew through the gate as if mocking her: it could go wherever it wanted.

"Whoa," August said. "I thought my heart had stopped."

Praveen looked at him suspiciously. "Really. Aren't you going to MIT to major in electrical engineering?"

"Right," August drawled sarcastically. "So I powered up the fence, ran into it, and nearly electrocuted myself to make you think I'm not the murderer. Damn, Praveen."

She narrowed her eyes. "How do we know you *did* run into it? You were just lying there."

A small rectangle was glowing beside August's shoe. Robin bent down and picked it up. It was a shattered cell phone, the back crisscrossed with flaps of reflective duct tape.

"August?" she said, showing it to him.

"You've had a cell phone all this time?" Praveen shrieked. "So you could call the other killer?"

"No, no, that's Jacob's," August said quickly. "I would know that odd phone anywhere. I found it on the ground behind the warehouse. It's broken."

"Jacob?" Kyle said. "He didn't come."

"Well, he *texted* me that he wasn't coming," August said.

Kyle took the phone from him and examined it. A vast spiderweb of cracks prevented anyone from seeing the display.

Robin was stunned. Her mind began to work. Was August lying? She'd been back there, too, and had never seen it. Had he been holding out on them?

Was Jacob Stein the killer?

The look Kyle gave her said he was thinking the same thing.

"Why are you up here?" she asked August.

He huffed. "Mick and Hiro were staggering around with that idiot crowbar. They kept stopping and arguing and Hiro said forget it and he started down toward the beach. And Mick stomped around and then he yelled and I totally bailed."

"You didn't tell them about the phone?" Kyle said.

"I don't know them," August shot back. "And I found it after I peeled off. I thought about going after them but I got distracted trying to make it work. Hacker, remember? Then I saw the gates in the moonlight and I went up to check them out. And I nearly died."

Wordlessly, Robin pulled the piece of green material out of her pocket and held it up to August's shirt. It looked like a match.

"I found this next to Jackson's car," Robin said.

Praveen and Kyle leaned in for a look. Praveen caught her breath, and Robin could see comprehension dawning on Kyle's face about why she had shown him the fabric in the first place.

"You bastard!" Praveen shrieked, throwing herself at him. He stumbled and fell and she fell on top of him. Grabbing him by the neck, she pressed down hard with all her weight, hollering, spit flying everywhere.

"Praveen, stop!" Robin shouted. She tried to yank Praveen away by her shoulders. Then Kyle pushed Robin, sending her tumbling into sticky, thorny bushes, and he hoisted Praveen up around her waist. She kicked and flailed. He set her down as Robin freed herself and scrabbled over to August, helping him up.

"Kill him, Kyle!" Praveen shouted. "He'll kill us! You know it's him!"

Kyle shook August by the collar, shoving his face into August's. "What did you do, you sick freak?"

August thrashed, arms, head, feet. *"Nothing!"*

Praveen pounded on Kyle's back. "Kyle, throw him against the fence. He's the killer, I know it."

"No, don't!" Robin cried, pushing herself between August and Kyle. Then she was shoved out of the way a second time as Kyle bulldozed August toward the fence. Praveen was helping. Together they backed him up and he grunted, struggling against them like a football player trying to hold the line.

"Robin, help me!" August pleaded. "Oh my God!"

Robin glommed on to Kyle again and tried to yank him away. The powerful muscles in his arms and shoulders moved beneath her fingers but he stayed as he was, on the verge of murdering August.

Praveen just hissed, pounding on August's chest with her fists. "The cell phone! Your shirt!"

"Look at my shirt! Look at it!" August begged them.

"Let him show us!" Robin yelled.

Kyle let go. August snaked his hands down his sides and pulled the ends of his shirt out of his dirt-encrusted tuxedo pants. Robin took the flashlight and ran the light along it. There were no rips.

"So, okay? There's nothing wrong with my freakin' shirt. I can't believe you people," August said. His voice was shaking. "So, what's it going to be, Praveen? Kyle? The sun rises and you're the last ones standing?"

Praveen turned away. "Shut up. Just shut up."

"Or what? You'll electrocute me?"

Fresh screams tore through the darkness.

"They're dead!" Beth shrieked. "They're dead!"

A resonant whooshing sound was followed by a sudden, intense flare that rose through the darkness, so bright Robin had to shield her eyes.

She lowered her hand.

On the roof of the warehouse, huge, flaming letters flickered:

DIDN'T FOLLOW THE RULES

24

DOWN FOR THE
BODY COUNT

ROBIN'S RULE #12:

*Bad things happen to
good people and there's nothing
you can do about it.*

Beth's voice rang out over the brick and stone and shell as Robin started down the hill. When Kyle tried to take her hand, she stuffed them both into her pockets. He had almost killed August and she just didn't want to touch him for a little while. They jogged, keeping pace with each other, as August and Praveen trailed slowly behind them.

Beth was hunched over sobbing. Robin wanted to rush forward but Kyle grabbed her wrist, nearly dangling her like a string puppet, and forced her behind him. He went up to Beth.

"It was the generators. They're . . . they're . . ." She

completely lost it, sobbing. Robin tried to get around Kyle, not to comfort her but to make her be quiet.

Flashlight on, August darted over to the two black shapes. He bent down beside one and reached out a hand. Then did the same to the other.

"What happened?" August asked Beth. She kept crying. "You have to tell me," he said sternly. *"Now."*

After she explained, he shook his head. "They were wired. The gas cans. So when Mick put the cap on . . . and Larson had the knife . . ."

"So they were *electrocuted*," Kyle said.

"August!" Praveen shouted, but Robin whirled on her.

"Back off, Praveen," she said.

Praveen's eyes grew huge. She stared at Robin as if she, not August, was in her sights.

"And Morgan. We found her. . . . Rats were eating . . ." Beth couldn't get out the rest before dissolving into more sobs.

AUGUST'S RULE #3:

Do unto others as they did unto Alexa.

Shit, August thought.

The flames on the warehouse roof lit up the scene: Beth crying, Praveen spinning herself back up into a frenzy, and Robin very carefully retrieving the knife from beside Larson's body. The fire gave off thick, oily smoke, but as far as he could tell, there was no blazing inferno. The warehouse was mostly brick, which was fortunate, as August realized that all their stuff was inside. Wallets and purses had not been on anyone's mind, and probably weren't on anybody else's but his.

"We need to figure out where the electricity is located," he said while Robin worked to calm Beth down. The group moved well away from the generators and the corpses. "That was used to do this."

"You already know," Praveen shot back. "There's a fence up there," she told Beth. "It's electrified. August did it."

Praveen aimed her flashlight straight at him, like she could kill him with it or make him disappear or something. All he could see was the brilliance of the light. He tried to wave her off but she kept doing it.

"I didn't electrify the fence," he said. "God, who do you think I am, some supervillain? Listen to me. There's working electricity here in the cannery. This is *huge*. We just have to find the source."

"Like you talked Mick into doing," Praveen said.

"I don't even know what you're talking about." He took a step forward. "Stop it!"

Kyle grabbed the flashlight from Praveen and clicked it off before stuffing it in the pocket of his jacket.

"He wasn't there, Praveen," Robin said. "Remember? We didn't know where he was."

"He was making sure Mick and Larson died," Praveen snapped.

"For the last time, I'm not the one doing this!" August shouted, spittle flying from his mouth.

"You're lying!" Praveen yelled. "Every word out of your mouth is a lie!"

Arms spread wide, she ran toward the cliff, weaving and bobbing as if someone had shot her in the back. For a moment August thought she had been hit. But Praveen kept running.

"Wait!" Robin yelled at her. "Oh my God, Praveen! Just *stop*!"

She watched in frustration as Praveen headed toward the rickety wooden dock and then into the warehouse. Praveen had been out of her mind most of the night, and now she'd just run into a building whose roof was on fire.

THEA'S RULE #5:

If you hide, you're less likely to get hurt.

Thea didn't know how long she shivered in Jackson's car, Inky clutched to her chest. Jackson had loved the dog even more than her. She kept petting the little thing over and over; if she made it out of this alive, she would take care of Inky forever. So many things had gone wrong so fast. None of this should have happened.

Jackson.

The blood gushing out of his throat.

The shadowy figure looming behind him.

She squeezed her eyes shut and Inky wriggled, sensing her panic. The sight would haunt her until she died, however soon that turned out to be. She had a terrible feeling it wouldn't be very long.

I didn't even get to hang out with Hiro, she thought.

There were lots of noises outside, the most terrifying of which had been Beth yelling that someone else was dead. At least, that was what it had sounded like. Maybe it wasn't even Beth. Whoever it was and whoever was dead, she wasn't going to look.

Inky whimpered. Thea could feel her heart pounding out of rhythm. So afraid of everything all the time. Jackson had given her power, real power. People were—*had been*—afraid of him. Her boyfriend. No one messed with her when he was with her. She'd loved knowing that, feeling safe with him.

Just not safe *from* him. His temper. Until now.

Thud.

Something landed on the roof.

The whole car shook.

Thea bit her tongue so hard it started bleeding.

"Woof!"

Thud.

The car shook again.

Inky barked.

This time Thea held his muzzle, muffling the next *woof;* then she panicked. Maybe that had been a mistake.

Scratching sounds came from outside the car, near her head.

She should get up; she should run. The car, which had offered her protection just a short while ago, was a trap. She was lying down like she was in a coffin and that's where she was going to end up. The killer knew she was here. Her only chance was to run or fight. She couldn't just let herself be butchered.

She felt in the footwell and her hand wrapped around the tire iron Kyle had made sure to give to her. She had a weapon. She could totally do this.

If she called for help . . .

. . . no guarantee that anyone would hear. That they would come.

Tears and sweat soaked her to the bone. She was so scared her fingers could barely hold on to the piece of metal and it started to slip. She readjusted her grip with one hand and tried to push Inky off with the other.

The scratching stopped.

Thea froze. Her eyes were huge as she listened hard. Could it have just been the wind? An animal?

Inky crawled back onto her chest, whimpering.

Crash!

Something smashed into the windshield, showering bits of glass down on the front seat. She cried out, dropping the tire iron, and then frantically felt for it. When she had it, she rocketed up and flung open the door. Her feet had barely hit the ground and she was running. The tire iron slid again from her clammy hand and she didn't stop to get it. She couldn't.

The car door slammed shut.

Running steps behind her.

Closer.

Closer.

"Please, no!" She tried to yell as loudly as she could, but the sound was cut off as someone grabbed her hair and yanked, causing her feet to skid. Pinwheeling her arms, she tried to reach behind, to free herself, even as she fell.

She hit the ground so hard it knocked the wind out of her and then she was being dragged backward toward the car. She could hear Inky barking and barking.

Suddenly, whoever had her let go. *Safe, safe, safe.* She struggled to sit up and glanced upward just as the tire iron arced down.

ROBIN'S RULE #13:

Show up when you should.

"Praveen?" Robin called as the group clumped at the warehouse door. She looked at Kyle. "Did you hear that? Was that a scream?"

"I didn't hear anything," he said.

"That was me, wheezing," said Beth. She doubled over

coughing, waving her hands in front of her face as she shook her head. "Let's get Praveen and charge the phone."

"Praveen?" Robin yelled as she stuck her head in the warehouse. The lanterns they'd left behind were still on. Smoke danced lazily in the light.

Kyle was beside her, clicking on the flashlight. "I'm sorry, Robin," he said. "About August. I lost it. I really lost it."

She nodded stiffly. "We're all under a lot of stress." Then she cracked a half smile up at him. "To put it mildly."

"I wish I'd taken you to the winter formal," he said. He wrinkled his nose, eyes glittering. "Unwritten rule. No dating the coach's daughter."

His change of subject caught her off guard. "I'm not the coach's daughter anymore."

"He'll get his job back." He tentatively brushed his hand against hers. She took it, held it. Made it as right as she could again. Even Beth had said she would kill the killer. Kyle was the captain of the lacrosse team and she had seen him in outright battle on the field. Lacrosse players had tons of testosterone; she shouldn't be so hard on him for doing what he'd done. "He's a good coach."

"It was just such a horrible shock," she blurted. "Someone *doing* that. And leaving him there. It changed our lives forever."

"One slipup," he said softly, "and it's all gone."

"You wouldn't know. You're the king at school." She didn't mean to sound bitter.

"Class president. Lacrosse captain." He sounded as if he were making fun of himself. "Praveen!" he shouted.

Something shuffled in the hall to the left of the stage. Robin's fingers seized Kyle's.

"Praveen!" she joined in, hefting the knife in her hand. If the killer could hear them, maybe he'd stay away.

They hurried together past the stage and were about halfway down the hall. Somewhere back here was where Larson had found Heather's earring. She shut her eyes against the image of Heather's body swinging from the rope. Her stomach began to rebel; she had to stop for a second. Kyle stopped, too.

In the space of that moment, she heard a soft groan. She darted forward; almost too late, the flashlight passed over a patch of darkness—a hole—and she wobbled at the edge as Kyle caught up to her and grabbed her forearm.

"Whoa," he said.

She heard another groan and leaned over. Aiming her flashlight downward, they saw a blur of contrast, a shape. Red, green. Praveen's bloody clothes. Around the shape, darkness was spreading like a sunset shadow.

Fresh blood.

"She's down there. Hurt. She must have fallen through." The floor creaked as she shuffled forward and craned her neck to get a better look. "Praveen! We're coming!"

Kyle put his hand out. "Move back. Don't put too much weight on the floor—the wood feels rotted."

"August! Beth!" she shouted.

They came running. Robin quickly explained what had happened.

August blanched. "The floor looked solid when I checked this place out. I even tested it."

"Uh-huh," Beth snapped. "I would never have let that happen. Outside is the wooden deck, right? There were concrete stairs going down. Circular stairs."

Kyle nodded. "Right. I saw those, too."

They all went to the dock. Wet ocean breeze slammed against Robin as they found the concrete stairs. She clattered down to the next level first and tried the knob. It was locked.

Kyle looked at August. "Key?"

"Are you kidding?" August threw himself at the door. Then he brought up his leg and tried to kick it in. He swore and limped out of the way as Kyle gave it a shot.

"How come the frickin' door isn't rotten?" Kyle muttered. "Like the floor?"

Robin cupped her hands around her mouth. "Praveen, can you get to the door? Can you open the door?"

If Praveen answered, Robin didn't hear her. Kyle ran his hands through his hair and dropped them to his sides.

"*Why* did I leave the tire iron with Thea?" he said.

We've left Thea alone too long, Robin realized. *And we need to find Hiro, too.*

Fresh panic bubbled through her body. She hurtled herself at the door. And again, jerking out of Kyle's arms when he tried to catch her, stop her.

"Damn it!" she shouted. "Damn it!"

A cracking, popping sound was followed by the door canting off the jamb; registering that it was giving way, Robin attacked it wildly, ramming it, kicking it, grunting as Kyle reached up from behind her and threw his weight against it, too.

The door flapped backward and Robin went sprawling headlong into the room. The floor was cement and it scraped the side of her face. She barely noticed it as she scrabbled forward like an insect, hands finding Praveen's head.

Her wet, sticky scalp.

"Praveen, okay, it's okay," she said in a rush. A light came on over her shoulder. Kyle was hunched behind her with a flashlight, panting. She realized she was panting, too.

Praveen's eyes were closed, her mouth open. She was lying in a pool of blood and Robin couldn't make sense of what she was seeing: arms and legs bent, one wrist disappearing underneath Praveen's back.

Robin forced her hand down onto Praveen's neck. She couldn't tell if there was a pulse or not. Bending forward, she laid her cheek right up to Praveen's nose. A very slight puff of air tickled her.

Still alive.

Robin pressed her shaking hand on Praveen's arm and very, very gently squeezed. She looked toward the ceiling at the hole. It was so far to fall.

It would break anybody.

"Oh God," August said from somewhere behind Kyle and Robin. "Look at her."

"Shhh," Robin whispered. "It's okay, Praveen. You're going to be all right."

"We shouldn't move her," Kyle said. "She could have a spinal injury."

"Oh, man, move her," August said. "Get her out of here. Do you smell the smoke? I think this place *is* burning. I think it's going to go up like a rocket."

"Let me get her." Kyle's voice was strained, gentle. He leaned forward, gathering Praveen in his arms. Her head lolled against his chest. She looked mangled and fractured. The muscles in his arms and pecs flexed as he pushed up from his feet and straightened. Robin cradled the back of her head as it draped over Kyle's forearm and together they stutter-stepped toward the door.

"I've got her," Kyle said, placing his foot on the first step. "I'll take good care of her."

"I know you will," she murmured.

25

SONNET

BETH'S RULE #5:

Don't trust anyone but yourself.

"I'll clear a space," Beth said as she ran just ahead of Kyle and looked back over her shoulder to make sure the others were coming. Praveen's head looked *crumpled*, like a rotting mushroom. It was sickening, frightening.

She opened the door and crossed the threshold. They couldn't stay in here for very long. If the fire was spreading, it was slow, but there was no sense in tempting fate any more than they already had.

She grabbed the rest of the tablecloths off the tables to make a little bed on the stage for Praveen. She found another tablecloth in a cardboard box, then looked in and saw a shiny staple gun. *A weapon*. She knew exactly what she could do with it. She wasn't going to share it or give it over to someone else. This night could turn into kill or be killed. She'd do it, if she had to.

The box also contained several coils of skull lights. She poked through them and felt a little thrill of terror when she discovered an envelope taped to one of the spirals. It read #3 THE HUNTED.

"No freaking way," she whispered.

Footfalls sounded outside. August was the first one through the door. Beth turned away and slipped the staple gun under her sweater, tucking the sweater into her skirt; then Kyle entered with Praveen, and Robin shuffled beside him, holding Praveen's head. Praveen was bleeding all over them. Her eyelids were purple. Her lips were blue. No part of her wrap looked green anymore.

Stiff-lipped, August moved past Beth to gesture into the hallway where Praveen had fallen. "I think the killer weakened the floor somehow. It was fine when I scouted this place." He waved Kyle forward like someone deciding where to place a new sofa. "Let's put her on the stage."

"Which I have already planned for," Beth bit off. She closed her eyes, murmured an apology to Praveen for being petty in Praveen's time of need, and cleared her throat. She opened the envelope and her eyes flitted over the words.

"There's a new clue," she announced. Would the killer get mad that they had totally skipped number two? She remembered vaguely something about Thea having found a bucket. Screw it. She had found this clue. She took a deep breath and then she read:

As you die,

Don't you wonder why?

Follow the rules,

You stupid fools.

Lights, camera, action—

See the coming attraction!

"Movies?" Robin said as she plumped up the table-cloths to make a pillow for Praveen. "TV?"

"Coming attractions," August said. "Movie trailers? I didn't see a trailer on the property."

"We also need to check on Thea," Robin said. "She has to get out of the car. And we've got to find Hiro."

"I'll get Thea," August and Beth said at the same time. Beth cast August a hostile glare. There was no way she would ever trust him again.

"Oh, for God's sake," August said, screwing up his pale eyes as if he gave a damn about what she thought of him. "Beth, please. You know me."

"I thought I did," she replied frostily, shutting out her conscience's reminder that *she* was the one who had betrayed *him*.

"I can go," Kyle said.

"Not with August," Robin said. Beth couldn't be sure if Robin was blushing, but Merida the Brave kept her gaze steady the same way she had when August had told her to take off her top and run around the cannery with her and Thea.

"Kyle and I will go," Beth announced, taking some control.

"Okay," Kyle said, turning his back on Robin. Robin didn't seem to care, but Beth knew a rift in the Force when she saw one.

They walked outside; then, taking a deep breath, Beth sprinted in the direction of Jackson's car. Kyle kept up. The moon made an unenthusiastic appearance and they left their flashlights off. They had almost made it to the car when the moon gave out like a tired, dying lamp.

She stumbled in the dark, swore, and Kyle steadied her. His flashlight clicked on too loudly as he swept it along the ground. Less than a minute later the light reflected off Jackson's lowrider. Guarded relief surged through her when she heard the dog barking. At least Inky was okay.

"Thea, it's us, Beth and Kyle," she whispered against the backseat window on the driver's side, loudly enough that her friend could hear her but not so loud that anyone else could. At least, that was her hope.

Inky appeared like a jack-in-the-box, barking excitedly, his button eyes shining vampire-red in the light from the flashlight, his baby fangs bared in his most threatening expression.

"Shhh, Inky, please." Kyle reached out and grabbed the door handle. Locked. "Thea, open up."

No answer.

Now Beth was scared.

Kyle took a step closer and shined the light inside. They both peered in.

Thea wasn't in the backseat.

A bloom of panic swallowed Beth up; she got out her own flashlight and shined the beam all around the inside of the car. Thea was nowhere, but there was glass on the front seat.

"Thea!" Beth hissed, raising her voice.

Inky scampered back and forth, barking, flinging himself against the windows, growling as if he had rabies.

Kyle looked at her somberly; then he laced his fingers with hers and together they ducked down and crabwalked to the other side of the car.

No.

Thea was lying flat on her back, staring blankly upward at the sky with eyes that would never again see.

No.

Blood trickled down her mouth from the side of her head, which had been bashed in, probably with the tire iron that was supposed to protect her.

On her chest was a stone, her hands folded around it as if it were a bouquet of flowers.

Kyle grabbed Beth and held her as she unraveled. She didn't know she had completely lost it until finally she heard Kyle whispering, "Beth, Beth," in her ear.

"The tire iron is missing," Kyle whispered. "We have to get out of here."

Beth sniffed and wiped her nose with the back of her hand. Then she knelt down to get the rock off Thea's chest and wipe the blood off her cheeks, when her hand touched something wet. She yanked it back and shined her flashlight downward.

There, on the ground, written in blood, were the words:

DIDN'T FOLLOW THE RULES

AUGUST'S RULE #4:

Live because Alexa can't.

August dribbled water over Praveen's head and dabbed at all the bloody places with a napkin. He hoped he wasn't hurting her. The smoke was thickening. They had to get out of there pretty soon.

"I swear to you, Robin, I am not the killer."

She poured some water on another napkin and cleaned off Praveen's cheek. "I believe you."

He wanted to kiss her. He wondered why she had decided he was innocent. And when.

"When my dad got hurt, I wanted to kill whoever hit him. I wanted to cut off his legs and torture him for hours. Days. I know the level of pain you're dealing with."

He cocked his head. "And . . . you wouldn't kill that guy today."

"I swear to you, August, it stops hurting so much when you realize how unconstructive hate is. It would never help my dad regain the use of his legs. Then I just started dealing with how things have changed."

So should he tell her that he knew Larson had hit her father? That he had put two and two together over the course of a month and was absolutely positive of it? Tell her now in case there was no later?

"I didn't want to go through life filled with hate," she said. Then she forced out a hollow gallows laugh. "Going through life now might not be an option."

"How did you get over it?" His gaze was still averted as he listened, as if he could glean a clue about what to say and what not to.

She was quiet for a while and he dabbed at Praveen like an archaeologist dusting a fossil. "I think the main difference is that I know people love me," she said. "I have my family."

"Alexa was my family." His stomach twisted. He could feel the tears and he swore to himself that he would not cry, not now. That would be the ultimate loser gesture—an inexcusable act of self-pity while the *Titanic* sailed toward the iceberg.

"Your parents," she ventured, and he shook his head.

August exhaled years of loneliness, then drew them back in with the smoke. "I thought Beth . . ." He made an erasing gesture with his free hand. "It's the wrong time to have this kind of conversation."

"Maybe it's the best time," she said. "I don't think you

or Alexa ever had a real friend. I mean, someone who was just a nice person and liked being around you."

"There really is no 'me,'" he said without thinking. "There's just what I can do for people." He was shocked. He had never consciously grasped that this was exactly how he felt about himself.

"I don't think that's true. Beth said you write poetry. You do that for yourself."

"It's bad poetry. Just ask Beth."

"What the hell does Beth Breckenridge know about poetry?"

He smiled faintly. "Thanks for that."

She inclined her head.

"You play Clue," he said. "I thought no one would figure out that's where I was going with the murder weapons."

"We don't have a gas can in our version at home," she quipped.

"There weren't enough murder weapons for the hunt. I thought a gas can was in keeping with the simplicity of the design." He studied Praveen. "Who the hell is doing this?"

"Jacob?"

"I don't see it. I think someone dragged him off and murdered him. All this talk about the rules. I think someone's trying really hard to make it look like I'm the murderer."

"Or else they really are obsessive about rules."

"I'll bet this is the last party you'll ever crash." He paled. "I don't mean it *that* way."

"I didn't know I was crashing. Beth neglected to mention it." She caught her lower lip. "You don't think *Beth*—"

"Are you kidding? She wouldn't kill off the cool of the school," he said.

There was a crackly sort of pressure sound from the roof, and embers cascaded like fireflies. August waved at them with a bloody hand and they winked out in ones and twos and threes.

"Time to go," he said. "We should get everyone's purses and belongings and put them outside."

They worked together, and when they were done, they eased Praveen into his arms. Her head bobbed against his chest as they walked out of the warehouse, probably for the last time. He gazed at all his elaborate decorations soon to go up in flames. Last party ever. He made a little promise to Praveen and Robin that he would do everything he could to keep them both alive.

"Shouldn't they be back from the car by now?" Robin said.

"And shouldn't we be moving on to the next clue?" he added. "'Lights, camera, action, trailer?' I mean, if we don't start looking, he'll know."

"It's like he's watching our every move. *With a camera*," she said slowly. A light went on in her eyes, and she looked skyward. "Do you think that's the clue? He could have put cameras up. He could be sitting somewhere watching us.

That's how he knows when to attack. And when to punish us for not doing what he wants."

She raised her chin. "Are you watching me, you bastard? Do you like seeing us die? Is that what gets you off?"

"Robin?" Kyle called from the darkness.

"Kyle! Here!" Robin turned on a flashlight and waved it over her head.

Beth and Kyle emerged from the shadows, silhouetted by the flashlight. Beth lurched forward, zombielike, and it was one of the most terrifying things August had ever seen. Sure, Praveen had gone in and out, but Beth was *Beth*. This was not Beth.

"Thea," Robin murmured. Kyle shook his head as Beth fell into Kyle's arms.

And brave Robin pressed her face into August's shoulder. In the distance, Inky barked and barked and barked.

26

CHEATER THEATER

HIRO'S RULE #2:

March to the beat of
your own drumming.

Footsteps in the darkness.

Crammed into his hidey-hole, Hiro clutched the sodden white envelope containing a copy of the same clue they had found around Heather's neck. His entire survival strategy was based on hiding until the sun came up. Sweat popped on his forehead. Had he been discovered?

"Damn it," he muttered.

Mick wouldn't put down that stupid crowbar. Any fool could see that it was a burden, not a weapon. Then he realized Mick was *afraid* to let go of it. Mick was arming himself against *him*.

Okay, sure, he had lost it. A couple of times. Who wouldn't? But to treat him as if he were the killer . . .

So yeah, he had split. Stomped down onto the mushy, waterlogged beach. The tide had gone back out, and the sand was covered with all kinds of weird crap that he stumbled over in his boiling, frightened anger. In his mind's eye he saw Drew falling from the cliff, heard his scream. His corpse was in the water now. Hiro would never, ever go swimming in the ocean again.

He had come to hate Drew. Drew the addict, the destroyer, the plagiarist. But there was also the Drew who had gotten Maximum Volume together, made the demo, connected with Pascha. Drew before drugs. He had been missing that Drew for years.

But I did not push him. And I didn't do anything to Stacy.

The tunnel had appeared; it looked like someone had taken a huge bite out of the stones, weeds, and dirt. His heart had gone *ka-thumm ka-thumm* as he weighed the wisdom of disappearing inside. Finally he'd made his move, less than thrilled to find a glowing lantern about ten feet in because that meant someone else either was there or had been. But he picked it up and that was when he saw a tattered white envelope dripping with what had to be blood. Shocked, he almost dropped it. Barely legible were the same words that had been attached to the envelope taped to Heather's chest: *You killed them, you sick bastard.*

He swore and inched open what was left of the

envelope. It looked like something had been chewing on it. He was so freaked out he almost dropped it.

It was the same clue as before:

```
Water, water everywhere but not a drop to
drink.
If you ever want to leave here, now's the
time to think.
On my words now you must dwell.
For your sins fetch from the well.
```

So did that mean no one had found it yet? Was there more than one envelope with the same clue? Was the killer's hunt just some random joke, and he was going to kill them all anyway?

Is this Heather's envelope?

Rattled, he dropped it. Then he thought better of it and picked it back up. It was so *bloody*. There didn't appear to be any other information on it.

Then he heard screaming, then *more* screaming, and then even *more* screaming. Then silence.

He waited.

He had begun to wonder if he was the sole survivor. But now someone was coming, and he wasn't about to stick around to find out who it was. He looked left, right, a useless exercise since he was essentially blind in the darkness, and eased himself out of the crevice. Ever so cautiously he tiptoed toward the mouth of the—

Wait, he thought. *Is this the right way?*

He stood still and tried to orient himself. It was pitch-black. He had kept the lantern but turned it off once he'd hidden himself away. Whoever had said that the tunnels were gross was correct. The jury was still out on the drug dealers. Hiro hadn't explored the tunnels very much. Hadn't zoomed around looking for weapons or a clue as to the killer's identity. He had just hid.

The footfalls were coming closer.

He turned his head in their direction. A gentle blur of light floated in the darkness. A flashlight.

He swore and went the other way. Toe-heel, toe-heel, trying so hard not to make a sound. Then he saw a light up ahead and knew that if he stepped into it, whoever was approaching behind him would see his silhouette.

Hiro put his hand on the tunnel wall and it curved to the right. He followed it with his hand and then his toe hit something hard. Flailing his arms, Hiro fought for balance, but he fell forward. His palms slammed down on hard surfaces with strange protrusions. He smelled oil and battery acid.

Oh God, the car batteries, he thought.

Suddenly the air was thick with the smell of blood. It made his stomach clench as he jerked back to his feet. His lids fluttered as he completely lost control for a brief second, and then he scooted back out the way he had come.

He didn't see the blurry light.

He didn't hear the footfalls.

That could be great news, or the worst. His breath was jagged as he poured everything he had into the soundlessness. Surely whoever was in here had heard his fall.

Shambling forward, he stuck his right arm out and brushed the wall with his fingertips and then lost contact. He panicked again, but shuffled on. The wall came back. It canted toward the right. He trusted it and made a turn.

The moon hung in the sky like a silvery disco ball.

He had reached the mouth of the cave.

Swearing with relief, he popped out like a rabbit. He didn't take time to breathe. He just hauled ass, going right because that was in the opposite direction he had come.

On the beach, cutouts in lunch-size paper bags revealed a candle burning inside each one. A luminaria, common in Northern California. About ten feet farther down, there was another one. And another one. And a glow-in-the-dark sign that read CHEATER THEATER.

He considered the clue in his hand. The killer had hijacked the scavenger hunt; possibly this cheater theater thing was the right way to go. Then again, he wasn't about to be herded to his death. Furrowing his brow, he put the envelope in his jeans pocket.

A noise.

He wheeled around, bracing himself to see some crazed maniac in a long coat and hood charging at him with a machete. Nothing. He looked in the opposite direction. He didn't know what to do.

Then, slightly ahead of "Cheater Theater," perched on an inlet of water, squatted a tumbledown building with shingled siding. It was on the way to the theater, so he hung a left and trotted over to it. Windows were blackened and broken. There was no light but he could see the outline of frayed ropes hanging in loops in front of some of the blackened windows and a half-open door. Moonlight poured in from a stove-in ceiling, revealing rusted blocks and tackle hanging from hooks. Something squeaked back and forth, back and forth.

He heard movement on the beach behind him. Drawing closer.

"Shit," he murmured, and darted inside the building. As soon as he did it, he was sorry he had. Now he *was* being herded.

A noise like shuffling shoes echoed behind him. He darted past a stack of dinghies and what looked like a wooden clothes dresser, the varnish peeling off, a drawer hanging open. Fungus was crawling up and over the edge. On the top of the chest, a porcelain-headed doll with no eyes lay on its side next to a moldy catcher's mitt. Some kids had left their toys in there a long time ago, maybe so long ago that they'd grown up and died of old age.

A large portion of the interior had no floor, and the ocean rushed in and swirled along pylons at a frenetic pace. An ancient, used-up skiff that looked as if it was being held together by rust bobbed in the water.

There was a growl. A *growl.* Like from an animal. Dog?

Hungry dog? Not like that crazy little Chihuahua, but something big. A coyote? There was food at the party; it might have drawn animals or . . .

He yanked the envelope out of his pocket. He didn't know whose blood it was.

A roar shook his eardrums. He turned only enough to see a flash of fur, claws, teeth. Mountain lion! He began to run. Running into boxes, slamming into a post; it gave way and birds flapped and dry rot and dirt showered him. He kept running; there was hot breath on his back.

The floor gave way beneath his feet.

KYLE'S RULE #3:

Never date the coach's daughter.

"We should put Praveen in the Maximum Volume van," Kyle said. "Out of harm's way." He had taken her from August, who sagged with exhaustion. Flames danced along the warehouse roof and Robin wondered how long it would be before the other buildings caught fire.

Beth sucked in her breath and quivered; Robin traded looks with Kyle. "Maybe after . . . Jackson's car . . . we should stay away from cars. Maybe we should put her in the little shed behind the warehouse."

"That's where I found Jacob's phone," August said. "Behind the warehouse, in line with the shed."

"The shed is close to Jackson's car," Kyle said.

"Nowhere is safe," Beth murmured in a strangely disembodied voice. Kyle knew that what she was missing was called "affect," an observable emotion. Praveen had shifted her affect into her intense scratching. But Beth was just lost.

"We have to continue the hunt," August said. "We need to keep the killer happy."

"Maybe we could put Beth in the shed with Praveen," Robin said, and a shadow crossed her features. He understood; it sounded kind of like they were stashing the two of them out of the way. Well, weren't they?

Beth gave her head a shake. Kyle's arms were getting tired. He had had a very long night.

Then Beth turned her attention to August. Tears spilled down her sooty cheeks. August's pale brows shot up as she took a step toward him, and then she glided up to him and as if it were his only option, August put his arms around her.

"Beth," he said. "Beth, I'm sorry."

She made a muffled sound against his neck and he looked at Kyle and Robin with consternation. "Maybe we can start looking," he said. "You find a good place for Praveen and then you can find us."

"That's not a good idea," Robin said. Kyle had to agree. But Beth nodded like a ventriloquist's dummy and August shrugged.

"I guess that's what we're doing," he said.

"Wasn't August the one who insisted we shouldn't split up?" Kyle asked as he shifted his weight. He headed for the shed, with Robin beside him, and she held the door while he carried Praveen inside. When Robin turned on the flashlight, monsters stared back at them—fun-house mirrors installed, no doubt, by August.

Robin gathered up all Praveen's tablecloths and then laid her on the ground. She murmured very softly and Robin caught her breath. She pressed her ear to Praveen's lips.

"She's asking for water."

Kyle shut his eyes. "Didn't think of that." He shook his head. "We shouldn't risk it."

"Wadder," Praveen begged. She moved a little, moaned.

Robin made moves to stand, but Kyle held up his hand. "I'll do it."

"No," Robin said. "I'm the one who wants to go. I should take the risk."

"I said I would protect you." A fleeting smile crossed her lips. "A kiss before I go," he said, moving in and placing his mouth over hers. When she exhaled, he sucked her breath into his lungs. It felt so final.

Goodbye, just in case.

"Lock the door after me," he told her, and then he darted out into the night.

AUGUST'S NEW RULE:

Move on.

August and Beth skirted the warehouse. The fire was grow-ing, and it bathed their section of the cannery in an orange glow. The pine trees to their left stood like tempting tar-gets, teasing the night winds to blow some burning embers their way.

"I wish that was the sunrise," August said while walking to the cliff that overlooked the sea. He stared at the moon and the black, black water, willing the sun to come. Beth remained silent. Her head was hung low, and he heard her sniffling.

"Yes, you were a bitch," he said, "and yes, you screwed me over. I'm still mad at you. But as God is my witness, if we get out of this, I will pay for your tuition to Oberlin."

They were silent for a moment. Then she said, "You have to stop bleaching your hair. You look like a Morlock from *The Time Machine*."

He actually guffawed and he took her hand as a little sliver of hope spread through him. Then a flash caught his eye and he looked down the steep embankment. There. On the roof of an old building. Some words had been spray-painted. And though they were difficult to read, he was pretty sure one of them said THEATER.

"Beth," he said, and pointed.

She went very still.

"Showdown."

At the exact same time, they made a move toward the ski-run path that led to the beach. August went first, Beth close behind. Down the steep embankment, and then, as they reached the beach, the tinny barking of Inky vibrated off the cliff face.

"Inky!" Beth cried, and she held up a hand, telling August to wait. He crossed his arms and stood there for a second, but just then, he heard someone calling his name and whirled around.

Hiro stood on the steps with something in his hand. August looked at Beth, who was running down to the water's edge. He would be just a few feet away; he lifted a hand at Hiro and walked over to him.

"God, where the hell have you been?" August said.

"I was hiding, okay? And be careful," Hiro said. "There's a mountain lion skulking around. Do you have a clue about Cheater Theater? I mean, is there a written clue and not one that you made up yourself?"

August blinked at him. "Wait, what? A *mountain lion?*"

Hiro nodded. "I fell through the floor and I guess it was too smart to do the same. But you can bet it's still around here. Do you? Have a clue?"

"Yeah," August replied. "It was hidden in some boxes in the party room."

Hiro exhaled. "Then I made a wrong turn and this is the right place. We're supposed to put these on."

For a moment, August shuddered as if someone were

holding him over a vat of liquid nitrogen. *Could it be Hiro? Is this a trick?*

But then Hiro showed him the thing in his hand. It was a cheap rubber devil mask complete with horns and a goatee. August looked at Beth again. The fire was building and there was light. Inky was leading her toward them. She'd be there any second.

He ducked inside the shack to see a room decorated with spray-painted stars on the walls, ceiling, and floor. Nothing had been cleaned up: their tormentor had simply sprayed over cobwebs, piles of trash, dried seaweed, a rat corpse. A rickety table like an old-fashioned school desk was positioned in the center of the room. On it sat five ugly masks with names written inside them: Hiro, Praveen, Beth, Kyle, and August. Robin appeared to be off the hook. He remembered that she hadn't actually been invited, so maybe she really was.

There was a piece of paper on the same table as the masks. It read PUT ON YOUR MASK AND PERFORM YOUR SCRIPT. FIRST NAMES ALPHABETICAL.

"That puts you first, August DeYoung," Hiro said. He handed August an ivory-colored skull mask. August regarded it anxiously.

"Maybe this is laced with poison or something," August said, examining the mask.

"Just put it on, okay?" Hiro snapped, glancing around the room. "We don't want to piss this guy off."

"He's probably pissed off at you for hiding. By the way, you're supposed to put yours on now, too."

"Not until after you read your script," Hiro began, and then August tapped the sign. Hiro frowned. "Maybe."

Hiro put on his devil mask. "It stinks," he informed August. Then he gestured for August to do the same.

"Beth should have been here by now," August said. He picked up his script. "Hold on. I'll get her."

"Oh my God," Hiro snapped. He stomped toward the front door. "Beth!" he called.

Then August heard the little dog yipping and finally processed what Hiro had said about a mountain lion.

"Beth, come here!" he shouted.

The hut exploded.

HIRO'S RULE #3:

Never let a girl pin you down.

Flames and cinder blocks and sheets of siding rocketed toward Hiro; in a miraculous split second, he dove into the sand and covered his head. Chunks of stone and metal plummeted around him like bombs. The worst pain he had ever felt spread up his back; he was on fire. Shrieking, he rolled over. Smoke rushed into his eyes, blinding him. He scrabbled to his feet and ran away from the heat as fast as he could. He kept going and going; he heard screaming, and another explosion racked all the bones in his body as he ran to the beach, his feet sloshing into the water before he fell gratefully into the ocean. The water surged over his back, cooling and stinging.

"Help," he said, but he wasn't sure he spoke aloud. He couldn't hear anything. As he pushed himself weakly to his knees, he raised trembling arms to pull off the mask.

Needles stabbed the backs of his hands. Again. Again. Into his fingers. He flailed, yelling, but the sound was muffled. He fell face-first into the water and the foul rubber mask pressed against his nose and mouth. He tried to draw in a breath but he couldn't. Then his head smashed down hard on sand and pebbles and there were more needles. He couldn't lift his head out of the water. Was someone forcing him to stay under? He couldn't breathe. Panicking, he sucked in and—

ROBIN'S RULE #14:

Where there's life there's hope.

"Kyle?" Robin said. He had been gone a long time just to get some water, and she was ill with fear for him. She hazarded one tiny step outside the shed.

An explosion bursting into the sky shook her off her feet. She fell against the shed door, then stumbled out and looked upward. Above the burning warehouse, a fireball whirled like a second, orange moon.

"Kyle!" she shouted.

She flew to the warehouse and looked in, seeing nothing but smoke, and called his name again. Then she raced to the cliff and looked down. Some kind of building had burst apart, and piles of rubble burned like dried leaves. Branches of the pines had ignited.

At the water's edge, Beth was shrieking and wrestling with something in the water. *The killer,* Robin thought.

"I'm coming!" Robin shouted.

Her heart beat helter-skelter against her rib cage as she jettisoned herself down the super-steep path. She slid and rolled, knowing she was getting cuts and scratches but not feeling them. Orange and red flames glowed on the sand, on the thrashing ocean, where a body floated. *Drew,* Robin thought, and she was afraid she was going to throw up. There was something very wrong with its head and something like seaweed was floating on top of it. Beth was at the water's edge, alternately pulling the body by the ankle and then doing something to it with a shiny object. Robin slogged into the water. Then Inky flashed behind her, barking and yipping as he wove between her legs.

"Robin! Robin!" Beth shrieked. "Don't touch it!"

Before Robin could stop herself, she crawled over to the body and flipped it onto its back. She stifled a cry at its unexpected ugliness until she realized that it was a guy wearing a mask.

Don't let it be Kyle, she beseeched every star in the sky, and then she gingerly placed her hands beneath the bottom edge of the pliant rubber and eased it up over a chin, and then a pair of lips.

She knew then that it was Hiro.

"Help me!" Robin yelled to Beth. "He's going to suffocate!"

Beth was crying wildly. Robin got Hiro onto the sand. The mask had been stapled onto his head. She ripped at the rubber and chunks of skin came with it.

"Was anyone else in that building?" she said as Beth continued to cry. Beth tossed the shiny object in the water, put her hands on top of her head, and collapsed in the sand.

Beth didn't move or speak again as Robin ran warily toward the fire. The heat kept her at a distance; she circled around to one side and peered into the flames. Her head throbbed; she braced herself to see horrible things, the worst things, worse than bludgeonings and drownings. For so much stone and metal, the fire was intense. Pieces of siding formed a tent, but it was filled with smoke and burning embers. There couldn't be anyone inside, not alive, anyway.

And then she thought she saw movement behind the fire.

27

THE NAME IN
THE ENVELOPE

BETH'S RULE #6:

Hurt others before they hurt you.

"Beth, please help me," Robin said, poking her head back around the haystack-shaped piles of burning debris. "Who else was in here? Do you know? I thought I saw someone moving. Someone might still be alive."

But Beth had had enough of death and fire. It was beginning to sink in that she had . . .

She had . . .

Done something to Hiro.

She was shaking and doubled over, holding her stomach. Icy sweat beaded her forehead. She hadn't known. She'd thought he was the killer.

But *she* had killed *him*.

Beth bolted.

"Damn it, Beth, help me!" Robin bellowed.

Inky bobbed and danced, and Beth kept her eyes glued to him like a homing beacon. Inky threw himself against her shins, so she bent down and picked him up. She looked back at Robin, who was still digging in the fire. Beth didn't see anyone else. Robin had just seen the shadows cast by the fire. Beth was sure of it. August wasn't in there. She hadn't seen him go in. The explosion must have scared him back up the path.

If she believed that, why did she have to stop and throw up? Why was she crying and scanning the smoky orange billows for August?

She reached the top of the path. Lights suddenly flashed on as if someone had thrown a switch. They were fastened to poles that were angled downward, revealing a figure standing at the railing of the deck.

Kyle.

"Robin!" She whirled on her heel and cupped her hands around her mouth. "Kyle is up on the deck!"

She hurried toward him but he didn't move. Kyle just stood there as still as a statue. In her arms Inky squirmed and yipped and Beth finally let him go. The little Chihuahua ran toward Kyle . . . but then he kept on going.

"Kyle," she said. "Have you seen August?"

"Beth," he said, but his voice was . . . different. He was looking at her with the strangest expression on his face.

Then Inky reappeared, trotting beside another figure.

Drew.

ROBIN'S RULE #15:

Trust your friends to have your back.

Kyle.

And electricity.

Robin left the burning debris and charged up the path, racing onto the lighted deck. Kyle was safe, unhurt. For a millisecond Robin couldn't register why Beth was losing it, but then her eyes focused beyond Kyle to the ghost standing behind him.

Drew.

He was holding a rifle like the one belonging to the big-game hunter zombie on the beach, and it was pointed at the back of Kyle's head.

"Surprise," Drew said.

Her heart stopped. There was a wild roaring in her head. She saw dots and blackness, but she forced herself to stay conscious. She tried to move, to speak.

All this time, Drew.

It was impossible.

"You're *dead*. They saw you fall into the ocean," she said, gasping.

"Looks can be deceiving." His eyes were dilated, his face very oily and wet. He was higher than a kite and Robin wondered if she could make it if she rushed him. She looked at Beth again, now huddled against Kyle, weeping hysterically. Robin needed her not to check out. They might make it if they rushed Drew.

Or he might shoot Kyle, or Beth, or her.

"Who fell from the cliff?" she asked. Not one of them. A stranger? Someone else who'd had the misfortune to cross his path?

"Let's go to the warehouse," Drew said. "We can talk there."

Robin's blood ran cold. *He's going to kill us. We're not going to get out of here alive.*

Unless we act.

"Put your hands on top of your heads. All three of you."

No, Robin thought. *This can't be how it ends. This can't be happening to us.*

"Do it," Drew said, "or one of you dies now."

"Do it, Robin," Kyle said quietly. He folded his hands one over the other on the crown of his head.

"Please, no," Beth said. "Please, Drew. We haven't done anything to you."

"It's not about you," he said, and he laughed silently, like a deflating balloon. "Put your hands on your head, Beth, or I'll shoot them off at your wrists."

He's so drugged up. We can take him.

Her brain went into overdrive, plotting, tossing out ideas, panicking. Her rib cage contracted, containing her terror. They headed along the deck through rolling smoke and fog and she looked up at the roof. She swallowed down

307

a yell as she spotted bright yellow and orange flames dancing in the tower. The warehouse was on fire.

Oblivious, Drew herded them toward the front door. The windows were glowing yellow coffin shapes. There was more light than when Robin, Thea, and Beth had pulled into the lot. All this time, they had had electricity and not known it.

To go into the warehouse was to die. She forced herself to think. Kyle had lost the baseball bat and the killer—Drew—had taken the tire iron. The knife, what had happened to the knife?

Too soon, before she had made any kind of plan, they were at the door, and Drew gestured with the rifle at Beth. It was wobbling in his grasp.

"Open it," he said.

"Okay, okay, I am." Beth clutched the doorknob with both hands. "It's *warm*."

Inky barked and whined, weaving in and out of Beth's legs.

"And shut that dog up or else," Drew said.

"We can't if we keep our hands on our heads," Robin informed him. "If you'll let me pick him up—"

"No." He pivoted and aimed the rifle at Robin. Every hair on her body shot straight up. She had never looked down the barrel of a firearm before, and it was terrifying. It was like standing still as a wildfire rushed toward you. Her heart knocked against her sternum and her knees turned to water.

"One, two . . . ," Drew said.

"I'm opening it. I am!" Beth said.

The door opened, light spilling across the threshold as Beth moved toward Robin. A tendril of smoke danced near them. Inky darted in, then backed up and tried to crawl up Robin's shins.

Drew tracked Beth's every move. Robin couldn't breathe.

"Go inside," he ordered.

"There's a fire," Beth said.

"Just a little one."

"Drew, please, let us go," Beth said again.

"Beth, shut the hell up or I'll kill you," said Drew. "Right now. I'll splatter your brains all over the side of this building."

"Go in, B," Robin pleaded.

"He *is* going to kill us," Beth wailed. "That's why we're going in here. He's going to shoot us."

Drew snickered as if that were the best joke ever. Then he waggled the rifle at Beth again.

All this time, Kyle had stood stock-still. But Robin could see his mind working. He was trying to piece together an escape plan, too. A plan of attack. She had faith in him. In *them*. They weren't dead yet, and they weren't going to be.

"Put your hands back on your head, and go into the warehouse," Drew said to Beth.

Beth began crying so hard she could barely move, but she lurched across the threshold and hobbled forward.

Drew gestured for Robin to go next. It was a nightmare to show her back to him. All he had to do was pull the trigger and she would be dead.

She walked inside, breathless with fear. The smoke wasn't thick, but it made her cough. Drew coughed, too, and she stiffened, terrified the gun would accidentally go off. Two pole lamps positioned on either side of the stage gave light to the room. The battery-operated lanterns were off.

Drew hadn't told Kyle to move. Robin figured he was doing it on his own, and she tried to reach out to him, sense him. Beth moved ahead of her, but barely, racked with sobs as she nearly tripped over Inky. The dog plunged ahead.

Robin's stomach clenched as Drew muttered, "Shut up, you stupid mutt." She kept walking steadily behind Beth.

She braced herself to see the coffins of Cage, Heather, and Stacy, but they weren't there. Drew had taken them away. She looked furtively around.

Three large red plastic gas cans were set against the wall beside the food table. They looked exactly like Kyle's missing can. A box of long kitchen matches sat on top of the middle one.

Robin started to lose it as the direness of their situation hit her squarely in the gut. Drew was going to burn the warehouse down. Probably shoot them all, then splash more gasoline on the fire and leave.

Had Kyle seen the cans, too? Her anxiety was boring

a hole in her composure. They had to make a move, and soon.

"I said shut the hell up!" Drew yelled.

"Beth," Robin said. "Stop crying. You have to stop *now*."

"Please, Drew, please," Beth sobbed. "Don't. We won't tell anyone."

"Like I could trust *you* to keep your mouth shut. Walk toward the stage," Drew said.

Robin couldn't feel the floor as she put one foot down in front of the other. She was walking to her execution. All this time, this whole night, she hadn't ever really believed that she would die.

Desperately Robin's eyes traveled over the food table. She tried to imagine taking Drew on with a wooden skewer. Hitting him over the head with a can of soda. He was ragged, on drugs. But he probably wasn't as exhausted as she was. She hadn't eaten for hours. She should have been slamming back water at the very least. Her mouth was very dry.

She scanned for knives.

Her breath caught.

There, on the corner of the table, were the baseball bat and the tire iron. Just lying there, begging to be taken. Was it a trick?

He must have brought them back into the warehouse. She couldn't believe he would leave them out in plain sight. If it wasn't a trick, then he must be incredibly cocky or so high he wasn't thinking straight. Either way, it put a chink in his armor.

A chink would give them a fighting chance.

You're crazy, said the voice in her head. *He has a* gun.

It might not be loaded. It might not work. It might not even be a real gun. She had to be willing to take that chance.

"Stop at the stage," Drew said behind her. How close was he? She couldn't say.

She stopped and slid a glance left, right; she saw Beth, who was barely able to stand up. But she couldn't see Kyle. He hadn't advanced as far as she had. She hazarded a couple of steps backward, and then he showed up in her peripheral vision, but just barely. She backed up again. He seemed to be doing something, fumbling with some object. She saw a flash of metal and almost shouted with joy.

He's got the knife.

"Stop there, little red Robin. Not one more inch," Drew warned.

She froze. If only she could see Kyle, communicate that she knew he was armed.

"Why are you doing this?" Beth said brokenly.

Drew laughed as if Beth had just told the best joke in the world. "Think of the publicity," he said. "All my band-mates dead. Jerks. Losers. They would have lost that contract for me."

Robin heard him walking, pacing.

"They wanted me to go to rehab. Can you believe it? If Samurai had heard that . . . *Idiots!*"

There was more pacing.

Kyle, now, she thought. Could she get to the table, grab the bat?

"That's *it*?" Beth shrieked.

"That's *it*!" Drew yelled. "Bang! You are dead!"

Robin heard a click.

And as Beth screamed again, Robin whirled around without a moment's thought. Drew was pointing the rifle straight at Beth. She rammed into Beth, sending her stumbling, and flung herself low at Drew, beneath the rifle's aim. He swung it at her and the long metal barrel caught her on the shoulder.

She grabbed it, yelling, "Kyle!" Her feet scrabbled on the concrete as Drew thrust forward. She kept her grip on the rifle and swayed backward, like someone trying to keep from falling off a cliff.

"Kyle!" she cried again, but everything was a blur as she kept hold of the rifle. Something inside urged her to let go and run. But if she let go, and he took aim, and shot—

Why hasn't he shot?

Prop gun, fake gun, said the voice in her head, but her hands were frozen to it. If she let go, he could fire.

Drew's face was contorted with rage. His nose was running.

"*Kyle!*" she shouted a third time, but she didn't dare

look for him. All she was doing was putting Drew on alert. Reminding him that it was three against one.

Make that two. Beth wasn't going to be any help at all.

She stole one quick look around and was startled to see that the smoke had grown thicker. It wafted like a blanket on a wash line in front of the lights. Then she was staring back at Drew.

He still hadn't shot the gun.

"Do it," Drew cried. His eyes were glittering, spinning.

She pushed the rifle barrel toward the ceiling and dove at him, aiming for his knees, catching him square in the crotch. He shouted in agony and slammed violently onto his back. She heard a crack—his head—and the rifle went flying.

She leaped on top of him. He struggled and groaned, arms windmilling, legs flopping against the concrete as she straddled him. His head rolled from side to side. She hit him over and over again with her open hands and then she made fists. She couldn't hear anything but the sound of skin slapping skin.

I hate you I hate you I hate you, she thought as she pummeled him. She started to rise on her knees but then she realized he might buck her off. She crouched and remembered Praveen going after August; she closed her hands around Drew's neck and threw her weight against them.

Her momentum was stopped when his fist came out of nowhere and clocked her on the temple. Her ears rang; everything went black. She sucked in smoke and coughed

314

but somehow she fought back, striking with all her strength. She unleashed every ounce of the rage and terror that had built up inside her, and even as he went limp, she kept it up.

I want to kill him.

His face was mottled. His nose bloody. His lips were slack. He looked almost like Cage, like he was wearing Hiro's surreal mask. He looked like death.

Because he was.

The killer. The one who had tormented and butchered them. Who had faked his own death so he could hunt them in safety.

"Die," she said in a low, dangerous voice, sounding not at all like herself, and she spat on him.

He didn't move.

She stared down at the glob of her own spit on his cheek. At the damage she had done.

I saved us.

Horrified, exhilarated, she scrambled off him. Her hand caught on something that was hanging out of his pocket. It was a ripped green handkerchief.

A perfect match to the fabric she had found near Jackson's car.

Quivering, she remained on all fours, hovering vigilantly over him. She studied his face, his arms, daring him to move. Almost but not quite hoping that he would. She leaned forward, wheezing, and yanked the handkerchief out of his pocket. *Evidence,* she remembered, and wiped her face on her sleeve instead. Inky hopped around her, batting at her. Robin panted, making primal, guttural noises like an animal.

I won.

It was not a game, but it was over. The long, horrible ordeal was done. When the sun rose, she would see it. She and Beth and Kyle.

Then she straightened and looked around for Kyle, confused and worried because he hadn't helped her. Maybe the rifle had gone off when she had attacked Drew. Maybe he was hurt.

That was as far as her mind would go.

"Kyle," she said.

"Here, Robin," he replied from behind her. Up on the stage.

She turned.

Surely she was dreaming; he was standing beside Beth with one arm around her shoulders and the other down at his side. Beth was sobbing, and he was rubbing her shoulder as if to comfort her.

"Robin," Beth ground out.

"What are you doing?" Robin asked. She took another look at Drew, then crawled to the edge of the stage and used it to push herself to her feet. Beth and Kyle just kept standing there, Beth in tears and Kyle so strange, so quiet, and so . . . She didn't even know how to describe it.

Her legs were shaking so badly she had to stop.

The floor felt as if it were rocking like a hammock. She reached out a hand to Kyle and Beth and said, "You're safe."

"Not quite yet," Kyle replied. "But I'm getting warmer."

She saw a flash of metal at his side.

The knife.

"Robin!" Beth shrieked. "Robin!"

Then Kyle raised his hand and it flashed again in the light.

The world stopped completely. Robin heard the crackle of fire, the pounding of her heart. She heard the ocean waves.

Then time caught up. It was groaning steel and flurrying embers and tears streaming down Beth's face as her mouth moved but no sound came out.

Robin shouted, "No!"

While Kyle plunged his knife into the center of Beth's chest.

28

DEATH SCENE

KYLE'S RULE #4:

Those who break the rules

must be punished.

Beth's eyes bulged.

Blood blossoming in the middle of her sweater now poured down her front as Kyle yanked the knife back out with a flourish.

"And another cheater pays the price," he said.

Robin's breath fluttered as she strained not to lose control. But she couldn't help it. She threw back her head and shrieked. He waited patiently. Then she held her arms out to Beth, who had fallen on her side. Her eyes were wide as she stared straight at Robin, begging for help. Her lips moved.

"Let me go to her," Robin begged. "She's going to bleed to death."

"I can tell you're upset. You're not really making sense. I obviously know that, Robin." He hopped off the stage and landed in a crouch. His fingers raked her hair and he yanked her head back savagely, exposing her neck. "After all, I'm the one who harpooned that little fish."

"K-Kyle," she managed. Her throat ached so badly that she couldn't draw a breath. He put the knife against it. She jerked. It was as hot as a fireplace poker.

"Robin," he said softly. "You threw me. I didn't plan on you. Plan for you. I wanted to let you go."

Her legs began to twitch as her sight grew dim. She snaked back her hand and grabbed his wrist. It was corded with muscle. He was so strong, and she was completely flattened.

"That was so amazing, the way you took him on," Kyle said. "He was such a waste of space. A frickin' druggie, totally out of control. His bandmates had no idea just how addicted he was. He would do *anything* for drugs."

She was going to black out. Her eyes were rolling back in her head.

Then Kyle's mouth came down on hers, and his grip on her hair loosened. She exhaled against his mouth and sucked air in through her nose. She breathed in the scent of him beneath the blood and smoke and thought about biting him to make him let go of her but that could backfire so badly. He ended the kiss with a sad sigh.

"So you gave him drugs." Her voice was hoarse. Her scalp burning.

"Mostly I just listened. Addicts, they get so paranoid. He was so mad at the band. He was right; they were planning to dump him."

Her eyes darted, trying to figure her escape. The bat was on the table, so far away. The knife was still at her throat. The smoke was thickening as a wave of embers filtered down from the ceiling. It was closely followed by a second.

She peered up at him through her lashes. He thought she was looking at him, but she was checking the ceiling. Brilliant flames flickered through the crossbeams. He didn't seem to notice.

"It was easy to get ready," he said. "Everyone trusted me. They didn't hide things when I was around. I had all August's spreadsheets. It was like I told you, a magic trick. There are clues and objects salted all over this cannery. Mostly in the tunnel. With the bodies. Morgan surprised us. Drew didn't hit her hard enough, I guess."

"Hiro saw Drew die," Robin said.

"One of August's mannequins. Drew threw it off the cliff. He yelled, I shouted out his name—everyone sees what you tell them to see. Just like everything else in this world," he added bitterly.

"Why?" she whispered. "Kyle, what . . . what happened to you?" Something had done this to him. Some disaster, some tragedy, something unpardonable.

"You don't know what pressure's like," he said. "And for

nothing. You make one mistake. One really stupid mistake. You break the rules. And then you're done."

She stayed quiet. As long as she kept him talking, he wouldn't kill her.

"It was when I lived in San Francisco. I used to hang out with this older kid. Eddie Clausen. Eddie was a hood, but nothing like Jackson White. He was rich. His parents had more money than some small countries." He went silent for a moment. "I was sorry about Jackson."

Her stomach churned. Of all the people to be sorry about, Jackson would not have been her pick.

"Eddie," he said. "He was a dealer. He took me with him one night. I didn't know what was going on. There were lots of drugs and tattooed guys with guns. And police."

Kyle? She couldn't see him that way.

"The police took us into custody. We rode in the back of a squad car, and when we got to the station parking lot, one of them walked Eddie away. I was still in the back. My hands were cuffed. Two cops came over and dragged me out and they . . . they started *beating* me. They punched me in the face, the head, everywhere. I couldn't defend myself. Pretty soon I couldn't even *see*. And they threw me in a cell with adult offenders and what happened to me . . . *what happened to me*, Robin!"

"I'm sorry," she whispered, but she said it so softly that she knew he couldn't hear her. That was probably good. He was going someplace in his past that didn't include her. Maybe he would realize she wasn't part of his twisted world. He would take pity. But how could he let her go? He had confessed to murder right in front of her.

"I still have the scars. And the nightmares," he said. "And Eddie? You might wonder what happened to him." He gripped her hair again and she thought he might pull her scalp right off her skull.

She tried to swallow. And breathe.

"*Nothing*. His rich parents bailed him out that night. They blamed the whole thing on me." His voice shook with barely suppressed fury. "Eddie had been dealing drugs for *years* before I met him. Stole money out of their wallets. Broke into their storage, took all kinds of stuff, sold it. He drank all the fancy wines and whiskey, but no one ever said one word. The maids covered for him. His parents just pretended not to know. But they knew. They had to know. . . ."

His voice trailed off. He didn't sound like himself. This was a guy she had never met before. A wounded, angry, damaged boy. She would have no hold over a guy like that.

"I told the judge. I told all of them. Everybody could see how beat up I was. Resisting arrest, they said. And Eddie . . . he lied. They asked him to tell his version. He said I'd gotten into a fight before the cops came and that I was out of my mind when the cops took us. And they *had* to hit me a couple times to make me settle down. He didn't look at me *once*. Maybe he was scared. I don't know. And he got away with *that*, too."

His eyes were shimmering with tears, and there was

spittle on his chin. And then all his features went hard and angry, like he was turning into someone else.

"Just like these kids, getting away with everything."

Robin could only breathe in little gasps and she was getting woozy. She knew she had to do something to save herself. She was so tired, so scared. She kept thinking this was some dream she was having, some insane prank.

The dry wood overhead crackled. Red and orange flames skittered along the rafters in tidal waves. Surely he must notice.

"My parents still hate me. I heard them *talking*." He choked back a sob. "They wanted to put me away. I have done *everything* and it's never good enough. It's not enough. And never will be. And all these people at the party tonight, they're Eddies. I hated them. I hated all of them. They were just like him. Breaking the rules. Getting away with it. Lording it over everyone else, the people who do it right and get screwed over anyway. I'm glad I killed them."

"I'm not like them," she gritted out. Her eyes were watering. The fire overhead was gaining on the wood. Soon chunks would begin falling.

"I know you're not, and that posed a real dilemma until I realized the simple, terrible truth."

"And what was that?"

He shook his head. "You're a rule breaker, too, Robin. After all, you crashed a party you weren't invited to."

He was so crazy. She sobbed, low and hard, but she had to think. "No, I'm like you. Beth was my Eddie. She dragged me here. I didn't know I wasn't invited. I didn't know it was wrong."

He shook his head. "August was snooping around. He was going to find out."

She tried to clear her throat. He wasn't making any sense. Her heart was clanging. *"Find out . . ."*

"The stupid gate." He huffed. "They think they know everything. They're so *cool*. August blows through enough money in a *week* to support my family for a year. I started working part-time at the country club, but I didn't tell anyone because I was so humiliated. I was a *dishwasher*. But I quit as soon as Alexa died. So they stole my job from me, too."

"The gate?" she said hoarsely. "You locked it?"

He was staring off into space. "They were always sneaking in. Doing whatever they wanted. And I had spent hours cleaning grease traps and throwing out garbage and I could hear them laughing and splashing around. And Alexa made some sleazy comment about only illegal aliens working there. So when Jacob left, I took her clothes and I . . . I was so *angry*."

She nodded, tried to show him that she understood. Her head was buzzing; she was so afraid of him. She had to help him out of his darkness. "I can see why you were worried that August would find out you locked the gate, because terrible things have happened to you, but L-Larson was right. She was high. You didn't kill her, Kyle."

His face went completely blank. He looked like the

mannequin they had found in the cave. The world roared around her.

He did *kill her,* she realized. *He really did it.* She couldn't catch her breath. Kyle Thomas was a cold-blooded killer. He was *insane.*

He almost seemed to hesitate. A sad look passed over his face and he cupped her cheek. "I can't let you go, Robin. You know everything."

"They'll figure it out, Kyle," she said quietly, hopefully. "Evidence—"

"Drew. His fingerprints are everywhere. And then there's the fire."

As soon as he spoke the word, a large chunk of wood swung away from the ceiling and dangled overhead. She traced the path of its descent and realized it would probably fall about a foot to Kyle's left. She kept her eyes glued to it, watching, mustering her courage.

The fire kept burning through the piece of wood. Her breath stopped. She pursed her lips and watched. Her eyes blurred and teared with the smoke.

The wood began to fall and she flung herself backward with all her strength. He grunted and jerked forward just far enough so that the brick-sized chunk smacked him on the head. Fire flared from the wood and ignited his hair.

Bellowing, he released her. She moved sluggishly, awkwardly, as she stumbled to the baseball bat. She grabbed it, Kyle rolling into a fetal position. The fire was out. She raised the bat over her head and staggered back toward him.

She arced the bat in the air and brought it down on his head, but she hit his hand and the bat bounced off. She tried again, smacking his shoulder this time. He brought down his hands and she saw bleeding welts on the crown of his head and forehead. With one quick jerk, he wrestled it out of her grasp.

There was pure murder in his eyes.

She backed up, then wheeled around to cross the warehouse floor. She could hear him shouting. The door looked so far away.

The flames on the ceiling leaped to the walls and began to slide down them. Tongues of fire lapped at old paint. The remaining coffins and their robot corpses combusted. The sign for PENALTY BABES evaporated.

He was coming after her. He was swinging the bat back and forth in front of himself, raging. Smoke poured down but he kept coming. Sections of the ceiling thudded, one, two, three, four, five, like missiles. He dodged them.

She reached for the doorknob.

Turned it.

The bat cracked against her left side, and she crumpled to the floor. He stood over her; a moment flashed before her eyes—their first kiss—and then she rolled to the right, the bat narrowly missing her.

The far section of the room burst into flames, engulfing the stage. And Beth.

Robin raised a hand.

The bat came down and hit the concrete. Then, with a

ferocious roar, Inky lunged forward out of the smoke and bit Kyle's ankle. It stunned him and he swayed, just long enough for Robin to wrap her hands around the bat and yank it away from him.

He fell to his knees. Raising her hand, she found the knob and pulled herself to her feet by sheer force of will.

She hit him.

And hit him.

And hit him.

Then Robin ran out of the warehouse down toward the path. She slipped and rolled, over and over, bruised and hurting. She came to a stop among the blazing pines and manzanita bushes. Her face was bloody, her hair bouncing in her eyes. She couldn't move. She couldn't breathe.

She had to get up. She had to move or she'd die.

And then she remembered Praveen. Unconscious. Alone.

Keep running, she begged herself. *Please.*

A shadow moved in front of her.

August.

His face was sooty and blistered and he yanked her into his arms and hugged her. He then took her hand and started to run.

"Praveen," she said. "Praveen is up there."

He shook his head. "We can't, Robin. Not if we want to live. We'll come back for her. I promise."

"No. We can't leave without her!"

As she spoke, the bell tower tilted, the bricks sliding away from each other, crashing onto the fiery roof. The flames were rising; they were at least five feet tall—no, ten—and then the roof collapsed. The bell tower slammed to the ground and circular blasts of shells jettisoned into the air.

The walls splayed outward. They would hit the shed. Robin bit back a wail and kept climbing back up the cliff with August. There were cuts and burns on his neck and hands. He was limping badly, but he didn't slow down.

The fire crawled over Jackson's body.

They made it to the shed, which had started to smolder. August bent over, picking up Praveen, and carried her firefighter style. The added weight significantly slowed him down.

"Get out of here, get out," he said. "I'll catch up."

"I'm not going without you," she shouted. "No."

He shook his head. The buildings were catching, one by one by one. The fish guts building, another shed. The heat sent them back toward the cliff. The wooden deck transformed into a field of fire. The concrete spiral staircase looked like a pinwheel in the inferno.

Together they hurried down the road with the traffic barrier, where Kyle had found his crowbar. The burning factory loomed above them, threatening to slide down the cliff.

"If it goes, get into the water," August said.

She nodded and they ran, Inky darting from out of nowhere again and nipping at their heels.

Their progress was so slow; Robin and August were

both spent. On the cliff, the factory fire lit up the night as it raged. Robin looked back over her shoulder, sure that at any minute Kyle would burst out of it and run them to ground. She was shaking, shivering, barely keeping it together.

Each step was torturous, and she kept checking Praveen to make sure she was breathing. They were the only ones left. They had survived. And they would never be the same.

They passed Hiro's body and the exploded structure and were now walking on a primitive one-lane road. They'd only gone a few feet when August stopped abruptly, hunched over, panting so hard she was afraid he was going to have a heart attack.

"I can't go any farther," he said. "If you see a car there, get the phone. Call nine-one-one."

"We won't have service," she said.

"We'll find some. Just go. I have to take a break."

He laid Praveen on the sand and fell down beside her. Inky licked Praveen's cheek. Looking back at the warehouse for a few heartbeats, Robin forced herself to walk on. Everything in her wanted to rest, too. But they had to get Praveen to a doctor.

And they had to leave this hellhole.

She didn't need a flashlight. Startled, she looked toward the ocean. Streaks of lavender and turquoise were glowing against midnight blue.

Dawn was coming.

Finally.

She stopped to catch her breath, watching the sunrise. Inky yipped and sweat hit the back of her hand as she reached out a hand to pet him.

In the gray light, a battered white car sat beside the road. As she approached, she saw a Maximum Volume sticker on the bumper. Her stomach did a flip. Warily she approached it, circling it to make sure there were no surprises on the other side. She thought of Thea and swallowed hard. Her throat was seared. Then she tried the handle. Locked.

She looked around for a rock and once she found one, started pounding on the driver's window. It didn't take too many times until the glass shattered and fell like a curtain onto the ground and the seat. She unlocked the door and looked around for a cell phone or a spare key. Finding neither, she popped open the trunk.

Cell phones, all of them, including hers. She grabbed for it, sobbing. There was no service, but at least she could walk to someplace that had it. Or they could take the battery out of this car and put it in one of the others they had a key to and drive out of here.

Suddenly Inky growled. Robin stumbled as she turned. It was that stumble that saved her life.

Kyle.

His downward swing of a charred two-by-four slammed into the car instead of her. His face was covered with black soot, his ocean-colored eyes glittering with insanity. She threw herself at his hip, knocking him off balance. Then she kicked him in the crotch and Kyle doubled up, moaning. The two-by-four was too unwieldy but she punched and kicked him the same way she had Drew. He couldn't reclaim the advantage; gradually he stopped moving and she got up, kicking him one more time for good measure.

He lay silent as she dug the car keys out of his pocket with a shaking hand.

She left him there, then drove back for August and Praveen.

August laid Praveen in the back and sat with her. Although the light was coming, Robin had turned on the car's high beams. She braced herself and locked the doors as they drew close to where she had dropped Kyle.

There, bathed in the headlights, Kyle was sprawled on the ground, unmoving.

And an animal was bent over him.

Chewing on something.

Robin shouted and hit the horn. The animal raised its head. There was blood on its muzzle. It stood for one moment as if mesmerized, and then it dashed away, disappearing among the pines the fire had not yet reached.

Kyle was hurt; it had taken a bite out of his shoulder. By tacit agreement, they picked him up and put him in the trunk. She looked down at his bloodless face, the wound, and then shut her eyes against a flood of emotion before slamming the trunk.

By then, the sun was shining on the water.

The beach smoked. The charred skeletal remains of the warehouse seemed to roar like a furious, defeated beast.

Then it fell silent.

As silent as a tomb.

The police met them at the ER entrance of the hospital, and the trunk was opened while Praveen was whisked away to receive treatment. A well-meaning man in blue scrubs told Robin not to worry. Her boyfriend would be up and around in no time.

Robin didn't watch as Kyle's gurney disappeared through the emergency room doors.

"You'll never see him again," one of the cops promised her. "He's gone for the rest of his life. Count on it."

Then Robin crumbled into August DeYoung's arms.

But she should have looked. She should have reassured herself that Kyle was well and truly gone. It felt like he was still beside her.

Like he would never leave her, ever.

EPILOGUE

14 MONTHS LATER

"It's the rope," Carter said. "Strangulation is the sixth most common form of murder in the United States."

For a moment, Robin saw Heather swaying above her in the factory. Then she gave her head a shake and banished the image. Chills ran down her back on that hot July afternoon.

Kyle's trial had taken place during the fall of her senior year. It lasted for months. It was on all over the news. Kyle had been tried as an adult, and he was serving sixty years to life. He confessed to planning all the murders, although Drew had carried out most of them. During his trial, Kyle had steadfastly insisted that he had not planted explosives in the Cheater Theater. He said Drew must have done it on his own, even though, he admitted, Drew swore that he hadn't. There wasn't enough evidence to find out what had really happened, and Robin guessed they would never know.

Now it was July, and Kyle was in a maximum-security prison.

The DeYoungs left Callabrese as soon as August graduated. Their restaurant was up for sale. Their mansion was empty. August was at MIT, and he emailed Robin at least four times a week. He kept talking about coming to see her, but so far, email was as close as he got. Praveen had lived, and her family had taken the DeYoungs and the Brissetts on a spa weekend in Mendocino, then quietly arranged to put ten thousand dollars into a college fund for Robin. After that, Praveen's family moved to London, and Praveen and Robin Skyped. But in truth, they really didn't have much to say to each other anymore.

Because of the heat, the Brissetts were playing Clue in the kitchen, with all the windows open. They didn't run the air-conditioning because it cost too much and there were still many medical bills to pay. Her mom insisted that the ten thousand dollars be used for college only. Robin had been accepted at UC Berkeley, not too far away, and a better school than any she had dreamed of attending.

Robin could smell the fresh earth of the vineyards across the highway. The vines were thirsty. The nights were so sweltering and dry.

"I think it was Colonel Mustard with the rope in the kitchen," Carter announced.

At Robin's feet, Inky raised his head, growling like a tiny machine gun. A branch cracked in the backyard. Robin smiled. Her father and mother were on a stroll.

Miraculously, Robin's father had kept his vow and walked at her graduation three weeks ago. He said that he would dance at her wedding, whenever that might be.

"It's okay, sweetie," Robin said, leaning down and scratching his head.

Ignoring her, Inky yipped again, and the front door opened. Jinny Brissett came in first, followed by her husband. Robin lifted her hand in greeting. Then she realized they had come in the *front* door. The noise had come from the backyard.

Robin crossed the room, scooping up Inky, and reached a hand toward the knob. She hovered there, hearing the crackle of fire and Beth's shriek, that long, horrible death wail as Kyle plunged his knife into the center of her chest.

Someone's out there. Someone's in our yard, Robin thought.

"Honey? What's the matter?" her mother asked.

Robin froze with her hand around the knob.

But Robin knew that Kyle wasn't there. He wasn't coming, ever.

But if he did—

I will catch you and I will kill you, she vowed, her chest tightening.

Then she opened the door.

Nancy's Acknowledgments

Thank you first and foremost to Debbie Viguié, my partner in crime, work, and fun. You are so wonderful. And thank you so very much to our brilliant and insightful editor, Krista Vitola, who helped *The Rules* become the book it is today. Thanks to Alison Impey, Heather Kelly, Colleen Fellingham, and the sales, publicity, and marketing teams at Random House Children's Books. Thanks to my family, especially Belle and Tutu and our vacation fairy, He Who Loses at *Firefly*. Thanks, crazymombuds: Amy Schricker, Beth Hogan, and Pam Escobedo. Thank you, Stinne B. Lighthart and Debbie Nelson. A high-paw-five to Julia Escobedo, who takes care of all the animals and never stops being sweet. I love you, Point Loma Public Library.

Debbie's Acknowledgments

First and foremost, I would like to thank Krista Vitola for her clear editorial guidance and her fantastic sense of humor! I also must thank my awesome agent, Howard Morhaim, who consistently works hard on my behalf. I deeply appreciate you both. Thank you to my husband, Scott, and my parents, Rick and Barbara Reynolds, for their endless patience in listening to me while every last detail of this book was carefully crafted. I must also thank Jason and Rita De La Torre, Traci Owens, and Audra Berreth for their continued friendship and support.

About the Authors

Nancy Holder is the *New York Times* bestselling coauthor (with Debbie Viguié) of the Wicked saga and has written more than eighty novels and two hundred short stories, essays, and articles. She has written novels, espisode guides, short fiction, comic books, and other forms of "tie-in" material for *Buffy the Vampire Slayer, Teen Wolf, Smallville, Hellboy, Beauty and the Beast,* Sherlock Holmes, Zorro, and many other "universes." She has also written Nancy Drew stories as Carolyn Keene. She is a charter member of the Horror Writers Association and has received five Bram Stoker Awards for her supernatural fiction and a Scribe Award for the novel *Saving Grace: Tough Love,* based on the TV show by the same name. In 2012 *RT Book Reviews* awarded her their prestigious Pioneer in Young Adult Fiction Award. Many of her short stories have appeared in "Best of" anthologies.

Nancy's latest book is *Futuredaze²: Reprise,* which she coedited with Erin Underwood and which contains short science fiction stories for young adults from such authors as Neil Gaiman, Cassandra Clare, Libba Bray, and Scott Westerfeld. She edits comic books and pulp fiction and teaches in the University of Southern Maine's Stonecoast MFA in Creative Writing program.

Debbie Viguié is the *New York Times* bestselling author of more than two dozen novels and the coauthor, with Nancy Holder, of the Wicked series. In addition to her epic dark fantasy work, Debbie also writes thrillers, including the Psalm 23 Mysteries, the Kiss trilogy, and the Witch Hunt trilogy. Debbie also plays a recurring character on the audio drama *Dr. Geek's Lab*. When she isn't busy writing or acting, she enjoys spending time with her husband, Scott, visiting theme parks. They live in Florida with their cat, Schrödinger.